THE DAY AFTER CHRISTMAS

NICOLA KNIGHT

Copyright © 2025 Nicola Knight

The right of Nicola Knight to be identified as the Author of the Work has been asserted by them in accordance with the Copyright, Designs and Patents Act 1988.

First published in 2025 by Bloodhound Books.

Apart from any use permitted under UK copyright law, this publication may only be reproduced, stored, or transmitted, in any form, or by any means, with prior permission in writing of the publisher or, in the case of reprographic production, in accordance with the terms of licences issued by the Copyright Licensing Agency.
All characters in this publication are fictitious and any resemblance to real persons, living or dead, is purely coincidental.

www.bloodhoundbooks.com

Print ISBN: 978-1917705424

For dear Finley, the brightest star in the sky.

And for Colin, the best damn kitten cuddler the world has ever produced.

We miss you.

THE DAY AFTER

'Twas the day after the day after Christmas, when all through the house, not a creature was stirring... they were all too full of cheese and chocolate.

'Argh... my stomach,' groaned Felicity, shifting her position on the sofa. 'I swear I'm never eating another morsel ever again.'

'Now do you get it?' her boyfriend James said from the other sofa, reaching for another Pringle. He was blond. Blue eyes. Broad. Built. All the B's.

'Get what?'

'The whole Christmas thing?'

'I'm starting to,' she admitted grudgingly, tipping the last Malteser into her mouth and hurling the empty bag in the general direction of the bin.

'I'm fairly sure that counts as a morsel,' said James.

'Oh, just shut it, you.'

'Er, rude.'

But James was giving her the biggest grin. Suddenly Felicity's stomach, which had been chock-full of Christmas cake just moments before, felt all empty and fluttery. In the best way.

Felicity simply couldn't remember ever being this insanely happy before. This man was like pure distilled magic.

Which was quite strange really.

Felicity was a bona fide card-holding badge-wearing grinch of the highest order and to even feel anything remotely approaching happiness during the Christmas season was nothing short of miraculous. For the past few years, all Felicity had done at Christmas was hide away at the animal rescue centre where she worked, where she didn't have to talk to another human and certainly didn't have to endure any – horror of horrors – festivities of any kind. And now look at her.

Even hosting their first Boxing Day dinner together in James's gorgeous house had gone better than expected. Her long-lost brother, Tristan, had brought along his boyfriend, Pete, who had turned out to be an absolute hoot and at least shared some of Felicity's lingering disdain for certain elements of the season ('never mind sprouts, piccalilli is the actual spawn of the devil'). Somewhat miraculously, her friends Sophie and Bex had been on their best behaviour too. Mostly, anyway.

Bex didn't even mention Adam, Felicity's ex-boyfriend, who Bex just happened to be marrying in a few months' time. Everyone else studiously ignored the subject in true British style and Bex, to her credit, was making an extra effort to be attentive and even helped cook the dinner, which was very un-Bex-like behaviour.

Despite Bex's attempts at "assistance" while carrying a glass of red wine in each hand, the bubble and squeak ended up a tad burnt, and there hadn't been any leftovers as such – always the nicest part of Boxing Day or so she'd always been led to believe – because Felicity and James had spent Christmas Day eating cheese and onion pasties, so it was basically just elaborate (veggie) sausages and mash. Nevertheless, the gang lapped it up. Her boss, Andrea, and her latest flame, Javier, the oldest guests by quite some way and also for some reason the randiest, spent most of the meal feeding each other forkfuls of food, which was positively disgusting, in truth. Felicity found that copious quantities of "nosecco" made it marginally more tolerable although she could have murdered a gin and tonic.

She let them play Twister and Trivial Pursuit and she didn't even complain about the Christmas TV choices. Not even once. Not even when they all begged to watch that ancient rerun of *Morecambe and Wise* where they make a choreographed breakfast in perfect unison in their matching pyjamas, right down to the dubiously sliced grapefruit halves. When someone put Wizzard on the Bluetooth speaker, Felicity didn't utter a single word of protest, and that was progress, she felt.

And now here were Felicity and James, covered in rescued cats and biscuit crumbs. Still in their pyjamas at 12 noon in honour of *Morecambe and Wise* with no intention of getting dressed or even moving very far for the rest of the day. Staring at Christmas movie after Christmas movie. Eating Quality Street chocolates for breakfast and lunch. Feeling a bit sick. All of which would have been perfectly normal for most of the British population, but for Felicity? This was her first proper Christmas since... well, since early childhood, if those even counted. Ever, basically. And in spite of her thirty-three years of, let's face it, total grinchiness, the truth was that she was having a great time.

'What's next then, Brooks? *Muppet Christmas Carol* or *The Grinch*? Or is that second one a bit too close to the bone?'

'And there's yet more rudeness from the man in the *Mulan* pyjamas.'

'What about *Arthur Christmas*? That's quite a sweet one,' said James. 'Lots of cool gadgets too.'

'I'm pregnant,' said Felicity, suddenly.

At that very moment, James was reaching across to the coffee table for his fiftieth Hazelnut in Caramel of the day. As she spoke those words, he fell face first off the sofa in shock and landed in a heap on the carpet.

'Shit. Sorry. Are you okay?' said Felicity, her face caught somewhere between a giggle and panic that this was a Bad Sign.

'I'm okay,' came a muffled voice from the thick carpet.

'Thank God. Sorry. I didn't mean to…'

James's head bobbed up. He had half a Pringle stuck to his cheek and his blond hair was even mussier than usual but his eyes… his blue, oh-so blue eyes were shining like the sun.

'Say that again,' he whispered.

'You have a crisp on your cheek.'

'That's not what you said.'

'I know, but you do. Want me to get it?'

He rubbed furiously at the wrong cheek and missed the crisp completely. Felicity guffawed.

'Come here. Let me get it.'

James made a big show of marching over to her on his knees until he was kneeling right next to where she lay on the sofa. Slowly, ever so slowly, he pushed a stray strand of Felicity's red hair behind her ear. She reached out and touched his cheek lightly, brushing the crisp away and staring into those incredible eyes of his.

'Say it again,' he said, his voice cracking.

In that moment, Felicity's heart swelled eight sizes.

'I'm pregnant,' she whispered, breathing a soft sigh of relief as his handsome face lit up all over again.

CHAPTER 1

FOUR MONTHS LATER

They were hands down the worst two people Felicity had ever met.

As she watched Adam and Bex at the bar, giggling together, Bex with a hand on Adam's arm, head thrown back in exaggerated laughter, she felt it deep in her gut. Sadness mixed with a weird kind of hatred that one could only feel watching their best friend and their ex-boyfriend in love.

'To the happy couple,' shouted someone from the other side of the room. As the crowd erupted for the eighth or ninth time into boozy cheers and half-hearted refrains of "Congratulations" by Cliff Richard of all people (that from the mums at the back), Felicity watched Bex turn slowly to face the room, one hand raised just a little self-consciously, her face aglow, her glossy black hair bouncing as she turned. Adam waved his hands about feebly, palms out, as if to say that was quite enough of that, but no one took any notice. Despite these protests, a smile lit up his dark features. You could see he was loving it.

If this was the engagement party, thought Felicity, as she watched them, the wedding itself was going to be torture.

'Urgh, whose idea was this?' said Sophie, plonking herself

down on the pub stool next to Felicity and patting her arm in solidarity.

'The worst thing,' said Felicity, 'is I can feel everyone watching me, you know, to see my reaction. They're desperate for me to cause a scene or something.'

'You should,' said Sophie, taking another sip from her glass, which was bubbling delicately. Her (usually very collected) "other" best friend appeared to be slurring her words slightly. Sophie was tall and willowy and usually very "together" but she seemed to be making an exception for today.

'Are you drunk?' said Felicity, raising an eyebrow.

'I might be. Catch me up. I highly recommend it.'

'From the looks of it, you've had too much of a head start.'

'Oh shush. Whose idea was this party again, anyway?'

'You've said that already.'

'I know, but I haven't had a straight answer. Was it yours?'

Felicity shifted uncomfortably in her seat. She had suggested something, now that Sophie came to mention it. Ever since Adam and Bex told her they were getting married she kept finding ways to overcompensate for the churning feeling in her stomach by being ridiculously overly nice and helpful.

'Well,' she said now, 'I am the maid of honour.' This with a sarcastic smirk. The most ridiculous thing of all.

'How did that happen again?' said Sophie, narrowing her eyes.

'I have no idea.'

Sophie swayed a little on the stool.

'You should tell them to stick it where the sun doesn't shine.'

'Sophie Flatman. That is a terrible thing to say.'

'S'true though.'

'True.'

The following Saturday there was even more hell to sit through.

'Teal or rose?'

'Hmmmm?'

'I said, teal or rose? Felicity Brooks, are you even listening to me?' Bex was already scowling.

'Sorry. Sorry. I'm with you. No need to full-name me.'

'Well, honestly, sometimes I wonder if your heart is really in this.'

'Of course it is. Look. I'm right here with you.'

She wasn't. Of course she wasn't. Felicity tucked her legs underneath her with a sigh, and attempted to focus, cursing overly emotional Past Felicity from New Year's Eve who had agreed to this fiasco in the first place.

'Right here with me, are you?'

'Sorry. Yes. I'm back in the room. Look. See? Teal or rose, wasn't it?'

Bex gave a little trill of annoyance. 'I'm asking *you*.'

'Right. Yes. So you are. Well… teal then.'

'I was thinking rose.'

'Rose then.'

'Do you think? I'm just not sure it'll go with the dress.'

Felicity rubbed her temples. 'When's Sophie getting here?'

'I've no idea. She was meant to be here at 10am sharp. I do hope she makes it in time for the lunch with my mother.'

Felicity looked at her watch before she could help herself. 10.25am. This was the longest morning in the history of the universe. *Hurry up, Sophie.*

'How's it going in here?' A deep voice made her heart do a little backflip.

Standing in the doorway of the lounge was her Penguin Man, James. Now known as PM or J for short, unless she was cross with him. Ridiculously handsome James with his sky-blue eyes and his unruly hair and his penchant for dressing as a giant penguin for parties. Not in *that* way you understand. There are groups for that sort of thing.

At the sight of him, Felicity couldn't help the smile that lit up her face. He sauntered over and flopped down into the oversized armchair next to hers, stretching out his long legs and running a hand through his messy blond hair.

'I'm not sure you wanted to do that,' muttered Felicity under her breath. She pulled her own auburn hair back into a ponytail with one hand, a sure sign that she was stressed. 'Run. For heaven's sake, run.'

But it was too late. Bex homed in like a missile. 'Ah. Perfect timing, James. You'll do.'

'Well, thanks. I'm very flattered.'

'Teal or rose?' said Bex, perching on the arm of the sofa, so she could wave her laptop screen in his face.

'Say what now?' said James, brows crinkling.

'Teal or rose? It's a perfectly simple question.'

'I… erm… teal, I guess?' James glanced over at Felicity.

'Teal it is. That's settled then.' Bex looked triumphant.

'Hey, hold on a moment,' said Felicity. 'When I said teal, you said rose.'

'Did I? I don't think so, darling. Anyway, *someone* needs to make a decision. It might as well be him.'

'I don't even know what teal is,' said James with a grin.

'It's that one there, darling, the bluey-greeny colour. How can you not know that?'

'Er, because I'm a bloke?'

'You really should educate yourself.'

'And yet somehow you'd trust my judgement over Felicity's?'

'She wasn't even paying attention.'

'Well, she's had a lot on her mind.'

As they bickered, Felicity felt a sudden need to go for a walk.

Where the hell are you, Sophie?

CHAPTER 2

The woman herself eventually breezed in at 11am, all fragrant and well-rested. Not a single bag under those perfect green eyes. So would you be, to be fair, if you had the kind of set-up Sophie had. Nanny for the children, cleaner for the house, gardener for the... well, the garden. She even had a personal trainer who came right to her front door and got her out of bed every morning at 6am. Felicity had never even set foot inside a gym.

Felicity loved Sophie, of course. Sophie was the friend who hadn't cheated on her with her ex-boyfriend for starters and also, Sophie was kind and dependable and you could call her when you were in trouble, and even though she probably *would* care which exact flowers went in the floral displays for the church, she'd do it in a kind of wafty nice way that didn't make you want to tear all your hair out by the roots.

This was what was running through Felicity's head as she sat down to lunch a couple of hours later at the fancy Swallowtail Hotel with Bex's unbearable mother and auntie and cousins while they went over the right sort of tablecloths for the venue. Sophie was sitting next to Felicity, animatedly suggesting all sorts of intricate crafty additions to the centrepieces, while Felicity was plotting her escape. This was not how her usual Saturdays off were spent.

'Let's see what the maid of honour thinks, shall we?'

At these ominous words, Felicity shook herself from her musing and tried to focus.

Bex's mother, Petunia, was peering at her from across the table over horn-rimmed oversized glasses that she thought made her look younger, but which really just made her look, well, ridiculous, frankly. Petunia was everything one might imagine a person named Petunia to be – twin set, pearls, short-bobbed and peroxided hair that really no longer suited her and a pinched expression of permanent disapproval.

Felicity smiled weakly. 'Oh. Sorry, yes, what were you saying?' She hadn't touched a single mouthful of the retro melon and mozzarella starter in front of her, couldn't face it. Sophie gave her a little nudge of solidarity with her arm, then discreetly swapped Felicity's plate with her own empty one. Felicity gave her a grateful smile.

'I was just saying about the place settings. Do we go with classic white tablecloths and then bring a splash of colour with the napkins? Or perhaps change it up a little and do it the other way round?'

'Do you mean, use coloured tablecloths and white napkins?'

'That's precisely what I mean.'

A little titter went around the table as if Petunia had said something a little bit naughty. Sophie guffawed loudest of all and Felicity threw her a sideways glance. She was so elegant and willowy and all those things… and yet she had the dirtiest laugh going.

'Sorry, I'm not sure I quite understand?'

'No, no, you're quite right, Felicity, that would be rather reckless. I think we go traditional.'

Bex nodded her agreement and Felicity tried not to roll her

eyes. Next up she had to try to care about whether the colour of the napkins matched the plates or the bridesmaids (now in rose, not teal, for the moment at least) but her thoughts were all over the place. One minute she was thinking about her mother, the next she was thinking about bloody Adam again. How was Bex marrying Felicity's ex-boyfriend, exactly? How had this come about? And why, dear God in heaven, why had she agreed to be a part of it?

I'm too nice. That's what it is.

Once upon a time, Adam the Ratbag had been Felicity's teenage love. He was the one whose name she scribbled all over her exercise books. He was the one she sighed over when everyone else was too busy swooning over celebrities. And he was the one who helped her when she had no one else in the world to rely on.

Shame, then, that he was also the one who grew into a big fat cheater. He'd broken Felicity's heart more times than she cared to remember.

In a weird twist of fate, she almost broke his in real life when she finally told him to get lost and he proceeded to have a genuine albeit mild heart attack right there in front of her. Reminding her not for the first time that it simply wasn't worth being honest about your feelings to anyone, ever. To cap it all off, somewhere in the midst of finally declaring his undying love to Felicity about three hundred times, he had accidentally or maybe on purpose proposed to her best friend Bex in a moment of – what, desperation? Or cruelty? It was unclear. Either way, it turned out they had been sleeping together on and off for years right under Felicity's nose.

My life could legit be a sitcom, thought Felicity, as the waiter brought the main course. It was the smallest vegetable lasagne she had ever seen, presented, for some inexplicable reason, on a shiny metal garden trowel.

'Oh yes, that's a nice touch,' drawled Petunia. 'Very earthy.

Perhaps the caterers would do something like this for us, Bex, darling. What do you think?'

'I love it. It's perfect,' said Bex, but she wasn't really looking. Her hair was tied in a plait which hung down over her shoulder, making her look like a real-life Barbie doll. She had already gone back to tapping away at her phone, which was ever more permanently glued to her hand since she morphed into *Bexzilla*, bride from hell.

What do you even need me for? thought Felicity. When she looked down at the trowel again there was only a single solitary mouthful of lasagne left. *That went down fast.* Perhaps she was hungrier than she thought or maybe it was just rage-eating. *What kind of psychopath serves food on a trowel? And why haven't I just told these people to get the hell out of my life?*

Later, Sophie took Felicity home. The April sun was low in the sky and despite the warmth of the afternoon, the air was starting to chill. Sophie turned up the heaters and it blasted full in their faces as they drove.

'I cannot believe the trowel thing, can you?' said Sophie, her eyes flashing with humour.

'Petunia is unbearable.' Felicity fiddled with the sleeve of her jacket.

'I know, right? I'd forgotten just how awful she can be.'

'You didn't forget. We've managed to avoid having anything to do with Bex's family since school.'

'You're right. We have. And now we actually have to spend a whole weekend with her mealy-mouthed mother and her revolting relatives at the wedding. What have we done to deserve this?' Sophie laughed, then stopped short when she saw Felicity's face.

'We haven't done anything,' said Felicity, her voice flat.

They pulled into the drive in silence.

And then…

'Are you okay?' said Sophie.

'Of course I am. Why wouldn't I be?' said Felicity.

'Why are you doing this, really?' said Sophie quickly as Felicity started to unpeel herself from the front seat of the expensive Range Rover. One of three that Sophie and her husband owned. *Who needs more Range Rovers than you have people to drive them?*

'Doing what?' said Felicity, frowning.

'This. All of this. Helping Bex. Sticking by her. Being her goddamn maid of honour for heaven's sake. After what she did?'

Felicity turned to look at her friend for a long moment.

'You keep asking me that.'

'I know but you never give me a straight answer.'

'You want a straight answer?'

Sophie nodded.

'Honestly? I have no idea,' said Felicity, slipping out of the car and shutting the door behind her.

But she did.

Of course she did.

CHAPTER 3

Felicity had had the perfect opportunity to walk away. When Bex told her that she and Adam were getting married, Felicity would have been entirely and legitimately entitled to kick them both out of her life forever. Hell, she probably could have sold the story to a dodgy women's magazine. At the very least, she probably should have slashed holes in their clothes or their tyres or put out an advert in the local paper or something else vengeful, and at the same time suitably petty, to make herself feel better. Instead, she had found a way to, while not exactly forgive them, at least come to an acceptance of the situation.

That way's name was James.

He'd been furious at first, of course, when Felicity told him how her friends had betrayed her. Hopping mad, in fact. Gradually, though, after many a late-night chat over tea and biscuits, they'd concluded that Felicity would regret it if she ended the friendship with Bex forever. Bex and Sophie were her oldest friends, after all, and, aside from her boss, Andrea, and now James of course, really her only ones. Felicity had no family to speak of, her only brother being rather a difficult case to say the least, and Bex and Sophie had been at her side through the absolute worst times in her life. Her adult life, at least. So, it followed that she should try and make it work, somehow, right?

That was when she was feeling rational and calm. But every so often, usually after a glass of wine, Felicity would do a bit of hopping herself. Bex had been sleeping with Adam. Of all people. Weren't there rules about that sort of thing? Some kind of Girl Code? Didn't breaking it basically make the whole friendship null and void?

In the end, it all came down to one thing. When Felicity first agreed to all this, to supporting Bex through the wedding (as long as she didn't have to spend too much time with Adam, that was the deal) it was because she was in love. She'd fallen head over heels for James the Penguin Man and it made everything else seem unimportant. When she fell pregnant, that sealed it. Nothing else mattered. It was just the three of them from now on and if Felicity's friend wanted to marry her noxious ex-boyfriend then at the time she couldn't have cared less.

Until it all went wrong.

Until their world shifted on its axis.

Now it was all she could do not to cry every single day.

Over dinner that night, James instantly knew something was up.

'What's she done now?'

'Who?' said Felicity.

'Bex, of course.'

'Oh. No. Nothing. I'm just struggling a bit today, that's all.'

Without another word James put down his knife and fork, stood up, pulled Felicity out of her seat and into an embrace against his broad chest. He manoeuvred her into the easy chair in the corner, still embracing her, and she snuggled close and swallowed back tears. There was a little chirrup from the floor beside them and up jumped little Holly, their youngest cat, immediately purring, and flopping straight down onto Felicity's chest as if she knew that's where the pain was.

'I got you,' James whispered into Felicity's hair. 'See?' He indicated the cat. 'We got you.'

Felicity nodded against him, stroking Holly absent-mindedly behind her ears. 'I know. And I'm so lucky to have you all and this house and my amazing job and everything. It's just...'

'I know,' whispered James. 'I know.'

Felicity took some deep breaths and tried to sit with her feelings for a moment or two. It wasn't easy.

They hadn't even been trying for a baby. When they met just a year and a half ago, James turning up at the door of the cat rescue centre dressed as a giant penguin, looking all soggy and yet somehow ridiculously sexy, with a tiny Holly kitten in his arms, Felicity had been in such a state of confusion over Adam it had taken her some time to let down her guard. To let this handsome Penguin Man into her life. But when she finally did, oh how they fell for each other. They were totally and utterly in love, such as Felicity had never known. And how completely delighted they had been when Felicity fell pregnant.

At least, James had been delighted. Over the moon. Cock-a-hoop. All that stuff. Felicity, meanwhile, had been rather more cautious. Stunned was the word, perhaps. She took three pregnancy tests just to be extra, extra certain, and then walked out of the French doors into the garden and blinked at the early evening moon as if she could find answers on its puckered surface.

James had given her a moment of contemplation, then followed her outside, wrapped his strong arms around her just as he was doing now and assured her in a low whisper that despite the past, despite her trust issues and her nightmare family, despite her appalling track record with men, she would be an incredible mum. She had even started to believe it too. Until the night she woke and knew something was wrong.

A scan confirmed their deepest fears and although Felicity

tried to tell herself it obviously wasn't meant to work out this time or perhaps it was for the best anyway given how new their relationship was, and all the other nonsense that people try and tell themselves in such a moment, she knew she would never be the same.

'Come on,' said James now, bringing her back to the present. 'Let's go to bed.'

She obediently let him lead her upstairs and she wriggled down amongst their three gorgeous, rescued cats as if on autopilot. James was snoring within seconds, but Felicity? Of course not. Felicity lay there torturing herself over the upcoming horror that was Bex and Adam's wedding and wondering whether she'd ever feel normal again.

CHAPTER 4

'Morning,' said Andrea the next day, as Felicity started her shift at Animal Saviours, the animal rescue centre where it all began. Felicity gave her a tight smile and headed into the break room to put the kettle on. Andrea, her enigmatic boss, complete with animal-hair-coated fleece and long grey plait, followed her in.

'Well, you're a barrel of laughs this morning,' she said, leaning on the counter to watch as Felicity poured boiling water over teabags, her face aching from lack of sleep.

'Aren't I always?' she said softly.

'These days, not so much. But who can blame you, eh?'

This was probably a moment where they might have hugged. Andrea being Andrea was not a hugger though, except when it came to random men off Tinder, and so they just stood in silence for a few moments, Felicity staring at the chipped mugs before her, wishing against all hope there were chocolate biscuits some-where about the place that hadn't already been snaffled by her boss.

'Ooh, I know what will cheer you up,' said Andrea, eventually.

Felicity didn't even look up. 'You've finally got Javier tied up?

I mean, pinned down? Ew… no, they both sound dirty. You know what I mean.'

'Ha ha, you know me, I do like my men tied up. But no, that's not it. In fact, I don't think I'll ever have him pinned down now. He says he wants to give it one more chance with his wife, the absolute snake.'

'You're joking? I'm so sorry.'

'Oh, I'll be fine, don't you worry. I always am.'

'Still…'

Andrea waved a hand as if she could wipe Javier off the face of the earth. A shame, Felicity had liked him too. He'd made them all laugh at Christmas with his crazy cocktail concoctions in honour of Andrea, like Wet Dog and Not Another Cat Please. He'd seemed to really be into Andrea, too, but then what did she know? Felicity had been too busy trying not to be sick that day to really notice anything else.

Andrea's gravelly voice drew her back into the room. 'It is about men though. One man, to be specific. We have a new person starting work this week.'

'We what? How can we afford someone?' Felicity felt suddenly numb. This was her happy place, her sanctuary. She was a bit hot and bothered at the thought of someone invading it.

'We can't. He's on… if you must know he got into some trouble with the police and so, well, let's just call it work experience, shall we?'

'Oh, great. So, he's on community service then?'

'Kind of.'

'This is not just any new person but a convicted criminal, is that what you're saying?'

Andrea waved a hand. 'It was just something minor, probably. Anyway, I know the kid's family and they asked if we would take him for a few hours a day. Something about trying to increase empathy.'

'Great,' said Felicity again, feeling anything but. 'He'd better be okay around the animals.'

'Oh yes, it's nothing like that. You'll like him. He's…' She cut off and glanced at her watch, an ancient Timex that barely looked like it would still be functioning. She'd had it for as long as Felicity had known her. Andrea never bought anything new if she could help it. Even her bobbly fleece was verging on antique.

'He's what…?' said Felicity.

'He's here,' came a voice from the doorway.

Felicity turned sharply. Leaning against the door frame was a young man with a crooked smile, openly eyeing her up and down. Although he was dressed a bit like a teenager in cargo pants and a black shirt, he was older than she was expecting. Perhaps early twenties, she thought, with glossy, dark, almost black hair and a cheeky grin that even then Felicity knew meant trouble.

Andrea waved a hand towards him.

'Perfect timing as always, Charlie.'

He nodded his head slowly, blue-black eyes flashing.

'Hi, Charlie,' said Felicity, trying to remember how to be a normal person. 'Welcome to Animal Saviours.'

'That's my line,' said Andrea, laughing. 'But that's saved me the trouble. Come in, Charlie, grab a drink, you can leave your stuff over there. And then Felicity here can show you the ropes.'

'Oh, I can, can I?' said Felicity, turning back to the kettle with a sigh. She was going to kill Andrea later for springing this on her. Charlie was still openly staring at her; she could feel his eyes on her back.

'You certainly can,' he said, under his breath.

Felicity gave Charlie the most lacklustre tour of the rescue centre she'd ever given anyone. But even she couldn't fail to soften when

they came to the dog room and she showed him the litter of retriever puppies that had been abandoned at the front door a couple of weeks before.

'Meet Lilo, Stitch, Mike and Sully,' she said, a little proudly, leaning over their pen, which was on the counter in the middle of the room. Charlie was standing awfully close, so close she could smell his cheap aftershave. It wasn't altogether unpleasant.

'Holy shit. Look at their faces,' said Charlie, eyes wide. Three little golden faces were staring back up at him, tails wagging furiously. And right at the back, there was a tiny black one struggling to get through the throng, whimpering.

'I know, right? Aren't they the cutest things you've ever seen? The little black one is Mike. I think he might be my favourite.'

Charlie let out a long breath. 'I've never seen a puppy this close before.'

'Seriously?' said Felicity.

'Seriously,' said Charlie, with a grin.

Don't be a bitch, Felicity, she told herself, as she reached in to pick up Mike and snuggle him to her chest. The other puppies were clambering over themselves to try and join him.

'Do you want to hold him?' she said, handing him into Charlie's arms before he had a chance to refuse. Their hands brushed for just a moment as Mike wiggled into his hands and Charlie bent his face down and the puppy instantly started licking him all over. He laughed as Mike's tiny stump of a tail thumped harder, and even Felicity found herself smiling.

'He suits you,' she said simply, and he looked up at her then, an expression of pure joy on his face, Mike still virtually attached to his chin.

'He's amazing,' said Charlie, looking her right in the eye. She felt her face heat and instinctively took a step backwards.

'They were dumped outside,' she said abruptly. 'Far too young to be without their mum. We've been bottle-feeding them, which takes ages but… well… it's not exactly a hardship to be fair. I'll show you how to do it in a bit.'

Charlie's brow crinkled. 'That's awful. Why would anyone do that?'

Felicity shrugged. She was getting more used to it by now although it still cut her heart a little bit in two anytime it happened. She put her hand down to the other puppies and gave their little heads a stroke. They responded by wagging their tails ten times harder.

'Who knows? It's money, sometimes, or just people not thinking through the consequences. Retrievers get big, after all. Or it could be puppy farmers, maybe they didn't come out how they wanted, or the right colours. They were probably trying to get chocolate ones, that's what usually happens.'

Mike was now licking Charlie's ear. He was giggling again. 'How could anyone leave this little guy?'

'I know. He's amazing, isn't he? They all are. But not all people are kind.'

Something must have passed across her face then because Charlie studied her for a long moment, as if trying to figure her out. Felicity was the first to look away, feeling inexplicably cross with him.

'So… Felicity. Tell me something.'

Uh-oh.

'Ask me whatever you like.'

'Have you got a boyfriend?' he said, too casually, as he gently placed Mike back down in the pen. The little puppy wiggled back into the group and then turned and continued wagging his tail furiously about in their general direction.

'Wow, you don't hang about,' said Felicity, tucking a strand of her long red hair behind her ear and then panicking about them sticking out and pulling it to the front again.

Charlie gave her another flash of that crooked smile. 'Life moves fast,' was his only response.

'Well, yes, yes I do.'

Charlie's eyebrows lifted.

Felicity went on hastily, 'I do have a boyfriend, that is. Not move fast. And anyway, I'm far too old for you.'

'I'll be the judge of that,' he said, his grin growing wider.

'Shall we move on?'

Charlie did a little mock bow. 'Lead the way.'

CHAPTER 5

As soon as Charlie had left the premises, Felicity marched straight into Andrea's office.

'Any chance you're going to explain what the hell you're up to?' she said sharply.

Andrea spun on her ancient office chair, its hinges creaking beneath the weight of her enormous purple fleece. For some reason today's sensation had a wolf howling at the moon emblazoned across the front. It was quite the visual treat.

'I honestly don't know what you mean.'

'Yes, you jolly well do. You're up to something.'

Andrea put a hand to her chest. 'I most certainly am not. If you're referring to that nice young man, I am just doing a favour for a friend, that's all. Why? How did he get on?'

Felicity clicked her tongue. 'He was… fine, actually. But that's very much not the point.'

'What is the point exactly?'

'I don't know. He keeps staring at me. I don't trust him.'

'I wish he'd stare at me,' said Andrea with a sigh. She turned back to her computer even though she only ever seemed to pretend to use it. 'Those eyes… my Lord.'

'You are old enough to be his grandmother,' said Felicity, not even attempting to sugar the pill.

'I do like them young,' said Andrea, almost to herself. 'One, they have more stamina. Two, they appreciate the wisdom and experience an older woman can bring. Three, they don't expect you to be their carer when they get old and saggy-arsed.'

'You are impossible,' said Felicity, but she could feel a smile tugging at her lips.

'Incorrigible, don't you mean?' said Andrea, her eyes still on her computer.

'That too.'

'So, Felicity, I've delivered you a gorgeous young man to help you around here. He's perfectly polite and seems good with the animals and he's super easy on the eye, and you're here in my office all angry and cross. What's the problem exactly?'

Felicity's shoulders sagged. 'I have no idea,' she admitted, eventually.

'Well, good. Off you pop home to your Penguin Man and we'll say no more about it.'

'Fine.'

'Fine.'

Felicity tried to ignore the feeling of uncertainty tightening her chest. Or perhaps it was good old-fashioned protectiveness. She loved Animal Saviours like it was her second home, she loved the way she and Andrea worked together so seamlessly, telepathically almost, and she loved that she could do the whole job with her eyes closed, practically. She was damned if some young upstart was going to come in and mess with the status quo. Even one that looked like *that*.

That night in bed she tried to tell James about their new arrival. He was irritatingly calm about the whole thing and the more he refused to be drawn in, the more irate Felicity became.

'So, what's the problem exactly? Tell me again?' he said,

massaging his temples with a finger and thumb. Felicity tried to ignore the way his arm muscles flexed as he did so.

'He's been in some trouble but we don't even know what he did, right? He might be an axe murderer or something.'

James laughed. 'Doing community service? Unlikely.'

'Okay, fine, I take your point. But we don't know what he *did* do. The thing is, I just don't trust him.'

James opened his mouth to say something, then shut it again rapidly.

Felicity scoffed. 'I know, you're going to say, "There's a surprise", like I don't trust anyone or something.'

'Well, you don't. But no, that's not what I was going to say. I was going to say you should give him a chance, that's all. Andrea has, after all, and she's usually spiky as hell about new people.'

Felicity leant over and kissed James hard on the mouth.

'Woah. What was that for?'

'Well, you're right of course, Andrea hates new people. She'd never normally welcome someone into our little inner sanctum so quickly.'

'She invited *me* in, let's not forget.'

James had briefly spent time volunteering at Animal Saviours as part of a sabbatical from work the previous year. It had started for the sake of his well-being but ended up being mainly so he could spend time with Felicity. Which in itself was a kind of therapy for both of them. Even now, she still missed him being around the place. And not just because he was in equal parts easy on the eye and good at moving heavy stuff.

'Yes, but that was so me and you could spend more time together, you know that. She's a devious one.'

'So...?' James lifted an eyebrow.

'So, the same applies now. I knew she was up to something.'

'What though? She's not trying to get you to trade me in for a younger model, is she?'

'I've no idea, but I'm sure as hell gonna find out.'

James was already reaching for his phone. 'We could start by finding out what he did. What's his surname?'

'You know what? I've no idea.'

'That might be a good place to start.'

'Roger that.' Felicity nodded, then stopped and punched James lightly on the chest. 'What's that look for?'

James shrugged, pulling her closer to him. 'Whoever this guy is, he's doing something right. I haven't seen you this animated for a long time.'

Felicity felt her face heating and not for the first time that day.

'Trust me, it's nothing to do with him,' she muttered.

James kissed the top of her head. 'Takes more than some upstart kid to threaten my ego,' he said.

'Ha ha. You? An ego?'

James ran his hand down her side and she felt her skin light up like he'd lit a fuse somewhere deep inside her.

'You're gonna pay for that, Felicity Brooks,' he said, pulling her on top of him.

'I sincerely hope so,' she said, all thoughts of Charlie's dimples swiftly forgotten.

CHAPTER 6

Two weeks later, Felicity sat in a kind of stupor as Bex had her wedding dress fitted and Sophie hovered around her, touching all the dresses on the racks and cooing.

Bex and Sophie had always been there for Felicity, her pseudo-family, as she liked to call them. Since school, the three of them were close-knit, heads together, virtually inseparable. Gradually, over the years, Felicity's other friends had drifted away, either fed up of her general grumpiness or put off by her refusal to let anyone get close. Although she had very little in common with either of them, these two were the only ones that had never abandoned her, never refused to take no for an answer. Listened endlessly to the same old sad stories about her absent father, her alcoholic mother, her totally miserable upbringing. Until she met Andrea, they were her only friends in the world. Her only family to speak of. Her only anything.

When she and Adam split up that first time, not long after she went to university, Bex and Sophie dropped everything to come up to campus and visit her. They sat up all night while she cried. Bex stayed on for two weeks, sleeping on the floor in her dorm room. Helping her pick up the shattered pieces of her heart.

Bringing her dodgy kebabs from the shop at the end of the road. Sophie and Bex had been amazing during that time. It never even occurred to her that they might not be good for her. That it was something you could pick and choose. That there might be other friends out there. Friends who didn't sleep with her ex-boyfriends for a start.

A fresh wave of nausea washed over her. No wonder Bex had been so keen for her and James to get together. It left her and Adam free to finally see if things were working between them. It left them free to get engaged. Eugh.

'You okay, Fliss?' said Sophie, who was now standing, hands on hips, staring down at her.

'Oh, yes. Fine. Sorry.'

Sophie flopped down into the chair beside her.

'Don't be sorry, you just look a bit pale, that's all.'

'I'm fine.'

Sophie squeezed her hand. 'Doesn't she look amazing?' she said, nodding towards Bex.

'Hmmm? Oh, yes. Beautiful.'

And she did. Bex's long dark hair was brushed to perfection, flowing down the back of a tight-fitted deep-red corset, overlaid with lace, leading into a long cream silk skirt. She looked like a model. Felicity had always felt slightly awkward next to Bex, never more so than now. She was shorter, rounder, paler. She made a mental note not to stand too close to Bex on the dreaded wedding day. Maybe she could be the type of maid of honour who stood at the back of the church instead? Was that a thing?

'What do you think, ladies?' said Bex, as if reading her thoughts, swirling to face them, dress following her movements with an elegant swish, swish.

'Teal is the way to go,' said Felicity.

'I meant about the dress.'

'You look stunning,' said Felicity and Sophie practically in unison.

Bex narrowed her eyes. 'Have you two been rehearsing that?'

'Only for half an hour or so,' Sophie said and laughed lightly.

'Well, thank you kindly.' Bex gave a low curtsey, then put her hand to her chest and giggled. As she lifted her head, something caught her eye through the enormous window behind them, and she squealed in delight.

'What is he doing here? Tell him to get lost, would you? It's bad luck, it's bad luck.'

She was still squealing and muttering about bad luck as she disappeared into the changing cubicle. Sophie and Felicity looked at each other, then turned slowly to peer out of the window. Sure enough, there was Adam, hands in his pockets, perfect grin on his stupidly perfect face. Not in the least bothered about bad luck, it seemed. Felicity's stomach sank towards the floor.

They intercepted him outside.

'You can't be here,' said Sophie, hand on his chest, pushing him gently back from the door as he laughed. 'Impossible man.'

Felicity hung back, feeling almost shy. It was the first time she'd actually seen Adam in person since he and Bex had got engaged. Although she knew it was inevitable she'd see him at some point, somehow she hadn't prepared herself for it to be today.

'Felicity,' said Adam, nodding at her, his hands still in his pockets, that infuriating look on his stupid handsome face.

'Adam,' she managed to squeak.

'How have you been?'

'Fine thanks,' she said, looking at the floor. A bit like the sun, it was always better if you didn't look directly at Adam, Felicity had found. Previously that was so she didn't accidentally sleep with him. Now it was more so she could resist the urge to stab him in the eye with a pencil. Looking back, it was hard to imagine what she'd ever seen in him. Once he had been the person who absorbed all her thoughts, who her universe revolved around. All she could see now was someone she knew she could never trust. Not even an inch. A shudder ran down her spine.

'Good. Good to see you.'

Was it her imagination or did his voice give way a little as he said it?

'That's quite enough of that,' Sophie cut in. 'Adam, you can't be here. It's bad luck.'

'That's nonsense.'

'It's not nonsense,' Felicity found herself saying. 'It's tradition.'

'Since when have you ever cared about things like tradition?' Adam's voice was cutting all of a sudden.

'I…' Felicity was speechless.

'It's *tradition*,' said Sophie, firmly. 'Now get lost.'

'I'm entitled to see my *fiancée* if I want,' said Adam, still staring at Felicity. She willed herself not to be cowed. To hold her shoulders back. To look him in the eye. But all she wanted to do was run.

'You are, yes, but just not right now, okay?' Sophie was clearly on a losing wicket.

'It's okay, it's okay,' came a voice from behind them. Bex had got changed in double-quick time and was back in her usual classy ensemble day clothes, Chanel or at least a decent imitation, hair only the teeniest tiny bit dishevelled. 'He's taking me to lunch.'

'Well, why didn't you say?' said Sophie, her voice a little frosty.

'I've gone for it, girls. That's the one. The woman's put it aside for me. Felicity, maybe you wouldn't mind collecting it once it's all adjusted.'

'It looked like it fit fine to me,' said Felicity, quietly.

Bex put a hand on her chest. 'Oh, did you think so? It was a little too big, what a pain. And I'd gone for the smallest one they had too, can you believe it?'

Felicity and Sophie murmured assent as Bex put her arm

through Adam's and they sauntered off together. She even managed to resist giving a smug smile back over her shoulder as she went, which, in the circumstances, was admirable really, thought Felicity.

'At least she's trying not to rub my nose in it,' she said, when Bex and Adam were out of earshot.

'You think?' Sophie said with a laugh.

'Nope. Since when did she turn into such a knob? Has she always been this bad?'

Sophie shrugged. 'I'm sure she can't have been, can she?'

'I mean, I know I'm not the best judge of character going,' said Felicity, with a wry smile, 'but I'm sure even I would have noticed that.'

'Come on, Fliss, we're free for the afternoon. Let's go do something fun.'

'Hide under a duvet?' said Felicity miserably.

'Nope. We're going shopping. Retail therapy is just what you need.'

'Even worse.'

'Where's your sense of adventure?'

'How is going shopping for clothes an adventure?'

'Well, that's exactly where you're wrong, my friend. You'll see.'

'I seriously doubt that.'

An hour later and Felicity was laden down with Sophie's bags of purchases, sitting on a chair in the changing room feeling like a long-suffering boyfriend.

'How is this meant to be helping, exactly?' she said, as Sophie came out of the cubicle and did the little back and forth wiggle-dance that only ever happens in a changing room.

'Go and buy something,' said Sophie with a laugh. 'Retail

therapy only works if you actually hand over some of that hard-earned cash.'

'Are you forgetting I work for a charity? I never *have* any cash.'

'Oh, Fliss, stop being such a grump. You never spend anything on yourself.'

'Sorry, just didn't bank on seeing Adam today.'

'Even more reason to treat yourself,' said Sophie.

Sophie did another twirl and the pink-and-cream skirt she was trying on swirled out around her. 'Also, sorry. I hadn't thought. I should have asked you. How was that?'

'Weird. Annoying.'

'He's still handsome though, eh?'

'How can you say that, Soph? When I look at him now, all I see is his Big Fat Betrayal.'

'Betrayal but also those dark eyes. That smile.'

'Like Tom Cruise, I always thought. Combined with Dev Patel, we used to say.' Felicity sighed inwardly.

'Who?'

'That handsome Asian actor?'

'Ooh yes. I can see why you guys fancied Adam, I must say. Pearly white teeth too.'

'Soph, you're really not helping. Get that one.'

Sophie looked down. 'Do you think?'

'Yes, it suits you. Not the top though. Too plain.'

'I do like the way it swirls.'

'And then please can we get going? I need to go and lick my wounds in peace.'

Sophie nodded. 'I just need to go to one more shop.'

Felicity let out a groan.

CHAPTER 7

Felicity had formulated a plan. Well, not so much of a plan. She was just going to ask him straight out. There was no harm in that, surely.

'Charlie…?' she wheedled, as she took off her new coat in the staff room the following week. Sophie's pestering had practically bankrupted her but at least she had something warm to wear at last. The weather had gone cold again even though it was nearly May. Because Britain. 'Can I ask you something?'

'Give the poor boy a chance,' said Andrea from her standard position by the kettle, chomping on a chocolate biscuit. 'He's only just arrived.'

Felicity shot her a look. 'Chocolate digestives for breakfast again? Tut tut.'

'Don't knock it till you've tried it. Breakfast of champions,' said Andrea through a mouthful of crumbs. Charlie huffed a dirty little laugh at that and Andrea and Felicity frowned at him.

'Hello?' he said, looking between them, eyes widening. 'Breakfast of champions? Haven't you two ever heard of James Hunt?'

'Who?' said Andrea.

'The racing driver?' said Felicity, even more baffled.

Charlie gave a little nod of affirmation. 'Total legend.'

'How have *you* heard of James Hunt, more to the point? Weren't you just born last week?' Felicity got up and flicked the kettle on to re-boil.

Charlie chose to ignore this cheap shot. 'I love motor racing. I especially love James Hunt; the man was an absolute icon. He had this badge on his overalls that said, "Sex: Breakfast of Champions". That's why I laughed.'

Andrea guffawed.

'Charlie! Didn't know you had it in you. I knew we'd get on, you and I.'

Felicity rolled her eyes. 'Please.'

Charlie lifted his eyes to hers. 'I suppose you'd rather have a chocolate digestive, would you?'

Felicity's face grew instantly warm. 'That is… well, I… that's none of your business,' she snapped, wishing she could think of some witty retort.

'Anyway…' he said, moving a little closer to her, 'didn't you have something you wanted to ask me?'

'Never mind,' she huffed, and left the room without even making a cup of tea, which always put her in a bad mood. And she'd totally messed up her chance to find out his full name. *Breakfast of Champions*, indeed, she muttered as she headed for cuddles with the Disney puppies.

An hour later Felicity was still grumbling to herself as she washed up puppy bowls. Mood black. And that's why she was so wholly and entirely unprepared for what happened next.

'Hello, Felicity,' said a distantly familiar voice.

Felicity whirled around from the sink to find a man standing in the doorway. Why did men always turn up at her work when she least expected it? What was wrong with them as a race?

'Can I help you?' she said carefully, as if to a stranger, although she had known almost immediately who it was, the knowledge starting deep down in her gut before it reached her brain, even. She had a sudden urge to laugh and cry all in the same moment.

And perhaps also vomit.

'It's me, Felicity,' said the man, who was still hovering uncertainly by the door.

Felicity couldn't find any words to reply. From somewhere she had picked up a tea towel and she began to twist it between her hands like she was preparing to use it in self-defence.

The man took one small, very tentative step into the room, palms outward, then stopped. Felicity couldn't help but stare. Struck dumb now as the reality of the situation hit her. He didn't look like Dean Martin anymore.

His features no longer fitted together on his face quite as perfectly as they used to, and she found herself squinting at him to try and picture the man she had once known. His dark hair was thin now but he wasn't balding and he was sporting an expensive-looking black leather jacket and washed-out jeans combo that belied his years. He was slim and looked to be in good shape, but his face was thickened and deeply lined, and the scent that had wafted into the room with him was unfamiliar, almost medical somehow. Her memories were hazy and she had so few photographs, but despite all the question marks and missing jigsaw pieces, still she knew. Just knew.

It was him.

For the first time since she was tiny.

The very first time.

Her father.

Felicity twisted and pulled at the tea towel as they stood and regarded each other for a long, agonising moment. She wondered if she might faint. Did people really do that sort of thing? *Holy shit. Is this really happening?*

'Aren't you going to say hello?' said the man, eventually.

'Is it… is, erm, I mean, is that what one says in this situation?'

'I'm not sure there are any rules in this situation.'

Her father – yes, against all the odds, against all human reason, that is who it was – took one more step further into the room. His voice was calm and deep, but he was tall and incongruous in this familiar, comforting space, and Felicity had an almost hysterical urge to laugh.

I mean, this just cannot be happening.

Instead, she cleared her throat. 'That's far enough.'

She was holding the tea towel out in front of her now as if it was going to provide some kind of protection from this unwelcome apparition.

'Fair play.'

Harry Brooks – oh yes, the apparition had a name – leant against the storage unit just inside the door and Felicity wondered how he could be so casual in such a momentous moment.

'How… how the hell did you find me?' she said, her voice dragging over the words.

Harry shrugged. Actually shrugged. 'It took some doing.'

'I would imagine so, given I didn't exactly want to be found. But then, you've had thirty whole years, to be fair.'

He shrugged again but the tiniest flash of pain showed on his brow. He said nothing in reply.

Felicity tried again. 'Perhaps I should have asked why, not how. Would that be easier? Why… why did you find me?'

Her father smiled a tight, tense smile and looked for the first time around the room. Felicity felt as though she had pins and needles running through her entire body.

'Isn't there somewhere we could talk, properly? Could you allow me that?'

'I'm working,' said Felicity.

'I can see that,' he replied simply.

'And besides…'

'Besides what?'

'Besides…'

Besides what?

Besides everything.

CHAPTER 8

*H*eart pounding, Felicity led Harry along the corridor to the break room and motioned to him to take a seat on one of the crappy white plastic garden chairs covered in cat blankets and dog hair. She sat down opposite him, her palms sweaty and clammy, wondering how the hell to handle this. They sat for a few moments in silence, both staring not quite at each other, past each other almost, as if awaiting divine assistance.

'Ah, you look great. It's so good to see you, baby girl,' said her father, eventually, slapping his hands on his knees in emphasis.

Felicity crossed her arms. 'No. No nicknames. Sorry. Just Felicity is fine, thanks.'

'Sorry. You're right. Of course. *Felicity.*'

'You and Mum had a lot to answer for with that name. And poor Tristan of course.'

Harry blinked at her. 'It's good to see you.'

'I wish I could say the same.'

'I appreciate it's a bit out of the blue.'

'Are you kidding me? I may look calm but trust me, I'm a human panic attack right now. Respectfully... What the hell are you doing here?' Felicity was seriously contemplating lying on the floor or doing star jumps just for something to do to escape the awkwardness and burn off this burst of nervous energy.

'Isn't it obvious? I wanted to see you.'

'After twenty-seven years, you just decided today was the day?' said Felicity.

'Seemed as good a day as any.'

'Well, it's not a good day. I'm working. And I have nothing to say to you.'

Felicity's jaw clenched painfully and she tried to think calm thoughts. Her father sat a little further back in his chair and regarded her thoughtfully.

'I can't get over how beautiful you are. You look just like your mother.'

'Please don't.'

'So grown up. And that red hair…'

'For God's sake. I am grown up,' she snapped. 'Or at least I'm attempting to be. You missed it.'

He flinched as if he'd been struck. 'Will you at least let me buy you a coffee?'

'I'm working. I've told you that.'

He began to wave his hand dismissively, then caught her expression and seemed to think better of it.

'This place is important to me,' said Felicity, answering his unspoken question. *And don't imagine I can just drop everything for you.*

'Fine. How about next Saturday? Just a coffee in town?'

'I really don't see what there is to talk about.'

'Only about twenty years' worth of your life that I need to catch up on.'

'Twenty-seven years, actually. And you're assuming, of course, that I want to tell you anything about my life.'

'Ouch,' said Harry, miming clutching at his heart.

'Ouch indeed.'

They stared at each other for a long moment then, a million unspoken words tumbling and whirling between them in the void. Mercifully, just as Felicity was beginning to hatch an escape plan, there was a noise from the corridor.

'Felicity? Are you okay?'

It was Charlie, standing in the doorway looking anxiously from Felicity to Harry and back again. She looked up at him pleadingly.

'Is this man bothering you?' said Charlie, and he sounded so much like a character from a movie that she suddenly, irrationally, felt the urge to laugh. His dark hair was flopping over his eyes so much he had to lift his chin to see either of them, like the shy girl in *The Incredibles*. But Charlie seemed to think it looked cool and who was Felicity to argue?

It was Harry who spoke first, and his voice was still so unfamiliar to her and yet *known*, somehow, that the laughter died on her lips.

'Now look here, son, this is a private conversation.'

'It's only private if Felicity says it is,' said Charlie, fists clenched, his face darkening.

Both men turned to look at her then and Felicity felt like she was having an out-of-body experience. She shifted in her seat. *This is insane.*

'It is private, but you can stay, Charlie. This gentleman was just leaving.'

'Is this your boyfriend or something?' said Harry, eyebrows raised.

'That is none of your business. But no. He's just a friend. A colleague, really.'

'Er, rude,' muttered Charlie under his breath.

Felicity stood up, hoping her father would take the hint. He took his time, but eventually, slowly, he got to his feet.

'How about that coffee then?' he said, ignoring Charlie, who had drawn himself up to his full height in the doorway (all five feet seven inches of him) as if preparing for gladiatorial combat.

'I don't think so.'

'You're serious?'

'We have nothing to say to each other.'

'I beg to differ.'

To his credit, Harry sounded a bit choked up. His dark eyes were wide and he had such an earnest expression on his face that she knew any normal human being would be conjuring up some form of feelings, like empathy or something, right now – but all she had was mild irritation. *I must be made of stone.*

She searched her feelings, but there were none forthcoming. She just felt numb, basically. Was she disassociating right now? Was that it? Was she going to come to her senses halfway down the motorway hard shoulder or something? This was all a bit surreal.

'Honestly, I just can't cope with this right now. Please go.'

Her father's face sagged. He suddenly looked exhausted. 'Felicity. Sweetheart. Please give me a chance.'

'No thank you,' said Felicity, and cringed at how childish she sounded. 'Thanks for stopping by.'

Now go.

She watched him leave, her body numb, her mind a blank.

'Who was that guy?'

Felicity edged past Charlie and headed for the toilets, ignoring his question. She locked herself in a cubicle and tried to slow her breathing to something like a normal rate. There were still no tears, which was weird. She had expected tears. *I mean, you would, wouldn't you? You would cry if your estranged father had turned up at your work out of the blue? Most people would.*

But no. There were no tears. Not a single one. In fact, her eyes were dry and tight as if she'd forgotten to blink for several hours. Her chest was tight too, and her breathing was shallow and rapid.

You need to calm down, she told herself but it didn't help. Herself wouldn't listen.

Someone tapped tentatively on the cubicle door.

'Felicity? Are you okay?'

It was Andrea.

'Charlie said some guy came by and… he's worried about you.'

'I'm fine…'

'Why are you hiding in the toilets then?'

'Er, I'm not? I just need a minute.'

'And why does your voice sound like that?' said Andrea through the door.

'Like what?'

'Like you're being strangled.'

Felicity gave a small cough in response.

'See? Like that.'

'I'm fine. Honest. I just need a minute if that's okay.'

'Okay…' said Andrea.

Silence.

'You're still there, aren't you?' said Felicity, after a beat.

'Yup. I'll just wait out here. Take your time.'

'Thanks.'

And with that, the tears came at last. Big, ugly, snot-filled sobs she just couldn't keep inside. So loud they drowned out the sound of Andrea asking if she was okay over and over again through the door until eventually Felicity opened it, fell into her arms and cried her heart out. When she finally stopped, she wiped her eyes and looked over Andrea's shoulder in time to see Charlie standing in the corridor outside, his face anguished and helpless.

CHAPTER 9

Did that really happen?

Felicity sat down heavily on the sofa that night and tucked her legs underneath her, gripping her mug of oat milk coffee as if her life depended on it. James was working late so Felicity had tried to practise a bit of that "self-care" everyone had started going on about these days, even though they apparently just meant things like washing your face and eating food, which Felicity was pretty sure were just the basics of everyday living. Surely it didn't warrant an entire industry to tell us how to do it.

She had her favourite flannel pyjamas on, her only matching pair in fact. They were pretty old and threadbare and it was a miracle she'd even managed to find the top and bottom on the same day. Yet they were cosy and soft and they smelt of her favourite tropical fabric softener. In other words, they were unbelievably comforting in that moment, and she stared at the tartan pattern and tried to get her thoughts in some kind of order.

But there was one thing she just kept coming back to.

I sent him away. Without even a second thought. What kind of person am I?

44

Hot tears pricked at her eyes again.

Just like that, she'd sent him packing. Her own father.

Never mind that he'd arrived out of the blue and nearly given her a heart attack. Never mind that he'd apparently never cared until now. He still didn't deserve that. Or did he? She was filled with irrational pity for the man. Perhaps she was his only hope in the world. Perhaps he was destitute or homeless. Maybe he'd been made redundant or split up with his partner or wife or husband or whatever. She hadn't even bothered to find out.

Felicity tried to picture Harry's face in her mind from when she was young, but it was strangely pixelated, like an old 8-bit computer game. The only image she had seemed to be a kind of hybrid of the dad she remembered from all those years ago and the one who had been standing in front of her this morning. Her past and her present clashing with a dissonance that left her feeling strange and uncomfortable. Both dads were strangers. Past Dad and Present Dad. She didn't know either of them. She didn't know if she wanted to.

Perhaps, she thought, things turning dark and bitter suddenly, it was the opposite. Perhaps he'd just be relieved now that he'd finally given it a go. Maybe he was heading back to a completely perfect and fulfilled life, feeling like he could tick a box on his bucket list or something. He'd reached out to his only daughter after thirty years and she'd sent him away. Now he had an excuse never to revisit that part of his life again. In a way, in that very act of rejection, she'd empowered him to continue being the most useless dad on the planet. For that is what he was.

Maybe I should have made it harder for him.

She'd made it too easy. She hadn't thrown something at his head or slapped his face or beaten her fists on his chest or screamed at him that he was a Giant Abandoner or any of the things she'd always pictured doing if her long-lost father ever crossed her path. She'd actually been relatively civil, in fact, which was surprising for many reasons, and she hadn't even asked him any questions about himself so not only was her stomach tied up in knots but her mind was buzzing with a zillion questions. Which, in some ways, was the same as it had been every day since she could remember. Now she just had new questions too. Where did he live? Who with? Why had he sought her out now of all times and what did he want?

That was it then. She had to somehow find a way to forget this day had ever happened. She could go back to just pretending her father had died along with her mother and that she was an orphan. That's how she'd always thought of herself, in truth. An orphan heart, is that what they call it when you don't trust a soul? The description certainly fitted.

But now, all of a sudden, this orphan had a parent who was very much alive and well and seemed to want to get to know her. Felicity had no idea what she was meant to do with that.

CHAPTER 10

*T*he following morning, Felicity had a day off, which was a bloody good job too as she'd barely slept all night for thinking about Harry. She lay in bed long after James had headed to his office, staring at the ceiling. Their little black cat, Bobby Charlton, came and curled up beside her, instantly purring, the vibrations against her side bringing her some much-needed calm.

Her father hadn't told her anything about himself. She hadn't given him the chance. She didn't know where he lived or anything about him. She had no way of contacting him even if she wanted to. Felicity chewed a fingernail for a moment or two. It would have to be by text, she knew that. Her brother never ever answered a ringing phone. She reached over to grab her phone from the side table, nearly knocking her enormous to-be-read pile onto the floor in the process. Bobby leapt up and jumped off the bed, indignant.

Felicity: Hey you

Tristan: Hey yourself

Felicity: How's things?

Tristan: How are things? I think you mean.

Felicity: Why are you such an arse?

Tristan: It's part of my charm.

Felicity: Doubtful. Anyway, I have some news
and I think we need to meet.

Tristan: Is it about Dad?

Felicity: Yes. How did you know that?

Tristan: He told me he was going to come and
see you.

Felicity: And you didn't think to mention it? Warn
me maybe?

Tristan: I've been busy, darling. Premieres to go
to. People to see.

Felicity: Arses to kiss.

Tristan: Very much so.

Felicity: So, here's the thing.

Tristan: Go on.

Felicity: I kind of sent him packing.

Tristan: I know. He told me. Harsh, Fliss.

Felicity: And I didn't even take his number.

Tristan: Awkward.

Felicity: Yes and so I was wondering...

Tristan: If I would give it to you?

Felicity: (gritting her teeth) Yes, if it's not too
much trouble.

Tristan: It's no trouble. Let me just ask him.

Felicity: What? Why do you need to ask him? I'm
sure he won't mind.

Tristan: Still, I'd feel better if I just checked.

Felicity: Go on then.

Tristan: I can't now, I'm going out.

Felicity (trying to stay calm) But you're talking to
me right now.

Tristan: I'll do it tonight. Don't panic.

Felicity: You won't. You'll forget.

Tristan: I promise.

Felicity: Why can't you just tell me now?

Tristan: Protocol, darling. What if he doesn't want
you stalking him?

Felicity: Forget it. I'll find it myself.

Damn her stupid brother. Damn ever even making the effort
to reach out to him in the first place. What had it even brought
her except more aggravation?

Felicity bit her lip harder. Picked up her phone again but a
quick Google search brought up nothing. She tried Facebook but
there was no one that looked even vaguely like her father. There
was nothing on Twitter, nothing on Instagram. Nothing on
LinkedIn. How was that possible? The man was like a ghost. And

then the reality bit. She had blown her one and only chance to talk to her dad after twenty-seven years. To maybe get some answers after all this time.

What if she never saw him again? And why was Tristan such a horse's arse?

CHAPTER 11

*E*ven later that night, when she and James were curled on the enormous squidgy sofa, both absolutely covered in cats, staring at an inane comedy show on Netflix, he spoke softly into her ear. A little shiver ran down her spine.

'Tell me something,' he said.

'Anything,' said Felicity.

'Your dad… when did you last see him? Before today, I mean.'

Tears sprang to her eyes without warning. 'The last time I saw him was when he walked out on us.'

'What, when you were six? You've genuinely not seen him again since then? Not even at your mum's funeral?'

'Yup. And no.'

'Wow,' he whispered.

'I know, and I handled it so badly,' she said. 'I was so shocked. I sent him away without even so much as offering him a coffee. I'm a terrible daughter, aren't I? No, don't answer that. I'm not sure I can ever forgive him for walking out on us like he did, but now I'll never forgive myself either.'

The tears began rolling down her cheeks. Apparently, she'd

opened up some kind of floodgate. It was all Andrea's fault. Stupid Andrea. Trying to be nice to her and all.

'Let's not forget who the bad guy is here,' said James, carefully. 'You know, he abandoned your whole family. When you and your brother were tiny.'

'How could I ever forget that?' said Felicity, trying not to sound cross.

'Just mentioning it in case you were somehow managing to feel guilty about someone else's appalling behaviour.'

Felicity smiled through the tears. 'Who me? Never.'

She picked up her phone.

Felicity: Any luck with that number?

Tristan… *tumbleweed*

She waited for a few minutes to see the ticks turn blue, then when they didn't she threw it onto the sofa in disgust.

'Bloody Tristan is bloody useless.'

'I'm so sorry,' said James, his hand on hers, his gaze steady. 'I wish I'd been there today.'

'Thanks. I do too.'

They sat for a moment or two with their own thoughts. James reached up and wiped her tears with a gentle hand.

It was a kind gesture, but Felicity felt suddenly overwhelmed.

'I don't want to talk about him anymore. Not yet anyway. Is that okay?'

'Okay. Whatever you say.'

'Thank you.'

She smiled into his face and wondered – not for the first time or even the three hundredth time, come to that – what it would be like to actually marry this man.

Cut that out.

He smiled back and ran a hand through his forever unruly blond hair.

Look at that smile. Honestly.

He always seemed to have a knack for reading her mind. She blushed automatically and he lifted an eyebrow.

'Surely you're not thinking what I'm thinking,' said James in a low voice.

Her face grew hot. 'I guarantee we're thinking completely different things right now.'

'I wouldn't bank on that,' said James, pulling her closer against him.

'Breakfast of champions,' she muttered, half to herself, a little smile on her face as she snuggled against him, eyes growing heavy. Though the spirit was willing, the flesh was most certainly not. She was completely wrung out.

'What?' whispered James into her ear.

'Never mind,' said Felicity, waving a hand, and seconds later she fell into a fitful sleep.

The next day was a Saturday and, mercifully, they both had a day off. After a leisurely breakfast of the ordinary variety in the ridiculously large kitchen in what she still thought of as James's house, Felicity made a coffee and took it up to the office, where even though he was meant to be resting she knew she would find him. Sure enough, there was James tapping away on the keyboard in front of his equally ridiculous Jack Bauer-type screen set-up.

Felicity felt a thrill run down her spine. No matter how much he claimed his job at GCHQ was boring, she never quite bought it. James Bond or not, it was still pretty sexy.

After a few seconds, the printer buzzed into life and coughed out a single sheet of paper. James handed it to Felicity and sat back down in the chair, looking triumphant.

Felicity stared down at the page, not comprehending.

'What is this, J?'

'That, my lady, is the phone number and address for your father.'

'What?'

'You heard me. Harry Brooks has a mobile phone and everything. Now you can call him whenever you're ready.'

'How did you…? How on earth…?'

'I had a name. That was enough.'

Felicity stared at the number on the page before her. She looked up at James who was still looking very pleased with himself.

'I can't believe you did that.'

'It was nothing. It's publicly listed so I didn't even have to break any laws.' This with a grin that showed off The Dimple to full effect.

'I mean it. I don't know what to say.'

She stared at him for a moment or two longer, eyes wide, tears prickling at her eyes even as a smile began to form. James smiled back, a huge, warm smile, as if he was delighted to make her happy, then stood up and walked across the room towards her. He took the paper from her hands, placed it carefully down on the coffee table, then pulled her to her feet.

'You don't need to say anything,' he said, his voice growing husky as he looked down into her face, his thumbs wiping her cheeks gently. She could feel the heat of his body, and his nearness made her entire body tingle.

'But I do. I need to say thank you.'

'It was nothing. Honestly.'

'Take me back to bed,' she said, surprising even herself.

James's eyebrows lifted to the ceiling.

'Promise you won't be thinking about your father the whole time?'

Felicity giggled. 'Not the whole time, no.'

'Gross.'

'Sorry, I mean, of course, I promise.'

'Then lead on, fair maiden.'

CHAPTER 12

$\mathcal{F}$elicity trundled to work on Monday with her head in a fog.

She was still completely exhausted, for a start. Emotionally and – ahem – physically too. Despite what had happened to them at the beginning of the year, losing their baby like that, despite the sadness she felt, for some reason the desire to be with James was stronger than ever. In a strange way it helped her forget the pain just for a little while. Or perhaps deep down she wanted to get pregnant again? Maybe that was it? She couldn't really work out what it was she really wanted. James didn't seem to be complaining, but truth be told it had been a while since she had been this… um… active?

James was rather – er, well, let's just say he was in good shape, whereas Felicity… wasn't. Fitness-wise, she was about as active as a sea cucumber. She'd never been overweight but when all was said and done, Felicity much preferred sitting down. If there was a biscuit involved, that was even better. She couldn't remember the last time she'd done anything you might count as proper exercise. When James came along with his muscles and his fitness club membership and swept her off her feet in his fancy penguin suit, she'd had no time to quickly pop along to Rothesay Road gym a few hundred thousand times to ease the deficit.

The upshot? Felicity was knackered, that was the technical term. Too much sex and not enough sleep. Not a problem she was really used to having. Not a problem she ever thought she'd be likely to complain about but still, here we were.

She was knackered, and she was befuddled. Confused. Bewildered, even.

She'd been carrying the piece of paper with her father's number on it all weekend as if afraid to lose it, but she had yet to summon up the courage to call him. She was so mad with him it was almost crippling in its intensity. Her stomach was in a permanently clenched state. And yet. And yet she wanted to see him. Maybe just once more. But not yet. All that wanting and wishing and pestering Tristan (who had never even replied, useless boy) and now she couldn't bring herself to actually do it. For some irrational reason she wanted James to be there when she spoke to him. Didn't want to be alone when Harry rejected her out of hand all over again. At the very least, he'd agree to a coffee, surely? Felicity knew she could be persuasive when she wanted to be. Maybe James would even agree to come with her. A blond titan for backup.

Ah, James. The thought of him still made her body respond in ways she never thought possible. Had all but given up on when he swanned (or should that be penguinned?) into her life.

When James knocked on the door of Animal Saviours on Christmas Eve with a tiny kitten in his hands, she had known, somehow, that he was going to be important. But she could never have known just *how* important he would turn out to be. Not just because he was gorgeous and sexy, although that all helped of course. But it was the way he gently eased into her life, like he could see her insecurities printed across her forehead. The way he insisted she trust him when that wasn't exactly her strong suit. The way he promised her he would win her trust even if it took him a lifetime. And so far, he had lived up to that promise. Always calling when he said he would. Always putting her first. Just being there for her. There was a lot to be said for it.

Felicity stared at the piece of paper for the fourteen millionth time. There was little point as she'd already memorised the number and put it into her smartphone, but still, it was comforting, somehow, the sight of those digits. Just sitting there on the page in their no-nonsense sans serif fourteen-point font. Taunting her with their practicality. Eleven little numbers that were all that stood between her and Harry. Who, for some unknown reason, had become someone she now simply had to see. Even if it was just to slap his face. At least it would prove he was real.

At that very moment, Andrea appeared in the doorway, Charlie looming behind her like a shadow.

'Felicity Brooks. I know daydreaming is fun and all but can we expect you to join us at any point? The RSPCA will be here shortly. Two rabbits have turned into six rabbits and a pigeon of all things, apparently. Can you get the extra basket from the storeroom?'

Felicity waved a hand absently. 'Sorry. Yep. I'll be there in a sec.'

Andrea wasn't so easily dismissed. She blustered into the room and peered over Felicity's shoulder, her long grey plait swinging behind her. She always smelt slightly musty, did Andrea. It had taken a while but Felicity had learnt to love her unique fragrance. Charlie flumped down into the chair beside her. His rather more enticing smell was something she was learning to filter out.

'What's that then? Been taking phone numbers behind old James's back, have we?' he said, that cheeky grin plastered all over his face.

'What? Oh, no. This is my father's number. Until the other day, I hadn't seen him in thirty years.'

Charlie let out a low whistle. 'That random guy was your dad? That's huge.'

'Yep.'

'Go on then. Do it. What are you waiting for?'

'Give me a minute.'

Andrea nearly snatched the piece of paper from her hand. 'Okay, fine. But if you don't do it soon, I'm calling him.'

'Don't you dare. Knowing you, you'll end up trying to sleep with him.'

'Why? Is he hot?'

Felicity's stare was like daggers.

'What? Sorry, not the time or place.' Andrea's apologies, which were rarer than hen's teeth, never really sounded like she meant it.

CHAPTER 13

A week later and she still hadn't called Harry. But something had shifted, that was for sure.

Felicity had gone from shamelessly sending her father away to desperately wanting to see him. She had no idea how it had happened. She had just that one conversation and her dim and distant memories to base an entire man on. There was not a jot of further information – except for a very ordinary-sounding address in Eastbourne – and before that all she knew was that he'd abandoned her shamelessly, leaving her with a mother who was next to useless, and a brother who seemed to have inherited the selfish abandoner gene. It was a miracle that Felicity had even made it to adulthood at all. And yet.

And yet there was this pull, like gravity. *Call him. Call him. Call him.*

She bit her lip one more time, then picked up her phone from the arm of the sofa and scrolled to Harry's name.

Come on then.

'Go on then,' said James, giving her a nudge, as if he knew instinctively what she was about to do. 'I'll put the kettle on.'

'No. Stay. Please.'

He sat back down beside her and put a hand on her knee. Felicity shut her eyes tight and tapped the button, moving the phone up to her ear. Then hastily took it away again and pressed the big red button.

'I can't bloody do it.'

'You can.'

'What if he answers?'

'That's kind of the point of a phone.'

'Dammit,' said Felicity, heart thumping big style now.

She tapped the green button twice and it picked up the last call. Felicity held the phone against her ear and prayed, but she wasn't sure if she was praying for him to answer or praying that he wouldn't.

'It's ringing, shush.' Felicity felt a bit sick.

'I didn't say anything,' said James, in a stage whisper.

And then, just like that…

'Hello?' came a voice.

'Hello, is that… is that Harry?'

'Felicity? Is that you?'

'Yes, yes, it's me.'

Harry let out a long breath. 'Oh, thank God. It's you.'

'Yes. It's me.'

'You found me.'

'I did.'

In the background, Felicity could hear muffled voices. Talking. Laughing. And music, playing softly, vaguely familiar. Old school Beatles or similar. Her mother had always loved to play rock and roll. Felicity wondered what Harry's "other" family was like. She felt strangely jealous all of a sudden.

Harry cleared his throat. 'I don't know how you found me, Felicity, but I'm bloody glad you did. I felt like such an idiot for not leaving my number but you seemed so… mad. You were so cross. I didn't think you would ever want to talk to me again.'

Felicity swallowed back tears. 'I am cross. Of course I'm cross.'

'Of course you are.' Harry sounded crestfallen.

'I will probably always be cross with you. But that doesn't mean I don't want to talk to you. I do. I really do. I'm so sorry.'

There was a long pause, following by a deep sigh.

'You have nothing to be sorry for, do you hear me?'

The tears were flowing now and Felicity could barely speak. James slipped an arm around her shoulders, which only made her cry harder.

'Please... can I see you?' she managed. Another pause. She looked down and saw she'd unknowingly ripped the tissue James had handed her into a thousand tiny pieces. Her lap was full of confetti. She heard a sniffing sound from the other end of the line, then some frantic throat-clearing.

'Of course. You can see me whenever you want.'

'Okay.'

'Okay.'

His voice changed. She could hear his smile and it was like the sun coming out.

'Are you working on Friday? Maybe I can meet you after work and take you for dinner?' He paused. 'Is that too much? Say if it's too much.'

Felicity exhaled. 'That sounds lovely. I finish at five.'

'Perfect. I'll be there then.'

'Perfect.'

'Bye, Felicity.'

'Bye.'

'See you Friday.'

'Will do.'

'Bye.'

'Bye.'

The line went dead.

There was a long silence. Then Felicity let out a noise that was half gasp, half giggle. She wiped at her cheeks as elation washed over her.

'That was my dad,' she said, voice wobbling.

James gave her arm a squeeze. 'That was your dad.'

'He's coming to take me out for dinner.'

'Brilliant. Proud of you.'

'Thank you for being here,' said Felicity, her voice raspy in her throat. And then, 'Buggeration.'

'What? What happened?' said James.

A wave of panic washed down Felicity's spine. 'Shouldn't I have asked him twenty questions or something? You know, to prove he really is who he says he is? What if this is all some kind of scam.'

She cast her eyes around wildly as if looking for a hidden camera. Tissue confetti fluttered to the floor.

'But I thought you said you recognised him,' said James calmly.

'I thought I did, but I was only six, right? I mean, I have these vague memories all jumbled up in my head but I don't really know, do I? He could be any old bloke. He could be an axe murderer, come to prey on me in my vulnerable state.'

'It's just dinner,' said James. 'Relax. If you like I can come?'

'Thanks, but I think I have to do this alone.'

CHAPTER 14

Charlie was transfixed by the new rabbits that had been dropped off by the RSPCA. He couldn't take his eyes off them in fact. Felicity could hardly blame him for that. They were mega-cute. Six miniature lops, huge fluffy feet and long droopy ears, and the softest grey fur. And a raggedy old pigeon with a twisted beak that Charlie instantly and very proudly named Half Pint.

Felicity smiled when she walked past their room and found Charlie staring down at the rabbits, long after his shift had ended.

'Don't you have a home to go to?' she whispered gently, walking up behind him.

'I don't know how either of you ever go home,' he whispered back and she could hear the smile in his voice. They stood side by side for a moment, staring down at the tiny balls of fluff who were lolloping their way slowly around the enclosure, nibbling up tiny morsels of dropped food and looking thoroughly at home already.

'When are you going to ask me?' said Charlie suddenly, not taking his eyes from the rabbits.

'Ask you what?' said Felicity, wondering what he was about to insinuate or whether he could read her thoughts.

'What I did, of course,' he said flatly.

'I always thought that was terribly bad form.'

Charlie laughed lightly. 'You watch too many movies.'

Felicity shrugged. 'That's certainly true, yes.'

They walked reluctantly away from the rabbits. When they reached the staff room, Charlie turned to her, an earnest look in his eyes.

'It's fine to ask me. I'd rather you did. I can feel you wanting to.'

'I do want to…' said Felicity. *Tread carefully.* 'But I really don't feel like I have a right to know, Charlie. It's totally up to you what you tell people.'

Charlie blew out a breath. 'I hacked into a retail site and ordered a lot of stuff on other people's credit cards. Expensive shit. Laptops, tablets, smartwatches. My parents' faces when it all turned up on a lorry. Priceless, basically.'

'Okay…'

As he spoke, Charlie's eyes were flashing with something she couldn't quite determine. Something like pride, perhaps. Or was it shame?

'The thing is, I don't even know why I did it. It's not like I needed the money. And I couldn't sell the stuff after that, so it all sat there in our garage, can you imagine? Until it got seized anyways.'

'You really don't know why?'

'I was just bored, I guess.'

Felicity forced herself not to look away. 'When I'm bored, I binge eat. Not so illegal but then again, a bit more punishing on the waistline.'

Charlie smiled weakly. 'I'll try that next time.'

'Next time?'

'Next time I'm bored.'

'Right.'

His brow crinkled. 'I do like to burn stuff too. My mum always said I was a pyromaniac even when I was a kid. Maybe I'll try that.'

Felicity tried to hide her shock. 'I mean, I was thinking something more like knitting?'

Charlie guffawed.

'Or crochet,' she went on. 'Crochet's ever so popular these days. Or cross-stitch, how about some nice wholesome cross-stitch?'

'Is that what you do?' said Charlie, taking a step closer to her.

Felicity's turn to laugh out loud. 'God, no. I'm crap at all that stuff. My friend Sophie is the crafter of the group. I can't do anything like that even remotely competently.'

Charlie lifted one eyebrow, his dark eyes flashing. 'So, what do you do when you're bored?' If he wasn't ten years her junior, she would have sworn he was flirting.

Felicity took a small step backwards. 'I told you. I binge eat. And I watch *Die Hard*. Or, you know, *Die Hard 2, Die Hard 3 – better known as Die Hard with a Vengeance – or Live Free or Die Hard... heck*, even *A Good Day to Die Hard* if I'm really desperate.'

'There are other films, you know,' said Charlie. 'You don't have to watch old movies all the time.'

'I'm aware. And also, ouch.'

Charlie chuckled softly. 'So long as you know.'

'But do these modern contrivances have Bruce Willis in a vest? That's the crucial question,' said Felicity.

'Who's Bruce Willis?'

'Thanks for making me feel like a dinosaur, yet again.'

'No problem.'

Felicity softened. 'Look, Charlie, you're working out your punishment, you've been honest about what you did. You'll get no judgement here, okay? Just enjoy being around the animals. They are loving having you around.'

Charlie's eyes widened slightly at her words.

'Sorry. Did I say something wrong?' said Felicity gently, putting a hand on his arm.

Charlie blinked at her. 'I'm sure you'll find this hard to believe, but no one has ever said anything like that to me before.' He shrugged. 'They don't say much to me at all, to be honest. Not since I was like thirteen or fourteen. I became invisible at that point.'

Felicity felt tears spring to her eyes and blinked them back hastily. 'Actually, I know exactly what you mean,' she said.

Charlie's eyes were like two dinner plates now. 'Really?'

Felicity nodded. 'You don't got an exclusive on crap childhoods, I'm afraid,' she said, with a half-smile.

'I'm sorry to hear that.' Charlie's forehead crinkled, which somehow made him even more attractive.

'Anyway, this is not about me,' said Felicity, waving a hand. 'The point is, the animals like you. And they are excellent judges of character, trust me.'

Charlie moved a little closer. 'And you?' he said, eyes soft.

Alarm bells.

'We like you just fine,' she said hastily. 'Just don't set fire to the place or anything. Let's get home before Andrea locks us both in.'

On the way out, Charlie put his hand on her arm.

'Felicity?'

'Yes, Charlie?'

'Thank you.'

'You're welcome.'

'I know what he did,' said Felicity that night as she snuggled against James's chest on the sofa.

'You do? Nice detectoring… er, detectiving… er… detectoristing? Anyway, nice work, Miss Brooks.'

Felicity giggled. 'Thanks but I didn't have to do any. He told me.'

'And?'

'It's not quite axe murdering.'

'Disappointing. Armed robbery?'

'Not exactly.'

'Embezzlement?'

Felicity blinked. 'I don't know what that is.'

'No one does,' said James. 'So, what then?'

'Theft. Online. Laptops and such.'

'Right. Makes sense.'

'He reckons he was just bored. But I still don't understand the shameless rule-breaking.'

'Me neither,' said James, his chest rising and falling steadily beneath her ear. 'You know I'm a total stickler.'

She smiled, inhaling the reassuring scent of him. 'I know, bless you. Never so much as stole a pick 'n' mix, did you?'

'I never did. Couldn't. The guilt would eat me up.'

Felicity thought for a moment. 'That was the weird thing. Charlie didn't seem that bothered. He claims he was just looking for something to do.'

'So? Maybe he was.'

'Yes… maybe.'

'You don't sound convinced.'

'I think there's something else going on. I'm just not sure why or what.'

'Detective Brooks is on the case.'

'Damn straight,' Felicity said, with a giggle.

'Well… be careful,' said James, his voice catching in his throat.

'I always am,' she whispered.

'No, you're not,' he said, and laughed.

There was a pause. Felicity's eyes were beginning to close when he spoke again, softly into her ear.

'Felicity…?'

'What?'

'Do you ever…?'

'What?'

'Have you ever thought…?'

Felicity lifted her face to look at him. 'Spit it out then, Penguin Man.'

He swallowed and she could see the muscle in his jaw clench. Sexy as the movement was, her heart gave a little lurch of anxiety.

'Have you ever thought about getting married?' he said carefully.

Felicity gave a little squeal which she tried – and failed – to cover with a cough.

'Sorry, just got something caught in my throat there,' she said, buying herself some time, pulse thumping. 'What did you just say?'

'You heard me.'

'James Cowley. Are you proposing to me right now?'

James shook his head frantically. A little too vigorously in Felicity's opinion.

'No, no, nothing like that. I just wondered…'

'I mean,' Felicity cut in, 'you could at least have hesitated for a second or two.'

'Sorry, I'm panicking,' said James.

Felicity's heart gave a little jump in her chest. 'It's not like I haven't thought about it.'

'You have?' James's eyes grew wide.

'Yes, of course I have. But after everything that's happened, I'm a little frightened at the thought of it. I'll be honest, I definitely wouldn't want to rush into anything.'

'Oh no, no, of course not.' Felicity could feel James's heart pounding in his chest.

'And,' she went on, 'I definitely wouldn't want the whole big wedding thing. Not just because of Bex and Adam, but regardless of that...'

James looked down at her, eyes fond. 'Because it's not really you?' he said, gently.

'It's not really me,' said Felicity, with a nod.

'Hmmm, I thought as much. I mean, not that I've thought about it much.' Now it was James's turn to get flustered.

'Are you... blushing?'

'I don't blush. Manly men like me definitely don't blush.'

'You are. You're blushing.'

'I most certainly am not.'

'James, please tell me you weren't actually going to propose to me just then.'

He shook his head even more strongly than before and something inside Felicity twisted like a knife.

'I can assure you, I definitely wasn't proposing. You don't need to worry about that.' He sounded a little... off, all of a sudden.

'Good.'

'Good.'

It was good. Wasn't it? Then why did she suddenly feel so sideswiped?

'Right then.'

'Glad we got that straight.'

Cue awkward silence.

Felicity put her head back on his chest and they both went back to staring at the TV with the distinct feeling that nothing was actually straight whatsoever.

CHAPTER 15

The next day at work Felicity threw herself into cat cuddles and taking the dogs for walks and tried not to think about the proposal that wasn't a proposal or the approaching meet-up with her long-lost father/potential weirdo stranger scam artist. She was so deeply not-thinking-about-it while she cleaned out the rabbit run in the corridor that she didn't hear Andrea calling her until her boss's voice was practically booming.

'Felicity? For goodness' sake. I've been calling and calling you. I nearly had to actually get up off this chair and everything. Can you please find Charlie something to do? He's hanging around my office like a bad smell.'

'Sorry. Yes, of course. Send him this way.'

Charlie stuck his head around the door frame and grinned.

'Hi, Charlie,' said Felicity, pulling fresh straw from a bale and laying it out in their little hutch bit, scooching the biggest rabbit gently over as she did so. Andrea and Felicity had named him Bugs because of his perfect grey fur and little white markings. In standard fashion, Charlie didn't have the faintest idea who Bugs Bunny was.

'I smell very nice – honest.'

'I'm sure you do,' said Felicity with a smile. 'Now come and help me get the lunchtime feeds ready for the kittens.'

The previous week they'd had a delivery of five tiny ginger kittens from a farmer down the road whose cat always liked "visiting" the neighbourhood females. They were so tiny they were still having milk replacer, which meant a lot of mixing up of powder and then the delightful task of having to hand-feed them. They'd named them all after vegetables for some reason Felicity couldn't quite remember now.

'It's a hard life,' said Felicity, scooping up the first kitten, the one they'd named Parsnip, and feeling its soft warm fur against her cheek.

Charlie was watching her so intently her face heated. 'Reckon you've got the best job ever,' he said.

'Reckon I might just have,' said Felicity, with the little body purring away in her hand. She passed it to Charlie. 'Here, you do this one and I'll have this' – she scooped another one out of the run – 'little dot here.'

'Carrot, I think that one is?'

'Is it? I thought this one was Carrot and that one with the white feet was Pumpkin?'

'Who cares?' Charlie practically gulped as he took the tiny body, holding it close to his chest and whispering in its ear.

'Told you they all loved you. You're a natural,' said Felicity after a moment.

'Do you think?'

'I can see it.'

Charlie flushed with pride as he stared down at the little kitten, his dark hair flopping over his face in a way that made her think of James, although his hair wasn't quite as unruly. He really was very handsome, even if he was practically half her age.

'You're staring,' said Charlie, after a moment, his eyes not leaving the kitten against his chest.

Felicity felt her face and ears grow even redder and inwardly cursed her red hair and pale skin for giving her away yet again.

'I was looking at the kitten,' she said primly.

'Sure you were.'

They worked in silence then, Felicity trying to remain professional as she showed Charlie the best way to hold the tiny kittens while they syringed the milk replacer gently into their mouths. As they fed the first two the other three were mewling from their box, impatiently scrabbling over each other as they waited their turn.

'You two all right in here?' said Andrea, passing the doorway.

'He's really getting the hang of it,' said Felicity.

'Good stuff,' said Andrea, and sailed out of view.

'You paid me another compliment,' said Charlie, gently placing down the first kitten and trying to select another from the undulating pile of fur balls in front of them.

'I'm nice,' said Felicity, giving her own kitten a last kiss on the top of the head.

'Oh, I know that,' said Charlie in a low voice. Felicity looked up. Was he blushing again? This was getting awkward.

She popped her kitten back in the box and began backing away. 'I'll let you finish up here, just make sure you don't miss the little runty one at the back, and don't drop any, whatever you do.'

'As if I would.'

'Thanks, so much… er… I'll see you in a bit.'

She practically ran down the corridor.

'He fancies you,' said Andrea, without looking up from a pile of sign-over papers, as Felicity walked into her office.

'Who?' said Felicity, trying to sound nonchalant.

Andrea rolled her eyes at this pathetic effort. 'Charlie, of course.'

'Nonsense.'

'He does. He keeps hanging around after work trying to get a chance to speak to you. I have to practically march him to the exit.'

'No, he doesn't.'

Andrea nodded emphatically. 'Yes, he does. It's become quite the awkward end to the day.'

'Why didn't you tell me?'

'I figured he'd get over it in a few days but it seems to be getting worse.'

'Oh, I'm sure it's not that at all.' Felicity's words rang hollow even to her own ears. 'He just seems to really like it here, maybe that's why he's hanging around. You should have seen him with those kittens earlier.'

Andrea looked up then, peering at Felicity over her grubby reading glasses, which made her pale-blue eyes even bigger.

'Want me to ask them to move him somewhere else? I can, if it's a problem.'

'Nothing I can't handle,' said Felicity, lifting her chin.

'Good.'

'See ya in a bit.'

'Will do.'

Felicity headed to the break room to find a jumper as it was inexplicably cold in the centre that day. She opened her locker and her mouth dropped open.

Sitting in her locker in the break room was a small shoebox. It was wrapped in pink paper with one of those cheap stick-on bows in red on the top.

A shudder went through her.

Last time someone had given her a mysterious box it had contained an engagement ring. A stunning Tiffany ring, no less. A stunning Tiffany ring that was meant for someone else. One of the many girls, in fact, that she had unknowingly played second fiddle to over the years. Cold prickled the back of her neck.

Surely Adam couldn't have left this here, could he? Surely all that was done now. She looked over her shoulder, half expecting him to be leaning against the door frame. He always had liked surprising her.

Satisfied there was no one around, she tentatively opened the box, and gasped. Inside was the most horrific thing she had ever seen. And she had been forced to watch *Hellraiser* as a kid. Twice. Her brother had a lot to answer for.

Slowly, ever so slowly, she drew out the item, a small wooden rabbit. It looked as though it had been hand-carved as its features were rather crudely drawn in felt-tip pen and in its tiny (creepy) paws it was holding a blood-red heart. On the heart was written, again in felt-tip, the words, *Be Mine*.

There was no way Adam would have ever left something so hideous even at the height of his stalking.

Felicity let out a sigh of relief, then bit her lip. If not Adam, then who? And why?

CHAPTER 16

Friday night came round faster than she was ready for.

At 5pm as she finished her shift and locked the big heavy barn doors behind her, her father (her actual real-life father!) was already waiting in the car park, moving from foot to foot as if he'd been there a while.

It was a balmy evening and Harry was wearing a pale-green shirt and chinos, making him look a little like he was going on holiday. As soon as she saw him, her body relaxed, shoulders dropping clear inches. It was really him. It was her father. She was sure of it now. Definitely not an axe murderer. She could feel it, somehow, a long-lost thread of connection drifting between them like a gossamer spider's web. Her heart gave a little lurch.

'Evening, Felicity,' he said, a little shyly.

'Evening,' she replied, her voice catching.

'Good evening,' came a third voice, and there was Andrea hurtling towards them across the gravel.

'I thought you'd gone home already,' said Felicity, weakly, even though Andrea had barely acknowledged her presence. She was homing in on Harry, her arms already outstretched.

'I forgot something,' said Andrea quickly to Felicity, a fixed smile on her face. And then, louder, 'Well, helllooooooo. You must be Harry. How delightful to meet you at last.'

As she pulled back from two ridiculously un-Andrea-like air kisses, Harry was openly staring.

'Erm. Hello. Yes, hello there. And you are...?' he said, his already deep voice suddenly a semitone deeper.

Andrea giggled, actually giggled, like a small child.

Felicity rolled her eyes. 'This is Andrea. She's my boss. She doesn't normally... I mean she's not normally...' Her voice tailed off as she realised neither of them was paying any attention to her at all.

'Ahem,' she tried, again.

Harry didn't even turn his head towards her. He and Andrea were standing, transfixed, as if neither of them had ever seen another human before.

'Sorry, darling,' he said eventually. 'What was that you were saying?'

'Never mind. And don't "darling" me. We're not there yet I'm afraid. Shall we go?' Felicity felt angry again all of a sudden. Protective, maybe even a little jealous. It was a strange feeling to be having about your own father.

'Oh yes, right, of course. Lovely to meet you, Andrea,' he said smoothly. 'I hope to see you again.'

'You can count on it,' said Andrea in her filthiest voice.

'No, you absolutely won't,' said Felicity, escorting Harry away and throwing Andrea a warning look over her shoulder. Andrea simply shrugged as if to say, 'What?'

Twenty minutes later, Felicity and Harry were in the dismal generic pizza restaurant on the high street, seated either side of a rickety wooden table on two rather uncomfortable stools, in a semi-awkward state of silence. Felicity sipped at her drink while they waited for their food to arrive, and steeled herself. Her father had made the effort to see her after all this time. He must have things he wanted to say.

After a few minutes, when he still hadn't spoken, she tried a little light sighing.

'Sorry,' he said, as if reading her mind. 'I'm just getting my thoughts in order.'

'Take your time.'

'Your friend Andrea…' he began.

'She's my boss,' snapped Felicity.

'Your boss is…'

'Don't say it.'

'Say what?'

Felicity sighed again. 'Don't say that you think she's surprisingly hot under all that cat hair and fleece.'

Harry lifted his eyebrows. 'She really is…'

'But can we not spend our first evening together talking about her? If you don't mind?'

Harry shifted in his seat. 'Yes, of course. Sorry. Forgive an old man a little distraction.' He let out a long breath. 'It's so good to see you, Felicity.'

'It's good to see you too,' she said, just stopping herself from saying "Dad" out loud. It was too weird. It was too soon. And she had to remember to be mad.

'We have so much to catch up on.'

'Tell me about it,' said Felicity. 'Starting with where the hell you've been for the last twenty-seven years.'

'On the south coast. Eastbourne, mainly.'

'With…?'

Harry bowed his head. 'With my soon-to-be ex-wife and our two children.'

Felicity nearly spat out her tonic water. 'I have more brothers? Sisters? What?' This was not something she'd even considered.

'One of each. Half-siblings, I guess. Sorry. Maybe I should have led with that.'

'You think? Woah. This is huge. How old are they?'

'Eleven and fourteen. Sammy and Zoe. You'd love them.' A pause. 'You are going to love them,' he corrected.

Felicity let this sink in for a moment. Harry had other children. She couldn't help the pang of jealousy that jolted through her. He'd been there for them. Why couldn't he have been there for her and Tristan?

'What else do you want to know?'

Felicity swallowed back the lump in her throat.

'And what do you do for work?'

'Um. That's an interesting question, shall we say?'

Somewhere in the back of her head, an alarm was ringing.

Harry must have seen her face change. 'Not like that. I'm not on the sick or anything.'

'I was thinking more criminal activity, actually,' she said with a chuckle.

Harry pretended to clutch his chest. 'Ouch. That hurts. No nothing like that either.'

'What then?'

'Well, let's say I'm a painter and decorator by trade.'

A fractured memory of a shabby front door resurfaced. There had been an argument. Her mother storming off. Red paint everywhere. Felicity screwed up her eyes to try and grasp more of the memory but it was just out of reach.

'You weren't doing that when we were little, were you?'

Harry's brows knitted together at that.

'No, I was a sales rep back then. I retrained about ten years ago. I enjoy it. It's a bit dull at times, fair enough, but it pays... well, some of the bills at least. This second divorce might bankrupt me though.'

Felicity could feel her palms prickling with sweat.

'You said she's a soon-to-be ex-wife? Do you still live together? I'm so sorry it hasn't worked out.'

Harry hung his head. 'Got what I deserved, didn't I? Eileen, her name is. She was a stunner when I met her but she turned out to be an absolute shrew.'

'D… I mean, Harry. That's a terrible thing to say.'

Harry turned to look at her, his eyes sparkling. 'Did you nearly call me Dad just then?'

Felicity huffed an awkward laugh. 'It just slipped out. Don't get used to it.'

'I liked it,' said Harry.

They smiled at each other for a moment or two. Felicity was the first to look away.

'I have to ask. Did you become a decorator because of the door?'

Her father's eyes grew wide. 'You remember The Door? You must have been just a nipper then.'

'That explains why I don't remember much. But I do remember the red paint.'

'Your mother,' said Harry, by way of explanation, sighing a little at the mention of her. 'That's right, your mother wanted a red front door and I made a total hash of it. She was furious with me for some reason.'

'I remember that much.'

'She was always very passionate about everything. She could convince anyone to do anything she wanted. And she wanted a lot of things. The moon on a stick and the sun too. It was frustrating at times but also exhilarating.'

'And from that one row, you thought you'd change career?'

'I told you, she could have sold ice to Iceland, that one. We rowed a lot but we always made up.'

'Gross,' said Felicity, with a grin.

'Not like that. I mean, a little bit like that but there was so much more to her.'

'I wish I'd known more of her, you know, what she was like before… you left?'

'I hardly dare ask what she was like afterwards,' he said, almost under his breath. Felicity had to lean in to hear him. 'I mean, I know things weren't good, I know that of course, but you were there. You saw it.'

She hadn't been prepared to talk about her mother yet. Tears sprang to her eyes.

'She was… damaged,' she said simply.

'I'm sorry,' said Harry.

'It's okay,' said Felicity. But it wasn't. Not really.

CHAPTER 17

Felicity's mother, Jocelyn, passed away when Felicity was a teenager, after years of alcohol and drug abuse and, they'd discovered much later, promiscuity too. She'd even cheated on Harry, more than once, perhaps, and yet when Harry left them, walking out at Christmas in the middle of a family dinner, Jocelyn went completely to pieces. Tristan had gone to search him out as soon as he was old enough to do so, leaving Felicity to mop up her mother physically and psychologically, as best she could. It had been the worst kind of childhood, one where she was forced to grow up way too fast and had no one to help her cope with the loss of her father, no male role models and barely a female one either. When Jocelyn wasn't drunk, she was sleeping it off or wallowing in her own misery. When Jocelyn finally died, sad as it was, the overwhelming feeling was relief.

Sitting across from her father now, who was arguably the reason for all this misery, Felicity knew she should be mad. She was mad. Perhaps it would be with her forever. But somehow, it was also good to be able to talk to someone from her own family. Someone who could understand. Someone who knew Jocelyn. Someone who knew.

That night, Felicity curled up against James and tried to explain what it had been like to finally spend time with her father. But the words were elusive. Bobby Charlton had settled himself under her chin and was purring for England. His soft black fur tickled her skin.

'Mainly, I just feel exhausted,' she said. 'Like I've been hit by not just a ton of bricks but maybe a whole houseful. If they use more than a ton of bricks to build a house, I really have no idea how many bricks a ton might be but I imagine it's quite a lot.'

James squeezed her shoulder. 'I'm not surprised. It must have been really emotional.'

'It's strange. It's like he's always been there and yet I know nothing about him, does that make sense? It's peculiar.'

'I can imagine,' murmured James. 'I mean, I can't really, but I'm trying.'

Felicity snuggled in closer. 'You are so lovely,' she said simply.

They sat in silence for a few moments.

'Felicity…' said James quietly. 'I've been thinking.'

'Did it hurt?'

He squeezed her side, making her giggle. 'Ha ha, you're hilarious, Brooks.'

'I know.'

'But I'm being serious.'

'Yikes. Not again.'

'I've been wondering if it bothers you that I used to share this house with my ex. You know, with Erika?'

Felicity stiffened at the name. Tall, glamorous and exotic-looking, Erika was everything Felicity was not. 'Well, now it does.'

'Sorry. I didn't mean to bring her up.'

'It's okay. But you only get one a year, right?'

'Right. Sorry. So… does it?'

Felicity turned to face him. His brow was crinkled with worry. She smoothed a hair back from his face while she thought it over.

'I mean, it's not something I think about on the regular or anything.' His eyes relaxed a little. 'But now you mention it, I suppose it's not ideal...'

James nodded gravely, his blue eyes wide. 'That's what I thought. I was just wondering—'

'But you love this place.'

James looked very intense. Felicity felt her cheeks growing warm. She loved it when he got all serious. 'I do. But I love you more. And I think...'

'Yes?' Her heart was pounding now.

'I think we should buy a place together.'

Until that moment, Felicity hadn't known how much it did bother her. But at his words, an invisible weight lifted from her shoulders. He was right. Erika's shadow was all over the house. The stark, minimalist kitchen, the Japanese wall art, the aesthetically pleasing but ultimately super-uncomfortable furniture. The only thing James had chosen in the whole place was this huge snuggly sofa they were now curled up on. It was incidentally also the only thing in the house that Felicity really liked.

'I think so too.'

James's mouth lifted in delight at her words and he leant in to kiss her hungrily, taking the breath from her body.

'Hold on, hold on,' she said, after a few lingering moments.

He chuckled against her lips. A low, rumbling sound that made her shiver with delight. 'Sorry, I just love kissing you.'

She put a hand on his Disney prince chest, muscles taut beneath, and leant back.

'Believe me, not as much as I love you kissing me.' He leant towards her again at that, eyes twinkling, but she pushed against him. 'But aren't you forgetting something?'

'What?'

'Well, how about the fact that I work for an animal charity and have no money whatsoever?'

'What about your flat?'

She had almost forgotten about her flat. Tiny, bijou, cosy. How she had loved living in that place.

'It was rented, remember? I didn't even get my deposit back because they said I'd, ahem, left it in a worse state than when I found it. Which, frankly, I find very insulting because I even scrubbed the oven for a whole half an hour.'

James laughed. 'Yes, but your idea of scrubbing an oven…'

'What is that supposed to mean?'

He just stared at her, eyebrows raised, until she had to admit, he was absolutely right. 'I hate housework,' she said with a shrug. 'You know this.'

'Me too,' he replied.

'So…? How are we gonna buy a house together with no money? And make sure we can still get a cleaner in sometimes?'

He waved a hand around. 'Because this place is going to raise quite enough for what we need.'

Felicity followed his gaze. It was an amazing house, a converted Victorian pile right in the middle of the most expensive area to live in the whole of Derbyshire, Chancery Downs. Or Chelsea Downs as the locals liked to call it because of the abundance of Range Rovers in the area.

'I can't ask you to do that,' she said softly.

'I want to,' he said.

'Doesn't Erika…?' Her voice died on her lips, the sentence unfinished.

James shook his head. 'I bought out her share when she… left. It wasn't much. She did all the furnishings and I paid for it all. That was pretty standard.'

'So she just wanted you for your cheque book?'

'Something like that.'

'Stupid girl didn't know what she had.' Felicity smiled, leaning in to kiss him. A haunted look passed across his face just for a second, and then he smiled and brushed her lips lightly with his.

'And I suppose you do?'

She nodded vigorously. She'd mercifully only come across Erika once in the flesh but she knew all she needed to know. Beautiful Erika was an idiot to let this incredible man go. Pure and simple. 'Hell, yeah I do.'

'Then let's go house-hunting, Miss Brooks.'

Goose bumps prickled down her spine.

'I'm getting on Rightmove right now.'

'Not… right this minute I hope.' James smiled, leaning in for another kiss.

She giggled. 'Not exactly right this minute… no way I can concentrate while you're doing that, PM.'

James laughed, his kisses moving down to her neck and making her forget her own name let alone where she lived. 'Sorry not sorry.'

'Can you promise not to mention your ex-girlfriend again for a bit?' breathed Felicity.

'I'll do my best.'

Everything went a bit blurry after that. In the best way.

CHAPTER 18

*T*he following day was Andrea's only day off of the week, which meant it was just Charlie and Felicity at the centre.

It'll be fine, Felicity told herself as she dumped her stuff in the staff room. She could handle this. She was a grown-up, right? So long as no actual handling went on, everything would be fine. Now, where was that boy?

'Charlie?' she said tentatively into the corridor.

'In here,' came a voice from Andrea's office.

'What are you doing in there? No stealing shit.'

'Would I?'

'Or setting fire to shit.'

'Come on. What do you take me for?'

'What are you doing then?' said Felicity. She rounded the corner and then let out a little scream. 'What the hell *are* you doing?'

Standing before her was Charlie, leaning on the edge of Andrea's desk, wearing nothing but a pair of boxer shorts. His tanned chest was smooth and firm and muscled and Felicity tried not to stare.

'Charlie,' she said as firmly as she could manage in the circumstances. 'Put your clothes on at once.'

'Don't tell me you don't want a piece of this?' Charlie waved a hand down his body, a wide grin plastered on his face.

Felicity tried to remain indignant. 'I most definitely do not.'

Charlie stood up, and moved closer to her, swaying seductively, not remotely put off by the fact she now had her hands over her eyes.

'Put some clothes on, what are you playing at?' She tried to sound light-hearted. Nonchalant. Carefree, even. And failed.

Nearly-naked Charlie continued towards her, not even perturbed when she started humming to herself and rocking back and forth to block out the sight of his approaching bare chest and dangerously-defined six-pack.

'Put it away. I mean it,' said Felicity, her voice getting more and more high-pitched.

Charlie smiled lazily. 'Come on, Felicity, you've been giving me the come-on for weeks.'

'I most certainly have not.'

'You have. You kept my rabbit and everything.'

Felicity had to resist the urge to laugh. Bless him. It was kind of sweet. 'You left me that… thing?'

'Of course I did. Made it myself,' he said proudly. His eyes were on her lips now. They were inches apart.

'Will you stop that?' she snapped.

'What?' he said innocently, moving his head towards hers. Felicity took a step back, breathing heavily. His cheeky lopsided grin was dangerously attractive but mostly she just felt absolutely baffled to find herself in this situation.

There was only one thing for it. Felicity put her hands over her eyes again. 'Charlie. Put your clothes back on right now,' she said in the loudest and firmest voice she could muster. 'Or I'll have to ask you to leave.'

He stopped moving towards her. 'You're serious?'

'Deadly.'

'Oh, man.' She felt rather than saw Charlie turn abruptly to the side. Felicity turned her head to the right and opened her fingers just in time to see his perfectly formed arse in his boxers as he bent to gather his clothes.

'Oh my God, my eyes,' exclaimed Felicity, no longer even pretending she wasn't looking.

'But I thought… I'm so sorry. I…'

'Just go and get dressed. I can't talk to you about this while you're… like that.'

'I'm going, I'm going,' Charlie shouted frantically, retreating down the corridor, clutching his clothes against him.

'In fact, Charlie, I don't think I can talk to you about this at all at the moment. Why don't you go home? I can handle things here today. We'll talk tomorrow.'

Charlie stopped and turned towards her, looking so sad that Felicity's heart twisted in her chest. He was a good lad deep down, she felt sure of it, and she hated being responsible for that face. 'Aw, Felicity, at least let me stay and help you.'

Be firm. 'No. I think you need to leave. Thank you.' Her cheeks were burning, partly with fury and partly with mortification. At least, that's what she told herself.

Charlie disappeared and came out of the staff room a few minutes later, fully dressed and looking sheepish.

'You won't…?' he said as he came towards her, forehead still wrinkled into a frown.

'What?'

'Tell Andrea? Or James?'

Felicity laughed then. 'Oh, no. Don't you worry about that. James definitely doesn't need to know any of this.' She was turning the handle to the front door now, thinking, *James is getting told the minute I get home.*

'Thanks,' said Charlie, huffing a sigh of relief.

'I mean, I probably should.'

'Do you think he's gonna wanna smack me about?'

'Yes, most likely. At the very least. Wouldn't you?'

Charlie shrugged. 'I s'pose so. Is he quite violent then, your fella?'

'You'll find out soon enough I imagine.'

'Oh, please don't tell him. I said I was sorry.'

'You probably should have thought of that before you decided to do… whatever this was.'

'I know but…'

'Bye then,' said Felicity, ushering him towards the exit.

'Bye…' came his plaintive little voice as she slammed the door behind him.

Her heart lurched as she turned back into the centre.

How did she always get herself into these pickles?

For some reason that she couldn't quite name, Felicity didn't tell James at all in the end, which, as it turned out, was a bit of a mistake.

ouse-hunting is not all it's cracked up to be, thought Felicity two weeks later, as they wandered down the road after their fourth completely miserable traipse around a hovel masquerading as a place they were supposed to want to live in.

All those programmes on TV. All those times the people turn down an absolutely gorgeous house because the kitchen doesn't have an island or the garden doesn't face west or whatever it might be. And we can't even find one that doesn't have rats, she thought.

'Well, that was the most depressing one yet,' said James, as they got into his vintage red Mustang, which had needed a run out. It looked ultra-cool but sounded like a jet engine and definitely wasn't doing the environment any favours. They had to speak really loudly to have any chance of a conversation.

'You're telling me. Why do people think a bath in a bedroom is ever a good idea? Who the hell wants to have a bath in an enormous airy room to start with? Brrrrrrr.' She mimed being cold. 'And those potty individuals seem to have actually got rid of the existing bathroom to do it. Madness.'

'To be fair I'd happily sit and watch you in the bath all day,' said James.

Her body flushed with heat. 'I do wish you wouldn't say things like that while you're driving,' said Felicity, running a cheeky hand along his thigh.

James let out a yelp. 'You really don't want to do THAT while I'm driving, that's for sure.'

'Spoilsport.' Felicity's hand stilled but she didn't remove it. James had always been really broad and muscly but his thighs were something else entirely. One of her favourite bits of him, in fact. If she was allowed a favourite bit.

'Anyway, it wasn't the bath in the bedroom that bothered me. It was the bizarre 1950's kitchen that they've clearly ripped out of somewhere else and tried to bodge into the space. The house was only built a few years ago, why didn't they just leave the one they had? How bad can it have been?'

'And it smelt of mice droppings. Did you notice that?'

'Well yes, there was that.'

Ten minutes later they were pulling up to the final viewing of the day. A little white painted cottage on the outskirts of town. Felicity's pick, this time. She thought it had potential. James wasn't so sure.

Waiting for them at the front gate was an extremely dapper-looking man with a perfectly groomed handlebar moustache. He was wearing a cravat and leaning on the bonnet of a long-nosed and very expensive-looking vintage Jaguar like something out of a comedy sketch show.

'I'm always worried when the estate agent is doing better than I am,' whispered James as they got out of the car. Felicity snorted.

'Hello there,' said the man in a nasally voice, introducing

himself as "Quentin" of all things. 'Ready to take a look at this little gem?'

'You bet,' said Felicity. It was a sweet-looking place, right along the road from one of their favourite pubs, with a little picket fence along the front and a large garden with a pond to the rear. Felicity had been studying the photos in great detail.

The estate agent couldn't have been less bothered about the sale.

'Er, yes, so here you have three bedrooms and a little upstairs office,' he was saying as they walked along the path to the front door. When they arrived he stepped to one side.

'You can go in first,' said Felicity politely, waving a hand.

But he shook his head. 'It's not huge so I'll just wait outside and you two head on in, okay?' said Quentin, getting out an ancient-looking mobile phone and jabbing at some numbers to make a call.

'Um, okay,' said Felicity, ducking her head under the lintel and walking into the hallway.

'That's not a great sign,' said James, following her in and closing the door behind him. 'But at least we can take our time.'

They were standing in a narrow hallway. Doors led off in all directions and straight ahead of them was a poky staircase leading upwards. Quite a change from what they were used to but James was being very game about it.

'Come on then, which way are we going first?'

Felicity felt a surge of excitement and started pushing doors open, shouting out the names of the rooms as she went as if James couldn't spot a dining room or a kitchen for himself.

'Ah, so this must be the lounge,' she said pointlessly as they entered a reasonably-sized room on the left side of the hallway, full of oversized sofas.

'What gave it away?' said James with a chuckle, but Felicity ignored him.

'Oooh, and this is the kitchen here.'

'I love how you're pretending you haven't already committed the floor plan to memory.'

'Shush, you. I just love Rightmove all right? Nothing wrong with that.'

'I'll be the judge of that.'

The kitchen was at the back of the house, and was surprisingly spacious given the size of the cottage from the outside.

'It's got drawers and everything,' said Felicity, opening and closing cupboards at random. The kitchen seemed reasonably new and well-fitted and had pleasing soft-close mechanisms on all the drawers and cupboards.

'Uh-huh,' said James. She could see he was rapidly losing the will to live.

Felicity didn't even give him the chance to flag. 'Come on, this way.' She led him back across the hallway to a smallish dining room, which had a hatch through to the kitchen. It was all very 1980s. Harmless and a little bit bland.

But when they got upstairs, they were in for a shock.

'Erm. Felicity? Can you come here for a second?'

At the top of the stairs, they had each gone the opposite way. Felicity had been admiring the small but functional bathroom, so she backtracked and peered over James's shoulder where he was standing in the entrance to one of the bedrooms.

'What the hell has been going on in there?' she said.

'I don't know, exactly,' said James, 'but it's making me feel rather uncomfortable.'

'You and me both,' said Felicity, scratching the back of her neck.

They stared for a while in silence. The room was a reasonable size but the carpet had been removed, revealing a blood-red floor in some kind of vinyl. And across the vinyl around the door were a series of deep gouges as if someone had been trying desperately to get out. The scratches went across the floor, up the door lintels, and right up to the top of the door frame. Making matters much, much worse, the room was completely empty and full of the overwhelming stench of dog hair and urine.

James and Felicity exchanged a look and backed out of the room without another word.

Downstairs, Quentin was still on the phone. He nodded when he saw them and ended the call.

'Ah, back already? What did you think? It's definitely got potential, hasn't it? Owner is open to offers.'

James didn't muck about.

'What on earth was going on in that top room?' he said, a mix of humour and disgust on his handsome face.

'Which room is that?'

'What do you mean which room? The one that stinks of dog? The one that looks like it used to house the Hound of the Baskervilles? That one,' said Felicity.

To his credit, Quentin didn't waver for a second.

'Oh yes, I should probably have mentioned that on your way in. Useful room, eh? The woman who lived here before used to breed puppies and that's where she kept them, I believe. So you have plenty of space if you are thinking of doing the same.'

James and Felicity both replied at the same time.

'How big were these puppies, exactly?' said Felicity.

'Just exactly how enormous were the puppies?' said James.

'Ooh, jinx,' said Felicity, then turned to Quentin, eyebrows raised. 'We're more cat people,' she said, putting her hands on her hips.

He shrugged. 'No idea I'm afraid. Can't stand animals of any kind. I can find out for you, if you like?'

Figures, thought Felicity.

'No need,' said James, already walking to the car.

It wasn't until they were a mile down the road that they

started cackling like a pair of old wives. 'Puppies. Puppies indeed!' said James when he was finally able to talk again.

'It was like a horror film,' said Felicity.

'We didn't even get to the basement. Has it got a basement?'

'It has, as it goes. Goes right under the house.'

'I knew it. That's where the bodies are hidden.'

They both guffawed again.

'Sorry,' snorted Felicity. 'It's not funny, but seriously, why didn't they mention it?'

'What do you mean?'

'On the listing. Why didn't they warn us? Everyone who's seen it must have thought the same thing. Love that they didn't even bother to mark the "Room of Doom" on there at all. No photos, nothing.'

'Hah,' said James. '"The Room of Doom".'

That set them both off again. When they finally stopped giggling, James grew serious.

'House-hunting is exhausting.'

'You got that right.'

'You know what we need? We need a break.'

'What exactly did you have in mind, Mr Penguin Man?'

'You'll see.'

CHAPTER 20

*A*nd true to his word, she did in fact see, the very next week when James came home with an envelope.

Not just any envelope. An envelope containing two plane tickets to Guernsey, the tiny island off the south coast of Britain. Not just any island off the coast of Britain either, but an island that also happened to be Felicity's childhood home.

When she opened it, Felicity squealed like a small child.

'Guernsey! Really? Are you serious?'

'I'm serious.'

'And how did you swing this with Andrea? I never take a holiday. I mean, apart from that one time I did take a holiday of course.'

The previous year Felicity had thrown caution to the wind and set off for Guernsey on a solo mission to rediscover her roots. It had proved to be momentous in more ways than one.

James beamed at her reaction and her insides did a little jig. 'It's only a long weekend this time I'm afraid, but work's all sorted. Andrea has Charlie coming in for extra shifts and I've got so much holiday left to take I'm constantly being nagged by HR. They practically cheered when I booked it.'

'Ah, that's nice,' said Felicity absently, trying not to think about Charlie in his boxers.

'What? Oh, no. No, it's not because they want me to have time off. Not for my well-being or any of that stuff. Only to save on admin. It stops their precious system from sending them constant reminders.'

'Ah.' Felicity flung her arms around his neck and kissed him on the cheek. 'Still, who cares? We're going to Guernsey. I'm so excited to show you around, you're going to love it. Where are we staying?'

James's cheeks grew a little bit rosy at that. 'It's a surprise,' he said eventually. 'Which means, I haven't actually booked anywhere yet but it's next on my list.'

'Don't worry,' Felicity said with a grin, 'I know just the place.'

'This one really is a keeper,' said Andrea, during break time the next day.

Felicity couldn't stop the smile that pulled at her lips. 'He really is. What on earth did I do to deserve such a man?'

'Thoughtful, kind, loves cats. Tick, tick, tick. Plus he's damn sexy,' said Andrea, stirring a third sugar into her coffee.

'Stop that.'

'What?'

'That.'

'Well, he is. What was it Adam called him again?'

Felicity's face flushed with sudden heat. 'A blond titan.'

'Yup. That's it in a nutshell. You must have done something pretty damn good in a former life, Miss Brooks.'

'I know, I know.'

Andrea turned and smiled at her. 'Or maybe the universe just decided it was finally your turn for a reward.'

'Aw.'

'I'm serious. You've had way more than your fair share of misery. You deserve it.'

Felicity didn't know what to do with that.

'I'm not used to you being sincere.'

'Ha ha, don't get used to it. The RSPCA inspector's on his way, best get a wriggle on, miss.'

'Yup, yup, I'm going,' said Felicity, rinsing her cup, glad of the distraction.

But as she went through the paperwork with Tony the inspector for two new feline arrivals – Bill and Ben, a pair of adorable Siamese cats she knew would be super easy to rehome – Felicity just could not stop thinking about what she was going to do to James when she got home. She'd forgotten all about Charlie and his shenanigans. In fact, she hadn't even asked Andrea where he was. It was only on her way home that she wondered if she should have told Andrea what he did.

When Thursday morning came around Felicity was almost apoplectic with excitement. She'd even been organised enough to pack her suitcase two days before, but then when it came to the morning they were due to go, she panicked that she couldn't remember what she'd put in there. James came into the bedroom to find her empty cabin bag on the bed and clothes and other sundries covering practically the entire surface of the floor, Felicity sat cross-legged in the middle of it all, stroking Gennie, Holly's mum, who had curled up on her legs the second she sat down.

'What on earth happened in here?' he said, pretending to be horrified, a smile tugging at the corners of his mouth.

Felicity bit her lip. 'I'm really sorry, I couldn't remember what I'd put in so I had to get it all out again and now I'm not sure if I've got the right stuff.'

James sat down beside her amidst the chaos and gave Gennie's soft ears a scratch.

'We're only going for three nights,' he said gently.

'I know that, but what if we go out for dinner? Or go walking? Or what if it rains? Or snows?'

'It's June.'

'I know that too.' Felicity put her face in her hands. 'I hate packing.'

James put his arm around her and pulled her to him. She inhaled his clean linen scent.

'I know you do, Felicity, but the thing is, we have to leave in half an hour.'

Felicity let out a wail and James squeezed her tighter to him.

'So what we're going to do,' he went on softly, 'is I'm going to pack this bag for you, okay?' Felicity nodded against his shoulder. 'And while I do that you are going to find some clothes to wear for the plane, okay?' She nodded again slowly. 'Because if there's one thing I do know, it's that you are not going to want to be boarding that plane in your underwear.'

He was right, of course. Felicity snort-laughed, looking down at where she was sitting in just her bra and knickers.

'You normally like this outfit,' she said with a giggle.

'That is my second favourite outfit of yours, in fact,' said James, his voice getting lower.

'And what's your first favourite?' said Felicity, trying to look vaguely coquettish.

James looked at her for a long moment, his sky-blue eyes flashing suggestively, then glanced down at his watch. 'I'll tell you when you're dressed. Come on now, Crazy Cat Lady, it's time to catch a plane.'

By some miracle, some blond-titan-shaped miracle, they did in fact catch the plane on time. Felicity had even less clue what was in her cabin bag now than she had had before but at least, she reasoned, as they took their seats on the tiny turboprop plane, she wasn't still in her underwear sitting on the carpet at home.

'And Sophie knows when to feed the cats, right?' she said, as the plane started moving towards the runway.

'I love how you start a conversation halfway through,' said James, kissing her forehead. 'Yes, Sophie is on the case. Stop worrying.'

'I'm trying. Sorry. Still not used to this whole travelling thing.'

Felicity's childhood had been so traumatic, so horrendous, that holidays were still rarer than a penguin (man) in summer.

James kissed her again. 'I know that. But you did it. We're here, we're on our way.'

Felicity smiled. 'Last time I was on one of these, I had a small accident with some toothpaste.'

'What?'

'Never mind. I'm glad you're here,' said Felicity then, tears rushing to her eyes. 'You make me so happy.'

James looked a little choked up himself. He stared at her for a long moment, as if he knew what he said next was going to be important. Felicity held her breath. Was this the moment? Was this it? Was he going to pop the question?

'Naked,' he said, quietly.

'What?' said Felicity, with a start. That was not what she was expecting.

'That's my favourite outfit of yours,' he replied, in a low rumbling tone that went right through her. Heat flooded her body from top to toe.

'Fancy you waiting till we got on the plane to say that so I couldn't do anything about it,' she whispered when she'd got her composure back.

He adjusted his baseball cap on his unruly blond hair and sat back in his seat with a smile. His next words were barely audible.

'You wait till I get you in that hotel room, Miss Brooks,' he said softly, closing his eyes. 'You are gonna get it.'

It was all Felicity could do not to climb into his lap right there and then. She was almost grateful when the stewardess came round to offer them some tiny peanuts. How things had changed since her last trip to Guernsey. This weekend was going to be very different, that was for sure. Little did she know quite how different or what it was going to lead to.

CHAPTER 21

The next morning, after a very – ahem – active night and an enormous breakfast at the Bella Dame Hotel, James and Felicity were finally ready to explore. And Felicity knew the first place she was going to take him.

The sun was beating down on their heads as they poured themselves into their tiny hire car, essential for the equally tiny Guernsey roads, and headed across to the west side of the island. The sky was blue and the sun's rays sparkled off the sea every time they got a glimpse of it. James could not stop making noises of appreciation as they went.

'It's so…'

'What?'

'Just…'

'What?'

'…it's beautiful.'

'Yup.' Felicity felt an irrational sense of pride.

'It's like England, Devon or Cornwall maybe, with that amazing coastline, and then also a bit like France and also it looks a bit like a model village in places, do you know what I mean?'

Felicity, who was concentrating on driving through the narrow stone-walled roadways, nodded. 'I know just what you mean. It's like a miniature snapshot of what I imagine England used to be like.'

James snapped his fingers. 'That's it, exactly. But also a tiny bit French,' he said, as they passed a stone farmhouse with blue-painted shutters. 'Why is that?'

'It was part of Normandy originally I think,' said Felicity, cursing under her breath as she spotted a car coming down the narrow track towards her and had to pull into yet another passing place. 'But it's been partially under the UK government for hundreds of years. They still use the French language for official business, though, which I always think is kind of cool.'

Felicity had known very little of her first home until she visited the previous year, her first trip since she was a child in fact, but she'd spent months since then googling everything she could find about this mysterious and beautiful island. It was lovely to finally be able to share it with someone else. Especially, she reflected as they drove, someone as wonderful as James.

'So where are we going exactly?' said James.

'You'll see.'

'Is it…?' said James, his voice tailing off.

'It might be,' said Felicity with a grin.

And sure enough, a few minutes later they were pulling up outside her childhood home in the St Peter's region of the island. Known locally as Le Manoir, the house was a large white building set back from the road, with huge mature trees all around it and high iron gates. Last time, she'd managed to have a sneaky little poke about in the grounds. It was still, to Felicity's knowledge, completely empty ever since the bank reclaimed it from her family due to unpaid bills, a thought that still filled her with shame. What she wasn't expecting to see, however, was the large *For Sale by Auction* sign on the fence.

'Woah,' said James, stretching his long legs out of the tiny

Fiesta and staring through the iron gate towards the house. 'This is incredible.'

When he didn't get an answer he turned, a frown on his face, to see Felicity still staring at the for sale sign.

'This wasn't here last time,' said Felicity, feeling inexplicably choked up all of a sudden.

James gave a low whistle. 'Shit.'

'Yup.'

'They can't sell it. I haven't had a good trespass yet,' said James, pulling open the gate.

Felicity swallowed. 'Apparently they can.'

James took her hand. 'Well then, we'd best go in and get it all out of our system now.'

'Lead on,' said Felicity, with a smile, although her insides had turned to scrambled egg.

Up close, Felicity could see the house was looking even more sad than it had before. As they crunched up the driveway they could see the cracks in the plaster, crumbled bricks and peeling paint on the windows. It still had a certain haunting beauty.

James was in awe. 'It's so lovely. I can't believe you grew up here.'

'I can't believe someone else is going to buy it.' Felicity's voice caught in her throat at the thought.

They peered in through the windows, where old, abandoned furniture was dotted at odd angles amongst the dust and leaves scattered across the floors. It still had that feeling of stepping inside a Victorian novel.

'It looks like the sort of place where someone might be trapped in the attic, you know?' said James.

Felicity wiped her eyes, momentarily impressed. 'Do you mean like in *Jane Eyre*?' she said.

'Do I mean what?' said James, running his hand over a window frame like he knew what he was looking for.

'It's a book. A really famous one. Where a guy has his mad wife locked up in the attic. Ringing any bells? No?'

James shrugged. 'Nope. Sorry. I was thinking of a horror film I watched once.'

'Never mind,' said Felicity.

Just as they were turning to leave, they heard a noise that stopped them in their tracks. It was coming from the back of the house. It sounded like a person was being strangled but also was somehow being very loud about it.

'Oh my God, there is someone locked in the attic,' said James, only half joking.

The noise came again, astonishingly loud. It almost sounded like laughter. Sad laughter.

Realisation dawned suddenly. 'Is that what I think it is?' said Felicity, already moving towards the source of the sound.

'It sounded like...' said James, close on her heels.

'A donkey,' said Felicity, as she pushed open the back door to reveal exactly that. There, in the old kitchen at the back of the house was a small brown fluffy donkey, yelling its little head off. Mercifully, its enormously loud bray softened to a series of gentle huffs when Felicity and James appeared.

They exchanged glances.

'Why can I never have a normal holiday?' said Felicity, keeping her voice low so as not to startle the poor creature.

'You love it,' said James, his eyes wide.

CHAPTER 22

Felicity resisted the urge to immediately ring Andrea. 'Right then. Erm…'

The donkey edged closer.

'What is he doing here? He's very cute but I'll be honest, I don't know anything about donkeys,' said Felicity with a shrug.

The room was a state, with a thick layer of dust covering everything, but it was hard to tell if the donkey had just arrived or had been living there for a while as there was no sign of droppings or any water or food anywhere around.

'I do,' said James, and Felicity looked at him in surprise.

'You do? How come?'

'You don't have to sound so shocked.' He laughed softly, rubbing the back of his neck. 'My parents never let me have any pets but my Great Aunt Barbara had donkeys when I was a kid. I got to go to the country to visit her, once or twice. Donkeys are officially the best.'

Felicity blinked. 'You know about donkeys? What are you, Old MacDonald or something?'

James chuckled, his eyes still on the donkey.

'No, nothing like that. She just had a donkey… kept like a pet, I guess? She was called Jessica. Jessica Rabbit to give her full title.'

'That's extremely cute,' said Felicity. 'Also, nice to see the legacy of *Who Framed Roger Rabbit* is still going strong.'

'What can I say? It's a classic.'

'Debatable.'

'And we had a couple of pygmy goats. We named them Billy and Gruff – geddit?'

As he spoke, James bopped down to its level and the little donkey came straight over and stood next to him. Slowly, James reached out a hand and gave its soft head a little rub. The poor creature had the most enormous brown eyes and a tiny splodge of white hair on his forehead. He was thin and his coat was dull and covered in dirt. He smelt… interesting. A little bit of urine but also comforting, musky and sweet, with undertones of hay.

'Hello, little guy,' said James.

'I think he likes you,' said Felicity, heart melting.

'It's always a bit hard to tell with donkeys, as they don't really show a lot of emotion. But yes, I think he might.'

'He's so cute.'

James looked up at her. 'What is he doing here?'

'And why was he making that awful noise? He sounded so upset.'

'It's a heart-breaking sound,' said James, 'but actually they tend to be mostly silent when they are distressed. They have great hearing, though, as you can tell by the ears. He probably heard us wandering about.'

'What a clever boy,' said Felicity, reaching out a hand and giving the donkey's soft head a rub.

'Poor chap,' said James. 'He really shouldn't be on his own like this.'

Felicity turned and looked out of the door as if the answer would be in the garden. But all she could see was the wide lawn stretching across to the neighbour's fence and… oh yes, there they were. Clear donkey tracks, meandering left and right across the space. The grass was so churned up in places it was impossible to tell where they started.

'He must have come from somewhere. Let's go ask the neighbours.'

They left the little donkey mooching around the kitchen, both feeling rather guilty as they closed the door on him, and went up and down the street, knocking on doors, but no one knew anything about a little brown donkey. It was as if he'd appeared out of mid-air.

'Reminds me of our first animal rescue,' said Felicity as they left the last house in the road.

'When was that?' said James.

'Ha. Very funny.'

'Sorry, couldn't resist.'

Felicity smiled to herself. She still remembered the first time she looked into those blue eyes of his, penguin hood hiding his blond hair from view. Despite her concern for their new furry friend, a little thrill of excitement ran through her body at the memory.

As they walked back up the gravel drive, James looked over at her as if he could read her mind.

'Not the time, Brooks. We have a donkey to save.'

The intensity in his voice just made the little thrill even more thrilling.

'Right you are. What do we do next then?'

'You're the animal saviour.'

'I know but you're the donkey expert.'

'Not really. I know they like their ears scratched and I know where you find the donkey button but...'

'I'm sorry. The what now?'

'The donkey button. Touch a donkey gently on its forehead and its ears will go back. Didn't you know that?'

'Why would anyone know that?'

James waved a hand. 'It's a thing, trust me. Anyway, I know that but I don't know what you're meant to do if you find a random donkey on a mini-break.'

'What kind of secret agent are you anyway?'

'No kind,' said James, laughing. 'We've been through this about a zillion times. I work for GCHQ not MI5.'

'I know you say that, but I'm still not convinced.'

'Whatever.'

They opened the back door into the kitchen and there was the little donkey, staring at them expectantly, as if he knew they'd be back.

'The point is,' James went on, 'what on earth are we gonna do with this little guy now?'

But Felicity was too busy touching its forehead. 'His ears really do go back. That is the cutest thing I've ever seen.'

'Told you.'

'Can we keep him?'

James actually laughed out loud. 'Are you kidding? What are we gonna do, pop him in our hand luggage?'

'Why not? He's so ickle.'

'He is pretty ickle, but not small enough to fit in your case I'm afraid,' said James solemnly.

The little donkey blinked his big eyes at Felicity and she threw her arms around his neck. She was already sold. The donkey lifted his chin and ever so gently rested it on her shoulder and Felicity's heart melted into a puddle.

'Look what he's doing.'

'He likes you.'

'He's properly cuddling me. Oh, James, I actually think I love him.'

'Ha ha, that didn't take long.' James sighed and ran a hand down his face. 'Okay, how's this, maybe we ring round and see if there's a rescue centre on the island?'

'That, Mr Penguin Man, is actually a sensible plan.'
'I have my moments,' said James.

CHAPTER 23

*A*fter a few false starts and some overly long conversations with several people on the island who simply refused to believe that Felicity and James had found a donkey in the first place, or for some reason thought they were making a prank call, they finally managed to get hold of a lady called Valerie who was, according to the local RSPCA centre, the closest thing the island had to a donkey expert.

To her credit, when they explained, she jumped straight in the car and was with them within half an hour.

Valerie was sturdy and square-shaped and Scottish but there was something in her brisk manner, and the way her ancient wax jacket was covered all over with animal hair, that made Felicity miss Andrea. She smiled to herself as Valerie approached them along the driveway, her grey bob swinging in time with her arms as she marched. Or maybe bustled was a better word. Felicity already knew you didn't mess with Valerie.

'Greetings,' said Valerie, as she approached.

'Hello,' said Felicity. 'Sorry… this is an odd one.'

Valerie waved away her comment. 'Och, odd is what I do. There's never a dull moment when it comes to animals.'

'Tell me about it,' said Felicity with a smile. 'I work at an animal rescue centre on the mainland.'

'Now, where is the poor little mite?' said Valerie, ignoring this completely.

James led the way. When she saw their new furry friend, Valerie crossed her arms over her ample chest and frowned.

'Nope. Not anyone I know,' she said. 'And she really shouldn't be here on her own.'

Felicity and James looked at each other.

'It's a girl?' said Felicity. 'We thought…' She stopped, realising they had no clue how to determine the sex of a donkey.

'Oh, yes, if it was a boy, you'd know, believe me,' Valerie said, laughing, as she bent down to stroke the donkey's soft brown nose, her eyes running over its body, assessing all the time.

There was a pause while Felicity resisted the urge to enquire further.

'He – she – had found her way in here somehow. But it doesn't seem like she's been here very long as there are no… uh, I mean, she hasn't made a mess or anything,' said James delicately. 'Well, except for that relatively new pile in the corner.' He wrinkled his nose.

Valerie straightened. 'Well,' she said, 'thank God you found her. Donkeys don't do well on their own.'

'That's what I said,' added James proudly.

Felicity gave him a sideways glance from her awkward position crouching on the floor, where their new friend was balancing her soft chin on Felicity's head.

'All right, calm down, Donkey Man,' she said with a laugh.

Valerie gave a snort, examining him. 'You'd better not be from Jersey,' she said mysteriously.

Felicity shifted position so she could sit on the floor and cross her legs, all the better to cuddle the donkey, who was standing with her eyes closed and bottom lip drooping, looking even more cute than before.

'From Jersey? No, we're both from England. Why did you…?'

Valerie tutted as if they were idiots. 'Jersey people call us Guernsey folk "donkeys". Didn't you know that?'

'That's a bit rude,' said James with a laugh.

Valerie smiled for the first time and she looked like a completely different – much friendlier – person.

'Well, it is but to be fair we are all stubborn as hell, and people always think donkeys are stubborn… so. Mules might be a better word although actually they are even sharper than donkeys. Don't miss a trick, mules don't. And anyway, we call that lot "toads", so we're even.'

James shrugged. 'I'd rather be a donkey than a toad.'

'Me too,' said Felicity with a nod.

'I'd quite like to be that donkey right now,' muttered James under his breath.

'Yes, I've got a new love now I'm afraid,' said Felicity, laughing, her fingers buried in the little donkey's fur.

'I can see that.'

'That's why people kept thinking we were prank-calling them,' said Felicity, recognition dawning. 'It's a Guernsey thing.'

'That'll be it,' said Valerie. 'Good job you found me.'

It wasn't long before they had to say their goodbyes. Valerie had brought a small trailer and after a little bit of negotiation and only a tiny bit of argy-bargy they managed to persuade the little donkey into the back with some ginger biscuits of all things. 'Their absolute favourites,' Valerie declared. And so it proved. She loaded without so much as a look back. Felicity felt bereft.

'Could we… I mean, if we ever came back would we be able to…?' Her voice tailed off. She felt a bit daft even asking.

'You want to come and visit her?' said Valerie, her stern voice softening.

'If that would be okay?'

'Sure, anytime. We've got thirty donkeys. Thirty-one, now. You'd love it.'

Felicity felt flushed with happiness at the thought of their rescued donkey having so many new friends.

'But I should warn you I won't be doing this forever,' said Valerie as she scribbled down her address and phone number. 'I'm getting far too old for this.'

'Surely not,' said James, his voice teasing.

'Flattery won't get you anywhere, young man.'

James looked chastened and Felicity bit her lip to keep from laughing.

'But…' said Valerie, pausing at the door to her car. 'Look, why don't you name her? She doesn't have a name as far as we know, although I'm damned if I know where she's come from. Would you like that?'

Felicity and James exchanged a long look.

'You go,' said James, his voice suddenly thick.

Felicity thought for just a moment and then she knew. 'Jessica,' she said, with a nod.

'Right you are,' said Valerie. 'Enjoy the rest of your stay.'

As she drove off with Jessica singing merrily away in the back of the trailer, James put his arms around Felicity and squeezed her tight.

'Thank you,' he said.

'I'm going to miss her,' said Felicity. And then, after a beat, 'How do you think Andrea would feel about expanding into the donkey-rescuing business?'

James laughed. 'We can but ask.'

CHAPTER 24

That night was Italian night at the hotel, and as they happily scoffed down the most delicious lemon risotto in the plush restaurant, the sea air still tingling in their cheeks, Felicity's phone buzzed.

> Valerie: Donkey settling in well. She's starving, poor thing. Rang round and can't find anyone willing to claim her. Come see her anytime.

> Felicity: Is tomorrow too soon? *smiley face*

> Valerie: Not at all.

> Felicity: Great, thank you, we'll just pop in.

> Valerie: That's fine, about 11 would be best.

> Felicity: 11 it is. We won't stay long.

> Valerie: No problem.

Her phone buzzed again.

'That Valerie's a chatty one,' said James absently, already

perusing the dessert menu in front of him while he was still eating his main.

But it wasn't Valerie this time.

Bex: Hi, Fliss, hope you are okay. How are the plans for the hen do coming? I keep getting asked.

Not even a kiss at the end. Felicity's heart bumped faster in her chest.

'I swear this wedding will be the death of me,' she said. Her tone was light but in truth, with every mention of the wedding she could feel her blood pressure rising.

'Trouble?' said James, taking a sip of his enormous gin and tonic.

'It's just Bex. She wants to know what's happening with the hen do. And truth be told I haven't even thought about it.'

James shrugged. 'Bar. Cocktails. Dancing. How hard can it be? You just go out in town and let your hair down, surely? Not too much, mind,' he added, waving his fork at her.

Felicity laughed. 'Is that what you think Bex would be satisfied with? A night out in town?'

'Why, what does she want?'

'I can tell you it's not that. She wants to be whisked away somewhere for a weekend. And not just any "somewhere". It has to be "Bex-worthy". I have no idea how I'm even going to afford it, let alone organise it.'

She let out a small wail and James covered her hand with his.

'You know what you need?'

'An enormous gin?'

'Well, yes, definitely, but also… Sophie. You need Sophie.'

Felicity's eyes widened.

'I do need Sophie. She will make it all all right. She'll know what to do. If I play my cards right, she'll even take it off my hands. She loves all the admin and that. Why Bex didn't make her the maid of honour is totally beyond me.'

'You really don't know why?' said James, his perfect brow line wrinkling.

'Do you?'

'I have a theory.'

Felicity's stomach twisted. She took a deep breath. 'Go on then, let's hear it.'

James hesitated for a second, then spoke, with pain in his voice.

'Well, Bex obviously just wants to torture you, doesn't she?'

'Does she?' said Felicity, eyes widening.

'I think so. She's known you for years and years. She knows you're not a… natural organiser, let's say.'

'Hey…'

'Sorry.' He winced.

In spite of the sinking feeling in her gut, Felicity laughed. 'It's okay. You're quite right of course. Go on.'

'Well, has it ever occurred to you that this is her way of making you pay for Adam being in love with you, for all those years? She's keeping her enemies close, for one thing, always a good strategy. And she gets to watch you try and organise all this stuff, being as exacting as she can be, knowing you'll be hating every second.' He lifted his glass and took a sip of wine, letting Felicity absorb his words. 'She's an evil genius, basically.'

'Well, we knew that already, didn't we?'

'True.'

Felicity swallowed. 'But surely she must think there's a risk I'll sabotage the whole thing. It's a gamble.'

James nodded. 'It is, but it's a calculated one. She's banking on the fact that you're far too lovely, not to mention intimidated by her to mess with her wedding. I kind of admire it in a weird way. Bex is calling your bluff.'

'Don't you dare say you admire her.'

'Okay, sorry, poor choice of words. But it's kind of impressive how much gall she has, given everything.'

'She can take her bluff and stick it up her arse.'

At that very moment, a waiter hovered into view. He gave a small cough when he heard the last line but to his credit he kept a straight face.

'Can I offer you any desserts, madam? Sir?'

'Oh yes, please,' said Felicity. 'I'll have whatever is the largest dessert you can find, with the biggest gin to go with it please.'

'Ooh. Same for me please,' said James. His cheeks were already flushed after the first gin. Felicity was feeling a bit tipsy herself but one more couldn't hurt, could it?

When the waiter had backed away, a bemused look on his face, James raised his eyebrows at Felicity.

'You okay?'

'Yup. I worked out a way to get my own back. I'm going to get enormously fat. Then she'll have to buy me a new dress and new shoes to fit my big fat maid of honour cankles.'

James laughed. Despite what she put away on a regular basis, Felicity was titchy by anyone's standards. 'Sounds like a fun challenge.'

'And that's why I love you,' said Felicity, suddenly filled with a rush of affection for this man who always managed to make her laugh, no matter the situation.

As the waiter put two gargantuan ice-cream sundaes in front of them, along with gin glasses the size of fish bowls, Felicity was conscious all eyes in the restaurant were on them, but she didn't care. Ice cream was always the answer, after all.

They ate in silence for a few blissful moments.

Then, 'What's a cankle?' said James.

Felicity snort-laughed into her gin glass. 'Trust me, you do not want to know.'

CHAPTER 25

At 10.45 the next morning, both rather the worse for wear, James and Felicity had their faces pressed up against Valerie's fence, trying desperately to get a glimpse of their little donkey.

'She did say eleven. I can't imagine she's going to want us to be early,' said Felicity, feeling irrationally excited just being there.

'Do you think Jessica is okay?' said James, a little frown line forming on his forehead.

'I expect so. She'll be so happy to have some little friends. Is it true they don't like to be alone?'

'Why are you asking me?'

'You're the Donkey Man.'

'Ha. Is that my new name? I think I preferred being a Penguin. Less smelly.'

'Are they? I think penguins are pretty stinky.'

'Ha. I suppose that doesn't come across on the documentaries. Well, I don't know much about donkeys other than what I told you, but I know they need to be kept together, they can die of sadness if they lose their best mate.'

Felicity's heart twisted. 'Do you think that's what happened to Jessica? She seemed quite happy, though, in a weird way.'

'She did but it's hard to tell with donkeys, they never seem to show how they're feeling. That's why people always think they're dumb. And why they get badly treated. Because they put up with a lot without complaining. I remember my aunt telling me Jessica got really sick once, and she only knew because her breathing got a bit faster. Thank God she spotted it in time.'

'That's so sweet and so sad that they are so misunderstood. Was she okay?'

'Yup, the original Jessica lived to the ripe age of forty-three. That's quite impressive, and also why we use the phrase "donkey's years" in case you didn't know.'

'You really are full of…'

'Also, never run from a donkey. That's the other thing I know.'

'What?'

'Especially a male donkey.'

'That's very disturbing.'

'Yup. And that's all I'm saying on the matter.'

'But I have so many questions.'

'I'm sure you do.'

Thankfully that was the moment Valerie spotted their eager little faces at the fence and finally invited them inside.

And straight into donkey heaven.

As it turned out, two farm gates were all that stood between them and direct access to a whole group of donkeys who were just wandering round an enclosed yard outside what appeared to be Valerie's house, a little scrubbed pink cottage with roses around the door and clutter piled up in every window. One in particular was full to the brim with ancient cuddly toys, bears and other stuffed animals, all faded and broken. Felicity's heart felt like it was being squeezed in her chest and she had to turn away.

The yard, though, that was immaculate apart from the

roughly ten donkeys pottering around in it, all colours of the rainbow. Well, all colours of the donkey rainbow at least, from white and spotty to brown to grey to even a kind of orange colour.

As they arrived the donkeys turned in unison and began to sing a greeting at the top of their voices. Or at least, what they assumed was a greeting. It was so loud, Felicity gave a little gasp, while James immediately started laughing.

Donkey heads were all around them suddenly, pushing against them, soft little noses searching their pockets for treats. In one horrifying moment one of them even reversed up towards Felicity who instinctively jumped backwards out of harm's way.

Valerie's turn to laugh. 'Don't worry. I know it looks bad but that's Eeyore and he just wants a bum scratch.'

Sure enough the little grey donkey didn't look like he was about to kick her. He was just standing, waiting expectantly. And when Felicity reached out and gave his hindquarters a tentative rub his lower lip began to droop and his eyes began to close.

'See? He loves that.'

Felicity giggled as the donkey backed into her even further. This was not what she was expecting at all.

'Speaking of tickling…' said James from his position between two donkeys, where he had apparently been conned into rubbing one ear of each. Every time he stopped one of them would give him a nudge until he started again.

'Oh. Yes, of course. Jessica. Yes, yes she's doing well, thank you. Would you like to see her?' said Valerie.

'Only if we can come straight back here afterwards,' said Felicity, who had already decided donkeys were her new favourites.

Valerie laughed. 'Of course. Donkey cuddles are good for the soul.'

'She's not wrong,' said James under his breath as they finally managed to extricate themselves from the throng. Valerie led them through another gate and down a little side path to what would have once been the garden for the cottage but was now, apparently, a little stable block made out of three or four old garden sheds all roughly nailed together. The stables were all empty apart from one, right at the end of the row, where Felicity could just make out a tiny head. At the sight of them, Jessica immediately started making little huffing noises.

'She recognises you,' said Valerie. 'Despite what that Jersey lot think, donkeys are super intelligent.'

'Yes, I'm getting that impression.'

'You're a natural with them,' said Valerie, flinging open the stable door and smiling as Felicity approached Jessica a little cautiously at first, and then threw her arms around her neck. The little donkey breathed in her ear and Felicity giggled.

'This was totally worth getting out of bed for,' she murmured into Jessica's soft coat.

'How is she doing?' said James, voice a little thick with emotion at the scene.

'She's great,' said Valerie, leaning against a nearby stable door. 'She's got an appetite which is a really good sign. I'll worm her later and give her a bath. No, I wouldn't advise that,' she said hastily when she saw Felicity's excited face. 'It's not as fun as it sounds.'

Felicity looked crestfallen.

'We brought her some gifts,' said James quietly. 'Ginger biscuits and some jam for jam sandwiches. I heard donkeys really love those.'

Valerie had the good grace to look mildly impressed. She even uncrossed her arms.

'He's a Donkey Man,' said Felicity, by way of explanation.

'Is that so…?' said Valerie, eyebrows raised.

'You bet,' Felicity said, with a grin.

James shifted uncomfortably under the women's combined stares.

'So, anyway, thanks for everything, Valerie…' he said, giving Jessica a final tickle, and backing away towards the gate, his face a little flushed.

Felicity giggled. 'Everything all right, Donkey Man?'

James ran a hand down his face. 'I'm really not sure you should call me that in public.'

'Valerie's not public, are you, Valerie?'

'Certainly not,' said Valerie, a full-on smile on her face now.

'Ahem. Anyway, let's get going, shall we?'

'Thanks for everything, Valerie,' said Felicity, pumping her hand. She gave Jessica one last hug, feeling extraordinarily choked up at the thought of leaving her behind.

'If you are ever back on the island,' said Valerie, gently, 'you're always welcome to visit. But don't leave it too long.'

'We won't,' James and Felicity sing-songed in unison as they made their way back out through the donkey throng.

'I want to live here,' said Felicity, under her breath. 'Donkeys are my new favourite thing.'

'I won't tell the cats you said that,' said James, as they jumped back in the hire car.

The rest of the weekend passed quickly in a haze of hiking and eating and talking about donkeys and enough nightly activity to make even Valerie blush. And all too soon it was time to go home, Felicity still daydreaming about donkeys on the plane, James daydreaming about living on a tiny island in the middle of the English Channel and eating seafood and drinking wine for the rest of his life.

As the plane touched down on the mainland just before lunchtime, Felicity's phone buzzed in her pocket.

Andrea (straight to the point as always):

Hope you had fun and haven't done your back in with all your holiday exertions. Please can you drop in to the rescue centre on your way home. Nothing to worry about.

Felicity's stomach dropped. Andrea never said there was nothing to worry about, which meant this time, there definitely was.

CHAPTER 26

'We'll just be a minute, hopefully,' said Felicity, as they jumped out of the car outside Animal Saviours. 'Then we can go grab some lunch.' Her heart was still pounding. Holiday glow officially gone. *What the hell had happened?*

James had been extraordinarily calm on the journey from the airport which had only made her more anxious.

'I'm sure it's nothing,' he kept saying in a weirdly measured voice.

'Don't you do your spy shit on me,' she muttered back as she pushed the heavy doors open, the smells and sounds of the animals hitting her right between the ears and nose.

'For the millionth time, I'm not a spy.'

'But my point is,' said Felicity with a smile, 'that's exactly what you'd say if you were.'

'Fair enough but you know me well enough now, it's not like I disappear off round the world all the time or anything.'

She shrugged. 'Maybe you're a sleeper agent.'

'Do you even know what one of those is?'

They were chatting easily back and forth as they made their

way down the corridor, which is why they didn't notice Andrea and Harry until they practically bumped into them. Felicity let out a gasp. They were locked in a passionate embrace right in the middle of the rescue centre.

Her boss and her father.

They sprang apart guiltily as James cleared his throat. Harry immediately covered his face with his hands.

'Erm, what the hell was that?' said Felicity, looking from one to the other.

Andrea tossed her salt-and-pepper plait over her shoulder in what seemed to be a gesture of defiance, blue eyes flashing, face flushed. 'What was what?'

Felicity pointed between them.

'That.'

The blood was pounding in her ears.

Harry, meanwhile, was practically sweating. 'It was nothing… it was just…' Andrea threw him a look and he stopped talking immediately.

'I mean, we just walked in here and you two were kissing so there's no point denying it.'

James snorted. 'Felicity's right. We did see that I'm afraid.' He pretended to rub his eyes. 'I don't think I'll ever unsee it, to be honest.'

Andrea folded her arms across her wolf fleece. *She was wearing a wolf fleece for God's sake. How did the woman do it?* 'Look, it was nothing.'

'Hey,' said Harry.

'Fine, it wasn't nothing as such,' said Andrea, rolling her eyes. 'But it's not why I called you here.'

'Thank God for that,' muttered Felicity, anger still burbling in her chest like lava. 'You do know he's still officially married, right?'

Andrea and Harry exchanged a glance.

'Ah, okay, you did know.'

'Of course I did,' said Andrea as she led them through to the staff room. 'You know I like them complicated.'

'That's for sure,' said Felicity under her breath.

James cleared his throat. 'So why did you call us here? And also, can we all agree we will never speak of what we have just witnessed?'

'Fine with me,' said Harry, sitting down heavily in one of the plastic garden chairs round the sides of the tiny room.

'And me,' said Felicity.

'You might want to sit down too, Felicity,' said Andrea. It wasn't like her to be considerate, something really was wrong.

Felicity stayed standing, too panicky now to sit.

'Suit yourself. The thing is, the centre is in trouble,' she said, not bothering to mince any words. 'Harry here was just... consoling me...'

James let out a little groan and sat down in the corner.

'Is that what you call it?' said Felicity, eyebrow raised.

'He was consoling me, because I've just had a letter from the bank,' said Andrea.

The blood drained from all Felicity's limbs at once. James pushed a chair forwards a few inches with his foot and she sank into it gratefully.

'The bank? Why?' Her palms were prickling. Was she having a heart attack? Is this what a heart attack felt like? How was anyone supposed to know?

'Why do you think?' piped up Harry. 'There's no money.'

'There's never any money,' said Felicity, looking between them. 'That's not news.'

Andrea's voice was strained. 'This time there really isn't any money. None. Not a bean.'

'But...' Felicity looked at Andrea, wondering for the first time if they should be having this conversation privately, but it was clear Harry already knew everything. How long had this been going on between them, exactly? 'But I thought you bought this place with your inheritance.'

Andrea sighed. 'I did, but a few years ago there was a teeny tiny blip in the finances and I may have taken out a teeny tiny' – she gestured with her fingers – 'mortgage.'

'Teeny tiny was it?' said Felicity.

'Well, not that teeny tiny,' said Andrea, handing Felicity a crumpled piece of paper from her back pocket. Felicity didn't miss the shake in her hand as she did so. 'I missed a few payments. So now they want it back.'

Felicity scanned the letter, but her vision was blurry with tears. Maybe it was a panic attack? Was that better?

'They want the centre?' she said, rubbing her face with her hand.

'I'm so sorry, Felicity,' said Andrea.

'What's going on?' said a voice from the doorway and they all jumped.

'Charlie, dammit, I forgot you were coming in this afternoon,' said Andrea.

Charlie was staring at Felicity, wide-eyed.

'Nothing,' said Felicity, blinking back tears and clearing her throat. 'Charlie, this is my boyfriend, James…'

'Woah, he's a unit,' said Charlie, reaching out a hand.

James stood and gave his hand a firm squeeze. 'Good to meet you too,' said James with a light laugh, but Felicity could tell he wasn't expecting Charlie to be that handsome.

'No wonder she won't even throw me a bone,' said Charlie.

'Charlie, for God's sake,' said Andrea.

James didn't miss a beat. 'Why would she go out for ice cream when she has knickerbocker glory at home?' He shrugged.

'That's the most British thing I've ever heard,' said Andrea, laughing a little too loudly.

Harry guffawed from the corner, but Charlie was frowning.

'What's knickerbocker glory?' he said. 'And can you teach me how to do it?'

Felicity couldn't help it. She snort-laughed at that. 'You'll find out when you're older,' she said. 'Now, can we get back to the matter at hand?'

Charlie looked suddenly nervous. 'You didn't tell them, did you?' he said, face paler by the second.

Felicity coughed.

'Tell us what?' said Andrea.

'What happened, you know, between me and Felicity,' said Charlie, putting his hands in his pockets.

'What did happen?' said James, moving as if to get out of his chair.

Charlie backed up.

'Nothing,' said Felicity, as loudly as she could manage without sounding shrill. 'Nothing happened between us. Nothing at all.'

James turned to look at her. 'Then why are you all red?'

'That happens to me all the time, J. You know this.'

'That's true, I do,' said James. He seemed more amused than anything else. 'Charlie. Do you want to explain?'

'Um. Looks like I've said enough,' said Charlie, trying to mouth an apology at Felicity, which felt rather less than genuine.

'You definitely have,' said Felicity through gritted teeth. 'James, I'll explain later, okay? But it was nothing, just a misunderstanding, that's all.'

'Fine,' said James, crossing his arms.

Andrea tutted. 'Charlie, give us a few minutes please. The dogs need doing if you don't mind.'

Charlie, still frowning, turned and practically ran out of the room, with just one quick glance at Felicity over his shoulder.

'The boy's got confidence, I'll give him that,' said Andrea.

'Hmmmm,' said James, his voice a low dangerous rumble. 'He'd best watch himself.'

CHAPTER 27

They talked round and round the issue until Felicity's stomach started to rumble.

'Go on, you two, you're still on holiday for one more day. Go get some food and we'll resume this tomorrow,' said Andrea.

'But you've only got thirty days according to this letter,' said Felicity. The letter in question was now soggy with sweat. She placed it carefully back down on the counter and hoped no one would notice.

'Come on, you need to go. We'll think of something,' said Andrea, following them to the door. Felicity wondered vaguely who the "we" was in that sentence.

Her train of thought was interrupted by the man himself. As they walked to the door to leave, Harry held up a hand.

'I forgot… er, something,' he said, in a pathetic voice, trailing after them.

'Oh, that's fine, let me help you find it,' said Andrea quickly, starting back down the corridor towards the staff room.

'Hold on. What did you forget?' said Felicity, eyebrows raised.

They both stopped short. Harry looked uncomfortable. 'Erm… I forgot my bag. I just need to pop back and get it.'

Felicity could have sworn she saw a naughty glint in Andrea's eye.

'Did you have a bag?' said Felicity. 'I don't remember a bag. Do you remember a bag?' She turned to James, eyebrows raised.

James grinned and turned to Harry. 'Don't worry, we'll wait for you.'

Felicity bit her lip.

Harry shifted from foot to foot. 'It's okay, don't worry, I'll… I can make my own way home.'

Felicity and James glanced at each other.

'Honestly, it's no trouble,' said Felicity.

'We'll just wait here,' said James.

Harry looked at Andrea for help.

'Oh, just bugger off home, you two, it doesn't take four people to retrieve a bag,' snapped Andrea, her face flushing.

'It doesn't take two people either,' retorted Felicity, but Harry and Andrea were already making their way back down the corridor. Surprisingly fast.

'None of this was on my bingo card for today,' said James.

Felicity let out a sigh. 'Let's go home.'

It wasn't until they got back that Felicity remembered Le Manoir was up for sale. With all the excitement of the day it had completely slipped her mind. Perhaps she ought to tell Harry. Once she had forgiven him for banging her boss, that is.

For now she had the future of Animal Saviours to deal with. This place was her lifeblood. A home, in many ways. A pseudo-family. They had to find a way to save it.

'Is there something you need to tell me?' said James, as they got ready for bed, ignoring their half-unpacked suitcases, exhaustion sweeping over them both.

'It's been a long day,' said Felicity, by way of an answer.

'I know.'

'Can we talk about it tomorrow?'

'Oh, sure. Yes. That's fine, I'll be able to sleep no problem. I mean, this lad has just told me something happened between him and my girlfriend, but that's fine. Any man would be able to sleep in this situation, I'm sure.'

Felicity sat down heavily on the side of the bed, wishing she could just hide under the duvet right about now. 'I should have told you at the time,' she said.

'Told me what, exactly?' said James, sitting down next to her.

Felicity looked into his clear-blue eyes.

'It really was nothing, okay? Don't freak out.'

'Well, now you're freaking me out.'

'I don't mean to. It was nothing.'

'Fine, it was nothing, whatever, but can you please tell me?'

Felicity took a deep breath. 'Charlie has a crush on me, okay? He made me this stupid rabbit toy thing and left it in my locker.'

James let out a long breath. 'So you've got another stalker. Is that all? I thought you two had...'

'Oh, God no,' said Felicity. 'But...'

'But what?'

'But he did try and seduce me. I mean, that's what I think he was doing. He's just a kid, James, honestly.'

James's jaw was clenching now. Felicity put a hand on his arm.

'When you say he tried to seduce you...?'

'Well, it was just me and him on shift.'

'And?'

'And he was in Andrea's office...'

'*And?*'

'And he was in just his boxers.'

'What the hell?' James stood up and started marching up and down the room.

'Calm down.'

'How am I meant to calm down?'

'Nothing happened, okay? I told him to put his clothes back on and that was that.'

'That was that?'

'I mean, yes, that was that. He put his clothes back on and I sent him home.'

James rubbed his face with his hands. 'So if that was that, why didn't you just tell me?'

Felicity blinked at him. 'I honestly don't know. I was meaning to.'

'Oh, well, that's fine then.' James uncrossed his arms. Then recrossed them again. Sweat prickled on the back of Felicity's neck.

'I was going to. I meant to. It was really funny, actually. I just didn't, in the end.'

'No.'

'No. I'm sorry.'

He sat down beside her again, arms still crossed, jaw still clenched, and she patted his arm gingerly.

'I'm really sorry. I should have told you.'

'Yes. You should. He wasn't… naked, was he?'

Felicity could have sworn she caught James sucking in his stomach as he said this.

'Are you clenching? You are, you're clenching!'

'Hey, he's a young lad, I'm sure he's got a great body.'

Felicity cleared her throat but elected to stay silent.

'See,' said James, jabbing at the air with a finger. 'That cough, right there. That says I'm right.'

'No, it doesn't,' said Felicity.

'So he has a disgusting body covered in boils or something does he?'

'Well, no, but…'

'I bloody knew it. I'm going to kill the useless little nutbag.'

'Don't mention nutbags,' said Felicity, bursting out laughing.

'Oh my God,' said James. 'You didn't see...'

Felicity shook her head. Her body was racked with laughter now and she couldn't speak for a good minute. After a few more seconds of this, James began laughing too.

'Nutbag,' she said, cackling.

'I'm glad we can laugh about this,' said James, still frowning and laughing all at the same time.

'I knew we would one day,' said Felicity.

He kissed the top of her head and relief washed over her.

'Of course we would,' said James. 'You just should have told me sooner, okay?'

'Okay.'

'And if he ever pulls anything like that again...'

'Yup. I know.'

'Right then. We'll say no more about it. Or about your boss and your dad, now that I think of it. What the hell is that about?'

'Like I said, it's been a long day,' said Felicity.

CHAPTER 28

The following morning Felicity felt weirdly awkward about going back into work.

She encountered Andrea in the puppy room, where she was busying herself with the very important work of cuddling three puppies at once.

'I was just about to feed them,' she said almost guiltily as Felicity entered the room.

'You're the boss, do what you want,' Felicity replied with a shrug. 'Oh, that's right, you did.'

'I have no idea what you are trying to say.'

'Really? So, you think having sex with my long-lost father is perfectly acceptable, do you?'

Andrea just laughed. 'Don't mince your words, Felicity. Don't sugar the pill.'

'Sorry. I didn't mean to say it quite like that.'

'Yes, you did.' Andrea popped the little gaggle of puppies back in the box and turned to prepare their milk.

'I just don't get why it has to be him, that's all. You know what he did to me. You knew what this might do to me. You must have.'

Andrea's face grew serious.

'I'd end it right now if that was what you wanted, Felicity.'

'Oh yeah, right.'

'I would. I mean it. Just say the word. You are...' Her voice tailed off.

'I am, what?' said Felicity, an edge to her voice she didn't seem to be able to stop.

'You're like my daughter,' said Andrea.

'Oh my God.'

'No, no, shit, I didn't mean because I'm... seeing your dad.' Andrea's face was ashen. 'Damn, I'm making this so much worse.'

Felicity was practically snarling by now, she was so cross.

'Hear me out, okay?' said Andrea. 'I meant you... you're the closest thing I have to a family. You feel like my daughter. And so you come first. If you want me to finish it with Harry, I'll do it.'

Felicity only stared at her.

'I'll do it right now if you want,' Andrea went on, picking up her phone.

Felicity took it out of her hands.

'Don't be daft. I don't expect you to do that.'

Andrea's shoulders dropped two inches. 'Really?'

'Yes, of course,' said Felicity with a sigh. 'I just wish you'd asked me first.'

'I meant to. I should have. It just...'

'Happened?' finished Felicity. 'Sure it did.'

'Honestly. I wasn't expecting it at all. But you're right, I should have asked.'

'Or ideally just not kissed my long-lost father in the first place.'

'That too.'

There was a pause.

'So what's the gossip then?' said Felicity, with a wry grin.

Andrea let out a little laugh, visibly relieved. 'Do you want... details?'

'God, no. Heaven forbid.'

'Because I'm happy to share…'

Felicity shrieked in horror. 'No. For the love of all that is good and holy, please. No details. I just meant, you know, is it serious? Because he's still married *and* he's a big fat cheater. You know that, right?'

Both Felicity's parents had had serious issues with fidelity, she had found out recently. She'd always assumed it was just Harry, but no, Jocelyn had also been at it with the local reporter when Felicity and her brother were only a few years old. Unbelievably, it had all gone *downhill* from there.

'I mean, you don't talk about it much, but I'd gathered something like that had gone on,' said Andrea, passing her a puppy and a tiny syringe of milk, Felicity avoiding her eye as she took the little bundle into her arms.

'It wasn't great. So just watch yourself, okay? Because I don't want to be mopping you off the floor.'

'I can handle myself,' said Andrea, tossing her head and picking up a puppy of her own. 'If he cheats, he dies.'

'Woah. I mean that might be a bit extreme.'

'Okay, fine. For you I won't kill him but I'll definitely be rather cross.'

'Fair enough.'

They were just about to move on to the last two puppies when the doorbell rang.

'I'll get it,' said Felicity.

'Thanks, I'll finish up here.'

'And stop daydreaming about my dad,' Felicity threw over her shoulder as she headed for the front door.

'But he's hot,' Andrea threw back.

'Ew.'

Felicity threw open the heavy front door to see a broad woman in an RSPCA uniform standing before her. Saskia was the local Animal Collection Officer and was always turning up with some animal or other that needed their care. Felicity had always suspected she was secretly in love with Andrea. But then, who wasn't?

'Saskia. What can we do for you this fine day?'

Saskia made a face. She had dyed deep-purple hair cut into a very cool pixie cut and tattoos on both hands. Felicity wondered, not for the first time, where she got her hair cut.

'I'm so sorry not to call. I just took an emergency case on my way home and thought it would be right up your *Straße*, if you know what I mean.'

Saskia also liked to throw foreign words into every other sentence. Felicity had no idea why.

'Go on then, give us a look,' said Felicity with a grin.

As everyone in the animal rescue world knew, "looking" was always code for "taking home and snuggling". At least she hadn't broken the number one cardinal rule and told Felicity its name. Once an animal had a cute name there was definitely no going back.

Saskia went to her van and produced a cage from the back. Inside was the scrawniest-looking excuse for a cat Felicity had ever seen. It was covered in tufts of ginger hair between raw pink bald patches, a couple of nasty-looking scratches, and on its head was a large sore that appeared to have been treated with a topical cream.

'He's been to the vets already,' said Saskia as if reading Felicity's mind. 'They said he should be fine with some decent food and love, but you just need to keep an eye on that nasty thing on his head.'

Felicity put a finger through the bar. The little cat immediately started rubbing his head against her hand. His purr was deep and rumbling.

'What happened to him?' she said in a low voice.

Saskia shrugged. 'Who really knows? He's super old and he was wandering round this estate on the other side of town. The person who reported him reckoned he did have an owner but they must have died or left as he's been on his own for a few weeks at least. The kids on the estate kept chasing him, poor boy.'

Felicity's stomach dropped at the thought.

'Does he have a name?' she said, tentatively. The little cat was lying on the floor of the cage now, his head resting on her hand.

'You've got a job for life there,' said Saskia, with a nod. 'They didn't mention one. Call him what you like. Think he's ginger somewhere under all that filth.'

'Maybe we should call him What-A-Mess. Remember that book?'

Saskia looked blank.

'Never mind.'

'Hey, Saskia,' said Andrea, coming out of the door to meet them.

Felicity didn't miss the slight flush that rose into the animal collection officer's cheeks.

How does she do it?

'Good to see you, Andrea.'

'How have you been?' said Andrea.

'*Tres bon, merci ma chérie,*' said Saskia with a grin. 'Brought you a little something.'

'I can see that,' said Andrea.

'Got room for a little one?'

'Do we?' said Felicity, turning to Andrea, her eyes wide.

Andrea didn't hesitate for even a moment.

'Course we do. Come on, Sas, let's go sort the paperwork. Felicity, I think there's a spare cage in the cat room for our new little friend.'

'How about Marmaduke?' said Felicity, lifting the cage and peering in. She could see the little cat's bones through his skin and he was crawling with lice. What on earth were they going to do if they couldn't save this place?

'*Perfetto,*' said Saskia.

CHAPTER 29

Saskia left an hour later, her face pale. She hadn't been able to resist giving Marmaduke a final little stroke on the way out. The elderly cat was already settled into a lovely cosy cage in the corner of the room with a bowl full of food, a soft blanket and as many cuddly toys as Felicity could find hanging about the place. He had tucked into his food with gusto, which was always an excellent sign.

'He's a sweetheart,' said Andrea, as they sat and ate their lunch.

'You told her, didn't you?' mumbled Felicity, her mouth full of salt-and-vinegar twists.

'About this place? I had to. We might not be here to take her waifs and strays soon.'

'That sounds like you've given up already.'

Andrea reached over and grabbed a handful of Felicity's crisps. 'Not at all. But it's pretty hopeless, you've got to admit it. Anyway, since when were you Little Miss Optimism? Actually, don't answer that. I know precisely when.'

'And what's that supposed to mean, exactly?'

'It started the day you met Penguin Man.' Andrea took another bite of her sandwich and grinned.

'You weren't even there. How do you know?'

'Fine, that week, then. You suddenly started seeing sunshine and rainbows everywhere.'

A shiver of pleasure ran down Felicity's spine. 'And what's wrong with that, exactly?'

'Nothing at all. I'm very happy you're happy. But I did enjoy Cynical Felicity a great deal.'

'She's not gone anywhere, I promise,' said Felicity. 'Just wait for Bex's wedding.'

'Ah, yes, the wedding from hell. I'm looking forward to it in a strange way.'

'You must be the only person on the planet then.'

'Will your dad be there? Asking for a friend.'

Felicity rolled her eyes. 'No, I don't think so. I haven't asked.'

'Maybe he can be my plus one,' said Andrea, her ice-blue eyes lighting up.

'If not, you can always take Saskia. I think she likes you.'

'Of course she does,' said Andrea, with a wink. 'She's not made of wood, is she? She don't cry splinters.'

'What are you on about?'

'She's only human, is what I'm saying.'

'Right. Sure, whatever. Anyway, stay away from my father, you hussy.'

'That ship has rather sailed, I'm afraid, dear Miss Brooks.'

'Yuck,' said Felicity, sitting lower in her chair and scowling.

'See, there's the grumpy Felicity I love.'

'If you keep banging my father you're going to see a lot more of her, I assure you,' muttered Felicity.

'Who's banging someone?' said Charlie, sticking his head round the door with a cheeky grin.

'Never you mind,' said Felicity and Andrea in unison.

'Shame,' said Charlie and ducked out of sight to dodge the biscuit Felicity threw at his head. He really was incorrigible.

That night, James and Felicity lay side by side in bed, staring at the ceiling.

'How much does she owe?' said James.

'Close to one hundred thousand apparently,' said Felicity. 'She said it was teeny tiny, the little liar.'

'One hundred thousand. In thirty days?'

'Twenty-eight days now.'

James scratched at his stubble. 'We need to hold some kind of a fundraiser. And not just any old fundraiser. It needs to be something really exciting and dramatic so people get behind it.'

Felicity sat up in excitement. 'Yes. That's a super idea. What about a car wash? You covered in soap suds, me with a sponge, I could get down with that.'

James laughed. 'Ooh, that is pretty tempting…' Then he shook his head. 'You need a lot of helpers otherwise it takes forever and you'll only make £4.50.'

'£4.50 in the hand is worth…'

'£5.00 in the glove?' finished James, with a grin.

'I don't think that's how it goes.'

'Still, the principle's there. It would be a start.'

'But you said we'd need a lot of volunteers.'

'You would. Good luck with that.'

'What about a sponsored something? You could run the London Marathon or sit in a bath of baked beans?'

'Oh, thank you very much.' James laughed again, this time grabbing her and tickling her stomach.

'Stop that.' Felicity cackled. 'You know I hate being tickled.'

'That's what makes it so fun.'

'I think you in those short shorts would be just the ticket,' said Felicity, still giggling.

'Oh you do, do you? Well, think of something else. My running days are long gone.'

'Wait,' said Felicity. His hands were still on her. 'Wait. I've got it.'

James finally stopped tickling her and raised his eyebrows.

'How about an open day at the centre? We could get a load of food vans on the car park and get Saskia along to talk about the RSPCA and introduce people to the animals. It would be really cool.'

James nodded, his blond hair even more ruffled than usual now. 'I like that. And what? You charge entry or something?'

'Yes, and maybe we have a raffle or a prize draw or something?'

'That's a bloomin' good idea.'

'I know, right? And then we get… we get a celebrity to come and open the place or sign autographs or something? That would get people along.'

'Do you know any celebrities?'

Felicity's shoulders sagged. 'Not exactly. But we can find one, right?'

'Exactly. You can always ask Tristan. He's a theatre director. He must know some famous types.'

Felicity rolled her eyes. 'He couldn't even give me our father's number. He'll never get his act together in time to help us.'

'Well, we'll have a think. Someone must know someone.'

'Let's do it. An open day would be super. Love that, Mr Penguin Man,' said Felicity, kissing his cheek.

'Hey, it was your idea, Crazy Cat Lady. You are a bloody genius.'

'I aim to please.'

❄

'Out of the question,' said Andrea the next day when Felicity cornered her in the office to tell her the plan.

'Oh, but seriously, it'll work! I know it will work. We never show this place off,' Felicity wheedled, waving a hand around.

Andrea scoffed. 'That's because it's a total dump that hasn't been properly deep cleaned in about ten years.'

Felicity screwed up her face. Then mimed rolling her sleeves up. 'Well, what better than an open day to give us just such an excuse. Come on, please let us? It'll be brilliant and we might make some money. We can get a load of kids to come pet the animals and, ooh, and we could invite the local press and get them to do a story, you know, save our local animal rescue centre-type thing. Come on, Andrea. What do we have to lose?'

'I can think of a few things. Our reputation. Our minds?'

'Oh, don't be so silly,' said Felicity, waltzing out of the room before Andrea could say no again. Then after a moment she stuck her head back through the office door. 'Don't happen to know any celebrities, do you?'

Andrea was sitting at her desk, head in her hands. She didn't look up. 'Nope.'

'Ah well, never mind, I'm sure we'll think of someone,' said Felicity.

'Animals, children and celebrities. What could possibly go wrong?' muttered Andrea.

She had a point.

CHAPTER 30

hree days later, they were no nearer to finding a celebrity or even anyone who had any links they could shamelessly exploit. Now it was more like what kind of minor C-list barely-a-celebrity would be available at such short notice.

They invited Harry and Tristan over for dinner the next day, hoping that some of the delicious Thai takeaway from down the road would be enough to butter them both up so they could ask them if they knew anyone. They only needed one of them to come good, after all.

'So, Harry. I need to ask a favour,' said Felicity when they were almost through the soup course. She was warming to this man, slowly. She couldn't think of him as her father quite yet, but if she didn't think about The Day When He Walked Out she could pretend he was just a new friend she'd made and that was sort of okay-ish.

'Name it,' said Harry, slurping his tom yum happily.

'And remember before you answer, please, that you are banging my boss and I'm allowing that to happen right in front of my eyes, more or less...'

'Gross,' said Tristan.

'Indeed,' said James.

'So you owe me. I'm serious.'

Harry nodded, his mouth now full of prawn wonton. 'I do owe you,' he mumbled.

'Yes, you do,' she said primly.

'So...?'

'So I was wondering if you happen to know anybody famous? For the open day. We were trying to think of a celebrity or an influencer we could invite along, you know, to get the numbers up, rally the troops to donate, maybe even get the press along.'

'This bloody open day,' said Harry, but he was smiling as he said it.

'I love that you're not asking me,' drawled Tristan. 'Theatre types not good enough for you, eh?'

'Look, you're an amazing director... er, I'm sure.' Felicity's words caught in her throat as she realised she still hadn't been to see one of her brother's rather worthy and overly long plays. She made a mental note to sort that out at some point. 'But we need someone a bit more well-known, I'm sorry.'

Tristan threw his father a look.

'Well, if it's well-known you want...' he said, nodding in Harry's direction.

'What are you talking about?' said Felicity. And then, to her father as hope rose in her chest, 'Do you know someone, Harry? Are you holding out on us?'

'In a manner of speaking...' said Harry.

'In which manner of speaking?' replied James.

Harry gave a long sigh and then threw Felicity a slightly pained expression.

'What is it? Is it your ex-wife or something? Please don't tell me she makes a living from YouTubing her car interior or something inane like that?'

Harry smiled enigmatically. 'No, it's not her...'

'Who then?'

He raised a chopstick.

'Well, if you must know,' said Harry, 'it's me.'

Tristan nodded firmly. 'It's him.'

'What?' said James.

'You're famous?' said Felicity, her chopsticks hitting the table with a clatter.

'In a manner of speaking,' he repeated, still with that mysterious smile.

'In what manner?' said James again, exasperated.

'It's complicated,' said Harry.

'It always is,' said Felicity.

As they dug into the main course, Harry explained. Or tried to, at least.

'I wasn't entirely honest about the painter-decorator thing,' he said.

'So you lied to me on our first meet-up? Is that what you're saying?' said Felicity. Her blood was thrumming in her ears. *What on earth was he going to say next?*

'He does do that, sometimes,' said Tristan. 'He did my lounge a while back. Very nice job too.'

'Can we get on with it?' said James. 'I would like to make it to dessert without any violence.'

'The truth is,' said Harry, 'I'm an author.'

'An author?' said Felicity automatically, her mind still whirring.

A slow flush crept up Harry's face.

'A bloody good one too,' said Tristan, proudly. It was the nicest thing she'd ever heard Tristan say about, well, anything.

Harry cleared his throat. 'Yes, I just wrote a couple of books, and it turns out they're very popular in the States… and…'

'WHAT? That's amazing. Wow.'

'Legend,' said James.

'Yes, well, I know. I wrote one about the history of rock and roll which went down well, and then I thought I'd have a go at something a bit different.'

'Just you wait for this,' said Tristan, eyebrows raised.

Felicity's thoughts were racing at a million miles an hour. 'But when I googled you, nothing came up. You're a ghost online. How can you have a successful book and also be a ghost?' Even as she asked the question the answer arrived in her mind. 'Oh. Of course. Silly me. You wrote it anonymously.'

Harry nodded. Despite his obvious discomfort, he was blushing.

'I wrote it, under a pseudonym, yes. My author name is… no, I don't want to say.'

'You bloody have to now,' squealed Felicity, phone in hand, prepared to google for England. James raised his to the ceiling, ready to race her to it. 'It's not "Barry Hooks", is it? That would be funny.'

Harry barked out a laugh but also looked like he was about to cry for some bizarre reason. 'Not that cheesy I promise. But you're not that far off. I called myself "Diana Edwards" and the Yanks, you know, they just lapped that up.'

That was all it took. Felicity and James immediately began tapping furiously at their phones. James won by a nose, and passed his phone to Felicity with a guffaw.

'Oh, bloody hell. Oh, my goodness. There you are.' She was staring down in pure disbelief at a shoddy-looking red-and-black cover featuring a scantily-clad woman and a half-naked and very oily-looking man, and the title *The Minx*. Felicity could feel the blood rushing in her ears and resisted the urge to get up and walk around the room.

'You think you know a person,' she said.

Harry laughed. 'Sorry. That was a bit of a bombshell, wasn't it? That's not me on the cover, by the way. Just my name.'

'I worked that much out.' Felicity shrugged. 'You write... romance? Very spicy romance, from the look of that cover. Wow. Maybe you and Andrea would be perfect for each other.'

Harry shifted uncomfortably, his lined face flushing slightly. 'I didn't mean to. It was a kind of accident. I was doing this writing course and they recommended trying to write in a totally different style from your default, pushing boundaries and all that, and, I don't know how to explain it but for a bit of a laugh I tried writing a sex scene from a woman's point of view and I really enjoyed it.'

James guffawed. 'I bet you did.'

Harry rubbed the back of his neck. 'God almighty. This is not something I ever thought I'd be discussing with my daughter and her... well, whatever you are, can I just say?'

'Clearly,' said James. 'And also, hey, I'm her... er...'

'He's mine,' said Felicity, quickly.

Tristan's eyebrows were now the highest anyone's eyebrows had ever been.

Harry went on, looking more and more uncomfortable. 'I loved trying to write as a woman. It was cathartic in some ways, after... everything that happened.'

Felicity frowned. 'So why not just own it? Write under your own name?'

'Do you know how few male romance authors there are out there writing proper spice? There's one or two of course, but mostly the men all use a pseudonym. There's something a bit creepy about it being a man, or at least some people might think so. Anyway, I changed the name on the cover and stuck it on "the book site", not thinking anything would come of it. It didn't do anything for a long time and then, I don't know, it just started to take off. It's still my biggest seller even all these years later.'

Felicity's finger hovered for only a split-second over the "buy now" button. 'This I have to read,' she said.

'I can get you a copy for free,' said Harry. 'You don't need to order it, love. I have hundreds.'

'He really does,' said Tristan, rolling his eyes dramatically.

'Too late,' said Felicity, with a smile.

'So how does any of this help us?' said James, when they'd retired to the lounge for brandy and cigars aka coffee and cake. 'You said it was anonymous.'

'Well, that's the thing,' said Tristan, leaning back in his chair. 'Harry's not famous but Diana Edwards certainly is. She has quite the following, shall we say?'

Felicity squealed. 'This is amazing.'

James waved his chopsticks as if he was signing his name in the air. 'Ah, I see. So, you come along to the open day and do a signing as Diana Edwards? Or at least, we'll advertise that it's her coming along and then it'll be you, not her. If that makes sense.'

'They want you to come out, basically,' drawled Tristan, clearly highly amused by the whole situation.

'I got that, thanks, son,' said Harry. He was still smiling but his eyes were lost in thought.

'Is it a terrible idea?' said Felicity at last.

'What? No, oh no, no, not at all,' said Harry. 'It's just, I've never been asked properly to do that before. And it would be in front of you guys.'

'No one's asking you to go on in drag, Father,' said Tristan, shifting in his seat and picking at the icing on the chocolate fudge cake Felicity had hastily bought after her own attempt went spectacularly wrong.

'That would be a good wheeze though,' said James.

'Trust me, no one wants to see these legs on display,' said Harry with a laugh.

'So you'll do it?'

'Fine, fine. I'll think about it.'

'Oh my gosh, that would be perfect,' said Felicity, excitement bubbling in her throat. 'Can't wait to get started.'

'Planning committee, assemble,' said James, raising a chopstick like an imaginary sword and pointing it above his head.

'Assemble,' said Felicity, joining hers to his over their heads. They glanced at Tristan and Harry, who then felt compelled to join in.

'Assemble,' roared Harry, who seemed to be quite excited even though he kept reminding them that he'd just said he'd think about it.

'Whatever,' said Tristan, holding his chopstick at half-mast.

'You love it,' Felicity said, laughing.

'He does,' said Harry, leaning forwards. 'Your brother used to practise being the Marvel characters in the shower. Very loudly, if I recall.'

Tristan made a noise somewhere between a guffaw and a scream. 'Nonsense. For God's sake, Dad, that cannot possibly be true.'

'It is, I'm afraid.'

Tristan crossed his arms. 'And here I thought you were a good one.'

'Good ones tell the truth.'

'Details, details,' said Tristan, but his arms remained crossed.

Listening to them talk, Felicity felt a pang of jealousy. The easy way they interacted was something she didn't know if she would ever have. That knowledge, that intimacy. That is what families are, mostly, when it comes down to it. Those shared expressions, the shared history, the experiences you have together during childhood that form and shape you, and not only you but also those around you. It was all permanently out of her reach now.

She could never go back and reshape those years. She didn't even know her father was a bestselling author. She didn't know he had a garage full of unsold books. She had so much to catch up on, so much she had missed, it was almost an insurmountable task. And it was all his fault.

A memory stung her eyes. Thirteen-year-old Tristan, packing a little suitcase, two bright-red spots on his cheeks clashing with his ginger hair, his jaw set in a tight line. Right when Jocelyn, their mother, had hit rock bottom, drinking all day every day and barely even acknowledging the children anymore, right when Felicity needed him most, Tristan had chosen to leave them both behind, and track down Harry. Felicity wondered now if he thought he was being brave. Perhaps he was channelling his inner Iron Man or the Hulk. Embarking on an adventure halfway across the country and seemingly oblivious to the devastation he was leaving behind him. Or, she thought a little bitterly, perhaps that's precisely why he left.

CHAPTER 31

*E*ven later still, as they all sat back with full bellies, minds racing from the revelations, all three men contemplating each other from across the room, she just came out with it.

'I went to Guernsey,' said Felicity, casually.

Tristan and Harry looked at each other, mouths open.

'When?' said Tristan.

'How?' said Harry.

'A year ago. By plane. And then again about a week ago, with James,' said Felicity, heat rushing to her face at the memory of their rather lovely trip. 'But I suspect you really meant to ask me why.'

'Yes, you're right. Why?' said Harry, studying her face closely.

'It was quite spontaneous really. I'm not sure why I went. I wanted to... *see something*, I suppose. I mean, I knew I wanted to see The House again and well, maybe try and find some answers.'

'And did you?' said Tristan, sitting forwards on the sofa.

'How was she?' said Harry. He meant The House.

'I sort of did,' said Felicity. 'She was in a poorly state, I'm afraid. She's empty. She's been empty since we left. It's up for sale now. So sad.'

'Le Manoir?' said Tristan, catching on a bit late.

'Yes.'

'Woah. I haven't thought about that place in a long time.'

'I've always wanted to go back,' said Harry thoughtfully.

'We found a donkey in it,' said James, out of the blue.

Felicity giggled. 'That's right, it wasn't completely empty. There was a donkey in the kitchen.'

'You're joking.'

'I'm serious. We named her Jessica after one James had as a kid.'

'Jessica?' snorted Tristan. 'I hate this trend for giving animals human names.'

'How did you ever come by a house like that?' said Felicity, ignoring her brother and turning to look at Harry. 'It's incredible.'

Harry's brow furrowed, and he took a long while to answer. The pause was just beginning to get awkwardly, embarrassingly long when he began to speak.

'It was my mother's,' he said. 'Jean, her name was. She was born and bred on Guernsey and she always used to tell me that house had been passed down through generations. Over centuries, even, I think. Unfortunately, at some point in the dim and distant past a relative had a few gambling-related issues shall we say? I really don't know how this was allowed to happen but a loan was taken out against it, and the payments were really high. The day we had to give it up was the greatest shame of my life. And it was all my fault…'

'What is it with people mortgaging their properties to the hilt?' said Felicity, lightly.

But Harry cringed into the sofa and Tristan patted his arm, looking ever so slightly awkward for the first time.

So, he does have feelings.

Harry's voice cracked as he spoke again. 'If I'd only stayed. That Christmas, I mean. If I could have stayed for a bit longer we might have found a way to make it work. We might have all stayed together. We might still have that amazing house.'

Felicity nodded but she couldn't speak. She was having another memory flash. A familiar one, this time, but it still stung like a bitch. Felicity's father standing up from the dinner table and walking out the door. On Boxing Day of all days. Felicity's heart went crunch in her chest, as a whole flood of memories hit her like a train. Tears sprang to her eyes as James reached for her hand.

'Don't be silly…' said Tristan, half-heartedly. 'I would never have met Pete if we'd stayed on the island and Felicity would never have met her, er, Penguin Man here,' he said, flashing James his best smile.

James grinned. 'That's me,' he said proudly.

'And I'd never have acquired all my deep-rooted trust issues, so there's that,' said Felicity. It came out more sharply than she had intended, and Harry winced.

'You're not even joking, are you?' he said, softly.

'Nope. I've never managed to trust anyone since. Poor James here is rather long-suffering, shall we say? There's nothing quite like your father walking out on you to shift your faith in humanity somewhat.'

Harry was staring at the floor. 'I'm so sorry,' he said. 'I honestly thought you'd be better off without me.'

'We really weren't. But, Harry…' said Felicity, her own voice breaking. 'We're not stupid. We know why you left.'

Harry let out a low wail. 'It doesn't matter, does it? I abandoned my beautiful children. How could anyone do that?' He put his head in his hands.

'It wasn't… well, I mean, you had your reasons, didn't you? It's still really crap, don't get me wrong. And to not be in touch after all these years, that's beyond shit. That's like inexcusable in every sense. But we sort of understand, I suppose you could say. Some of it, at least.'

She exchanged a look with Tristan. There was a moment of silence. Harry raised his head and stared at her from between his fingers, brows knitted together. What colour there had been had dropped from his face.

Felicity swallowed and went on, more softly this time.

'She was cheating on you, wasn't she?'

'What?' Tristan's turn to look like he was about to pass out.

'How did you know that?' Harry was practically whispering now, his face ashen.

May as well keep going.

'She was cheating on you with that photographer, wasn't she? I actually arranged to meet him the first time I went over there, last year. He's still on the island.'

'You did what?' Harry was angry now.

Backtrack, backtrack, backtrack.

'Erm… forget I said anything.'

Felicity could feel her ears heating up.

'Well, you'll bloody have to now, girl,' said Harry, with feeling.

Dammit. Just say it quick.

'Bisson. I met him. He's married now. He lives down the road from Le Manoir. He's got a lovely dog that likes Fanta.'

Tristan was looking from one to the other, his eyebrows drawn together at the top of his nose. Felicity remembered that look from when they were young. 'Sorry,' he said, 'but you're going to have to explain what the hell you are talking about. Did you say Fanta? As in, the drink?'

Felicity shrugged. 'It was Mum. There was a guy Mum was cheating on Harry with… oof, hold on… I'll show you.'

Felicity uncurled from the armchair and went to the bedroom to collect the old newspaper clipping she had been given which showed a garden party at their childhood home. Tristan was still burbling on about fizzy drinks in the space behind her. When she came back, the burbling had stopped and Tristan and her dad were both staring into space, each one looking like they needed a stiff drink.

'I think I have some brandy somewhere, if you need it,' she said, handing them the clipping. 'Take a look at this.'

Tristan stared at the photo and let out a kind of high-pitched squeak at the sight of The House in all its glory. Harry, however, was completely silent, his finger running over the picture of Felicity's mother there, right in the centre of the image, as if he was somehow trying to bring her back to life.

When Felicity finally got to the end of telling them all about her trip, these two strangers-who-were-no-longer-strangers stared at her as if she was an alien from outer space.

'Please say something.'

No response.

'Harry? Are you okay?' said James.

Harry shook himself out of his trance. 'I need a drink.'

Tristan rolled his eyes. 'You don't drink anymore, remember?'

'I'm beginning to regret that decision.'

'It was for good reason.'

'Still.'

It wasn't your average Saturday evening, that was for sure.

When they finally left, Felicity stared out of her window after them in a daze, James with a comforting arm draped around her shoulder. Her father and her brother, lit up by a single street lamp, jostling and chatting as they got into Tristan's car. Tristan was firing questions at Harry nineteen to the dozen, and Felicity couldn't help wondering if this was maybe what a proper, "normal" family felt like. At least, as "normal" as theirs could ever be. She didn't have many childhood memories that were worth keeping but for the first time in so many years she had blood relatives around her who she didn't either entirely hate or want to escape at the first opportunity. Who, on occasion, she actually quite liked.

Was this how other people felt about their families? A weird mixture of irritation and love? It was a strange but not entirely unpleasant thought.

CHAPTER 32

The next morning, Felicity woke up to a text from Harry. He wasn't sure about the whole signing thing. Felicity refused to panic. As soon as she got into work she went straight to see Andrea.

'Absolutely not,' said Andrea, when Felicity had explained exactly how much she needed Harry to be there that day. Though not *why*, exactly. Besides, surely he'd told her about his alter ego by now.

'Oh, come on now. Don't be like that. You know you're the best person to ask him. You have *influence*.' Was there a hint of a flush on Andrea's cheeks at that?

'I am not asking him anything of the kind. You want him at this open day of yours, ask him yourself.'

'I have, but he needs to hear it from you. He just needs to know how much this means to you.'

'You know I'm not good at all that emotional stuff,' said Andrea.

'So, you're not denying you have influence then.'

'I am neither confirming nor denying any such thing.'

'I think you just did,' said Felicity with a grin.

'Anyway, what do you want him there for?'

'Well, because he's famous. Sort of.'

'Famous?' said Andrea. Felicity began to feel a bit light-headed. 'Famous for what?'

'Hasn't he told you? What he does for a living?'

'He said he was in insurance,' said Andrea, frowning like a good 'un.

Awkward.

'Did he now? He told *me* he was a painter and decorator.'

'The little whatsit.'

'He has his reasons, trust me. Go and ask him again.'

'We haven't spent much time chatting, if you get my drift,' said Andrea, with a lascivious wink.

Felicity groaned and ran a hand down her face. 'Everyone gets your drift. The whole neighbourhood just got your drift. Please. No more drift.'

And you haven't even read his books yet.

Andrea's eyes flashed with something distinctly mischievous. 'Sorry, Felicity. But as your boss I feel I have no choice but to tell you that your father is an astonishingly talented lover.'

There was nothing else for it. Felicity stuck her fingers in her ears like a small child and ran for the exit as fast as she could.

'Was it something I said?' yelled Andrea from behind her, grinning from ear to ear.

That very afternoon, Harry texted back to confirm he'd be happy to do the event after all. He'd even found a few author friends to bring along. Felicity definitely didn't want to know how Andrea had persuaded him. She had to stay focused. There were only a few more weeks to pull this event together and save her beloved Animal Saviours. Exactly how hard could that be?

The following weekend it was time for the Dreaded Hen Do.

Felicity had totally dropped the ball, she knew she had. This was partly because of everything else that was going on, yes, but also because she was finding the whole Adam and Bex thing so difficult. It was as if she was paralysed somehow, everything about this wedding seemed like an extraordinary effort. In the end, after much panicking, Sophie had managed to save the day, pulling a few strings with some of her friends, all of whom seemed to be arty or crafty or sometimes both. They managed to arrange a pottery workshop for the daytime and a special meal in Bex's favourite restaurant in the evening and Felicity was fairly sure she'd be happy with that. She had to be, right? None of them could afford Ibiza or anything crazy expensive like that, and the fact that Adam and his mates were heading to Amsterdam for the weekend was neither here nor there.

'Is this what we're doing?' said Bex in a disappointed voice on Saturday morning when they arrived at the pottery centre.

'This is the first thing,' said Felicity confidently, trying to think of what they could do in the afternoon that she could book with one hour's notice. 'So just enjoy this first and then you'll see what's next.'

Sophie threw her *a look*, knowing full well there wasn't anything coming next, but Felicity chose to pretend she hadn't seen her.

'I can hardly wait,' said Bex, and her icy tone sent a shiver of anxiety down Felicity's spine.

'Come on, it'll be fun,' said Bex's friend Libby, sitting down eagerly at one of the wheels. Libby was one of the add-on friends whose details Felicity had managed to wheedle out of Petunia at the last minute, in a humiliating ritual that had involved her praising Bex's finer qualities for the best part of an hour and swallowing any last dregs of her self-worth.

Even Felicity wasn't sure she'd go as far as to say "fun". She was just wondering whether they'd forgotten about her booking entirely when an extremely handsome man came round the corner dressed in a *Great Pottery Throw Down*-style apron. He had dark, wavy hair, smears of white plaster across his forehead and on his sizeable forearms and he was carrying a small Bluetooth speaker. Immediately Bex gave a squeal.

'Are you the stripper?' she said, settling herself on a stool in the middle of the room and holding out her hand to him as if she was the Queen. The plastic tiara they'd given her was really coming into its own.

The extremely handsome man huffed a laugh and wiped his hands on his apron.

'No, ma'am, I'm very sorry but I can't say we offer that service here.'

He had a dreamy American accent. Things were looking up. Maybe this morning wouldn't be a total bust.

Bex scoffed. 'Come now. I know it's only ten in the morning but there's no way someone like you could be a potter. Do you want me to start the music for you? Where would you like me to stand? Or am I okay sitting?'

Horror rose in Felicity's throat as she watched the potter colour slightly and although she knew she should probably step in, something held her back.

Am I awful? Maybe I'm being awful. Do something, Felicity, before it gets any worse.

But before she could do anything, it did in fact get worse. Bex stood up slowly, dark tresses bouncing, dark-red lips pouting, and walked towards him, hips swaying. She put one hand on the tie of his apron where it was done up at the front and pulled.

'Do you want me to help you get started? Is this right?' she purred in her most seductive voice, leaning towards him.

The man actually looked quite tempted to kiss her for a moment, before he realised what was happening and started backing away, hastily retying his apron. His voice had risen a couple of octaves.

'Seriously, ma'am, this is your hen do I know, but we only

offer pottery workshops here, I swear.' He rubbed the back of his neck. 'Lord save me,' he muttered.

'Oh. That's… a shame,' said Bex, eyes still flashing. 'Well, why don't we just see where the day takes us?' she added, in a voice dripping with honey.

The potter waved his hands. 'Please. I'm just here for the pottery.'

'Of course you are,' said Bex.

'I am, honest to God. I mean, if you wanted something a bit more… racy,' said the man cautiously, 'you maybe ought to speak to your bridesmaids.'

All eyes turned to look at Felicity and her face flushed bright red.

Oh, thanks for that, Mr Pottery Man, great help you are.

Realisation finally dawned and Bex's beautiful face fell in dismay and flushed purple all at the same time. 'Sorry, so you're not actually a stripper?' She glanced around the room, her gaze resting on Felicity and Sophie, aghast. Felicity's skin broke out in a cold sweat.

But the man grinned shyly at that, and a dimple appeared in his left cheek. Two of the girls behind Felicity sighed audibly. 'No, ma'am.'

Bex was still staring at Felicity, her face more a shade of crimson now. 'Is this a wind-up? Are you trying to embarrass me, Fliss?'

Felicity shook her head firmly and Sophie stepped forwards.

'I organised this bit, Bex, and I can assure you this is a legitimate pottery centre with no strippers of any kind.'

She waved her hand in the general direction of the pottery throw-down man.

'But I thank you for the compliment, ma'am,' he said, throwing Bex a winning smile. 'I can honestly say that's never happened to me before.'

There was a long pause while everyone held their breath.

'I find that hard to believe,' breathed Bex in her most seductive voice and then laughed. 'Come on then, let's get potting or whatever you call it.'

The whole room breathed a sigh of relief.

'You got it, ma'am.'

Oh, thank the Lord, thought Felicity, who suddenly needed a sit down.

CHAPTER 33

By 10.30am everyone was ready at their potter's wheels while the extremely handsome man, whose name was Jack, they discovered, sat in the middle and showed them how to craft a vase using just a lump of clay and a lot of rather suggestive-looking hand movements.

Felicity smiled to herself as she watched. *Ironic that he'd probably make a great stripper*, she thought.

The other girls clearly shared her opinion as no one seemed very interested in actually having a go. They were all much more interested in the demonstration side of things, especially when he got to the part where he brought the neck in deftly, moving his hands firmly up and down the clay, and by 11.15am they had perfected the art of asking Jack to "just show us that one more time, if you could" so they could all enjoy the view.

At some point during the morning Felicity managed to excuse herself while they were all transfixed by Jack's muscled and very dextrous hands, and made some frantic phone calls to see if anywhere at all would be able to host a hostile hen and her eight companions who weren't even drunk yet.

Finally, inspiration struck and she found a nostalgia-themed bottomless brunch venue willing to squeeze them in at 1pm so long as they sat at the back and didn't actually drink too much. It wasn't ideal, but it would have to do.

'Is this what we're doing?' said Bex, ninety minutes later, as they shimmied into a booth in a tiny and very dark corner of the shabby-looking club.

'Yes,' said Felicity, trying not to grit her teeth. 'This is what we are doing now.'

'Lovely,' said Bex, curling a lip in disdain as her forearm stuck to the table.

'We should have brought Jack along after all,' said Sophie.

Libby and another girl called Karen tittered behind their hands like birds.

To be fair, it was a total dive; noisy, raucous and a little bit seedy somehow, but Felicity was banking on the Prosecco helping things along a little.

Plates of decidedly greasy-looking fry-up were delivered alongside cake stands full of stale pastries which the girls dived into frantically. Anything to line their stomachs.

'We're out of Prosecco I'm afraid,' said a voice next to her ear when she tried to order their drinks. 'We've only got wine but it's a little bit warm as the fridge has broken. So sorry.'

Although the words sounded apologetic, the waitress looked as though she couldn't have given less of a damn.

'I hardly dare ask if you do a vegetarian brunch option,' said Felicity, with trepidation.

The woman just blinked at her. Stale pastries and warm wine it was then. Dammit. Could this day get any worse?

Oh yes, it very much could.

CHAPTER 34

hen they got to the restaurant, five hours later, half an hour late for the booking and merry as their merry band could be on warm white wine, Sophie produced a shoebox full of cue cards from somewhere about her person and announced they were going to play the His and Hers game.

'I can't play any games right now,' said Bex, barely able to focus on the table in front of her.

'Me neither,' said Libby and Karen in total unison.

'I miss Jack,' said the one called Helen, another add-on with very severe eyebrows who Felicity was a bit scared of, truth be told.

'Ooh yes,' said Karen. 'We definitely should have made him come with us. Let's go back and find him.'

'I do love games though,' muttered Bex, apparently not to anyone in particular.

'I know you do, my love,' said Sophie, putting an encouraging arm round her shoulders.

'But I don't know the rules to this one...'

'It's okay, it's very easy,' said Sophie. 'We asked Adam some stuff about you and we're gonna see if his answer matches your answer. Does that make sense?'

'Go for it,' shouted Bex, her voice shrill. 'He's known me long enough, after all.'

Felicity shifted a bit in her seat. The previous week she and Sophie had sent Adam a tentative email with a list of questions about his (latest) beloved, half expecting him to refuse to play. She had been oddly jealous when he replied, and although he was very reluctant at first, his answers were warm and funny and even, occasionally, correct.

'Right. So. Listen up, everyone. The first question we asked Adam was, what is Bex's favourite clothing brand?'

'Reiss,' said Bex, swaying back and forth in her seat. Felicity had to stop watching her as it was making her feel a bit seasick and she felt sick enough already. She stared at the table, strangely invested in Bex's responses to the game all of a sudden.

'Yes, that's right. Well done, Adam.'

'I would have killed him if he got that wrong,' slurred Bex. 'Did he offer to buy me anything?' They all tittered politely. This was so unlike Bex, to be this drunk. Felicity was feeling a bit bad. *Maybe we should take her home.*

'What did Adam think was your favourite movie?'

'*The Lion King*?' said Bex.

'Nope...'

'Er, no, okay, hold on, he probably said something shooty like *The Bourne Identity* or *Deadpool*.'

'*Deadpool*, that's right.'

'But it's only because it's got that Ryan Gosling in it. He's delicious.' Several of the girls murmured their agreement.

'Reynolds,' said Felicity, under her breath.

'What?' said Bex, her eyes unfocused as she turned to look at Felicity.

'Reynolds. Not Gosling.'

'Right,' said Sophie hastily. 'Next one. We asked Adam what you would most like to eat on a Friday night.'

A couple of the girls giggled and nudged each other.

'Not like that,' said Sophie, rolling her eyes.

'Indian takeaway,' said Bex.

'Ooh, can you be more specific?' said Sophie.

Bex was looking rather pale. Even more so than usual, if that was possible. Her plastic tiara had slipped down the back of her head and she was now swaying quite violently on her chair.

'I like the one with the prawns,' she said, with a slight hiccough.

'Prawn bhuna. Close enough.'

'Bex, do you feel okay?' said Felicity, sliding a bit closer to her on the bench seating. 'You look a bit...'

And this, it turned out, was her fatal mistake.

Bex turned to answer her, opened her mouth and projectile vomited into Felicity's face, all down her front and all over the leather seating.

Everything happened in slow motion after that.

People around the restaurant started screaming. Bex stood up for some unknown reason and then vomited three more times onto the table in between dry heaving, giggling hysterically and saying, 'Oh my, oh Lord, oh my goodness,' over and over again.

Waiters and waitresses appeared out of nowhere, as if to help, but then were so mortified they just stood and stared at the scene of abject horror before them. Felicity, face and hair dripping with vomit, was so stunned she couldn't even move. She sat in horrified silence for a moment and then burst out laughing. What else was there to do? Bex looked at her and laughed too and then they were all laughing and it was a strangely warm and friendly moment until suddenly Felicity wasn't laughing any more. Sickness rose in her own throat and she pushed her chair back. Felicity stood and turned towards the toilets, then slipped in a pile of sick on the floor and fell down flat on her face. There was a gasp from behind her and then more laughing, this time from strangers; oh, the mortification. She lay for a moment right there on the restaurant floor, head aching from where it had met the cold tiles quite hard. The smell of vomit by this point was overwhelming.

Felicity clambered to a sitting position, using the table to pull herself up, groaning the whole time and putting her hands into even more of the piles of warm vomit around her. She staggered to the toilets, where she was sick into the toilet bowl, sat back, smelt the Bex sick in her own hair and then threw up twice more.

Sophie banged on the toilet door, asking her over and over again if she was okay but Felicity couldn't answer because more vomit. Eventually she managed to crawl to the door to open it, whimpering.

'Good Lord,' said Sophie. 'Let's get you home.'

It was all a blur after that.

No taxis would take her, and who could blame them? In the end Sophie called James. His mouth dropped open when he caught sight of Felicity but to his credit he managed to keep a straight face. Without a word, he took her arm, guiding her into the back of the car where she sat leaning her face against the half-open window, letting the cool air wash over her and praying to be magicked into her bed. It was the longest fifteen minutes of her life. When they finally got home, she waved feebly goodbye to Sophie with a grateful smile, then James steered her straight upstairs and into the bathroom, clothes still dripping with sick. She managed two showers in quick succession before climbing into bed, still whimpering. It was only later she even wondered how Sophie had got home.

The only one who wasn't horrified and appalled at her appearance was Gennie the cat, who climbed on top of her as she always did and purred on Felicity's stomach all night while she slept the sleep of the nearly dead. When she woke up the next day, even though she was now clean and smelt of petals, all she could think of was how Bex's vomit had smelt in her hair. She turned over and closed her eyes, blocking out the memory.

A few hours later she woke again to the smell and sound of fresh coffee being brewed on James's fancy machine downstairs. Her stomach groaned with hunger and she realised they hadn't even had time to have dinner at the restaurant before VomitGate saw the whole lot of them being turned out on their drunken ears. She was starving.

Felicity crawled out of bed, wrapping James's oversized and super-soft tartan dressing gown around her, and stumbled down the stairs just as James, wearing only a pair of soft grey tracksuit trousers, was putting a pile of home-made egg-and-hash-brown muffins on the table. Her absolute favourite breakfast. Her stomach groaned again. On any other day the sight of that muscled chest would have made her instantly hot and bothered. But not today. Today, she felt so rough she just wanted to find a corner to curl up in so she could die a slow and peaceful death. Still, she could vaguely remember that he'd been her knight in shining armour the previous evening. Best show some gratitude.

'Have I told you lately that I love you?' murmured Felicity, grabbing James around the waist and burying her face in his lovely broad back.

He reached one arm around to pull her against him.

'Not this morning,' he said and she could hear the smile in his voice.

'Also, how come you didn't run away screaming when you saw the state of me last night?' she said into his bare skin.

'I was tempted, I won't lie,' he said.

'Er, rude. Your poor car. I'm so sorry.'

'Don't worry,' he said, waving a hand. 'That's what car shampoo is for.'

'Was it that bad?'

'It was pretty bad.' A pause. 'What the hell happened?'

'I need to eat first,' she said. 'And I need coffee. So much coffee.'

James deposited her gently into a chair and passed a mug of steaming hot black coffee into her grateful hands. She clutched it like it was a life jacket. Which, in a way, it was.

CHAPTER 35

Three egg-and-hash-brown muffins and two coffees later, Felicity was finally ready to talk. Extremely fast. The story came out all in a rush.

'Slow down, Crazy Cat Lady. I see the caffeine is kicking in.'

'Sorry.'

'Start again.'

'Okay. So… Bex was sick in my face.'

'It was Bex? No way.'

'Yes, way. She was sick like right in my face, and then she was sick all over the table and I was sick in the toilets and it was a whole big vomit-fest basically.'

James laughed out loud. 'I mean, I guessed there was vomit involved somewhere along the line. But that is absolutely horrendous.'

'It really was. I actually don't think anyone's ever had a worse hen do since the dawn of time.'

'I've never seen Bex drunk enough to vomit, have you?' said James after a moment. 'I can't even imagine it.'

'Never,' said Felicity. 'She's always really restrained but she was properly giddy, like one step from falling down drunk.' She buried her head in her hands. 'I feel awful. I never should have let it get that far. It was the bottomless brunch that did it.'

'The what?'

Felicity's stomach roiled at the thought of the warm wine and she had to hold on to the table for a moment before she could speak.

'Basically, I'm the worst maid of honour in the world.'

'I'm sure that can't be true.'

'Oh, it is. We had a lovely day planned but when Bex thought the man at the pottery place was a stripper…'

James rolled his eyes. 'Oh my God.'

'Yup. We were all set to do crafting and then she got the completely wrong idea and at that point I thought what I'd booked was too tame so I panicked, right? And I rang round and found a bottomless brunch place… which is basically not as good as it sounds because they give you all the cheap nasty alcohol you can drink but they only give you one plate of brunch and not even a very good plate either. Nothing at all for vegetarians except for a rubbery egg and some stale croissants. Ew.'

She groaned as her stomach protested again.

James put a comforting hand on her arm. 'So essentially you just drank loads of cheap booze and had hardly anything to eat.'

'Essentially. And when we went to the restaurant, I… well, I don't even remember how we got there in one piece, to be fair, but when we got there it was really fancy and I realised we'd made a terrible mistake because we were all basically off our faces except for poor Sophie and I'd made a pledge with myself that I absolutely would not get pissed and I was totally sucked in by the whole bottomless thing, you know, and seriously what is wrong with me?'

'Take a breath.'

James patted her arm while Felicity covered her head with her hands again and moaned for a few more minutes. The caffeine was kicking in but all it was doing was beating her around the head with every mistake she'd ever made.

'And then we played His and Hers which was Sophie's idea but I couldn't really watch.'

'Why not?' said James.

'Because I kept remembering how weird Adam was about it.'

'Weird, how?' James's jaw clenched slightly like it always did when Adam's name was mentioned.

Felicity shrugged. 'When we sent him the same questions last week, he… I don't know, he was just really weird about it. Like he didn't want to play.'

'Well, perhaps he just didn't want to discuss his and Bex's sex life with his ex-girlfriend-slash-ex-fiancée or whatever you are. You can hardly blame the man for that.'

Felicity shook her head and then instantly regretted the movement.

'It wasn't questions about their sex life. God. What do you think I am?'

There had been a couple but Felicity wasn't about to confirm that to James.

'Okay, fine, whatever, I'm sure he still felt a bit uncomfortable about it, poor guy.'

'I suppose you're right. It just made me really worried for Bex.'

'We're all really worried for Bex. She's marrying a despicable individual,' said James. 'But it was her choice, remember? She was the one who cheated on you with him. And lied about it. And then asked you to help her plan the wedding.'

'And then vomited all over me,' said Felicity, with a weak smile.

James was getting into his stride now. 'Yes, and then vomited all over you. As if you deserved any more humiliation.'

'Thanks for that. Did I mention I fell over in it? Flat on my face in front of the whole restaurant.'

'That's not like you.'

'Hey.'

'Sorry. But it's true. About Bex I mean. I really think she owes you an apology, not the other way round.'

'I love that you're defending me but I should have taken better care of her yesterday. She trusted Sophie and I to look out for her.'

James pushed back his chair and stood up, his jaw muscles flexing. 'Felicity, I love you but you are wrong about this. She's the bitch here, not you.'

He turned and began loudly loading the dishwasher. Felicity watched him for a few moments, the way his muscles flexed across his back, the size of his thighs in those soft trousers. The way his fists were tight and his brow was all crinkled with fury.

'You look even hotter when you're mad,' she said, eventually.

He paused for only a microsecond, before continuing passively-aggressively loading the dishwasher for a few moments more. Then he said quietly, 'I'm not mad.'

'You are a little bit mad.'

'Fine, I'm a little bit mad. But seriously, Felicity,' he stopped and looked over at her, his sky-blue eyes flashing, 'are you really doing this?'

She knew what he meant.

'I can't have this conversation again.'

'I think you have to.'

'The wedding's coming up fast, James. I can't pull out now.'

James's mouth was set in a tight (but quite sexy) line. 'You don't have to do anything you're not comfortable with.'

'I do. Everything is arranged. I have to be there. She's one of my oldest friends.'

'She's a bitch.'

Felicity put her forehead slowly down on the table and took a deep breath. 'Seriously, I cannot keep having the same conversation about this.'

'Then don't. Just listen to me. I know we said you'd hang in there, and that they were your oldest friends and all that, but I've changed my mind. You think you have to be friends with them because you've always been friends with them and you've been through a lot together or whatever but seriously, you can walk away. People do that.'

'Do they?' Felicity said into the table.

'They do. Yes. I know you have trust issues or whatever and maybe you're scared you won't find other friends but you will, I promise you. You can find friends who don't treat you like shit.' He was sitting beside her now, his hand on her back.

She lifted her head slowly, wincing as her hangover headache started to kick in in earnest. He was looking at her with such concern she felt her heart thump.

'What did I do to deserve you?' she said softly.

'You won the boyfriend lottery, what can I say?' He grinned.

'I sure did.'

CHAPTER 36

James was right, she knew he was, of course he was.

Andrea and Sophie were her only true friends in the world, which was a bit of a sad state of affairs, truth be told, especially as one of them was also her boss.

'Felicity, are you okay?' said one of them now – Andrea, in fact – her brusque voice drawing Felicity back into the present. 'Only you've been sat in that chair for ten minutes now. Don't you have a home to go to?'

It was the end of shift and yes, Felicity very much did have a home to go to. One with a lovely man in it and three gorgeous cats and she knew she should be skipping home to them immediately, but something was holding her back.

'Andrea…' she said.

'Yes…?'

'Can I ask you something?'

'I think you just did.'

'You're hilarious,' said Felicity in her most sombre voice. *Go gently.* 'It's just… we were talking the other night and, well, we really need to get on and organise the fundraiser soon, just checking that's still okay?'

Andrea spun round sharply.

'Who's we?'

'Me, I said.'

'No, you said we. Who's the we, exactly?'

'I think you're missing the point.'

'It's Harry, isn't it?'

Felicity sighed. 'It might be, yes. And Tristan. And James. *We* were thinking we could do it in a couple of weeks' time, on Saturday 6th, maybe? Saskia and Harry – sorry, Diana – are all lined up and I've sort of taken the liberty of organising some food vans and we charge people to come and look round and see the animals.' She felt her face flush. 'And perhaps we might raise a bit of money for the bank?'

Andrea's forehead crinkled as she leant against the cheap Formica worktop.

'It's very sweet but we need a lot of money to make this work. I still don't think—'

Felicity cut her off. 'What have we got to lose? You never know, someone might make a big donation.' She tried to keep her voice steady. Chance would be a fine thing but they had to *try*.

'Well, I don't know. I suppose it's worth a try,' said her boss after a moment. 'Now tell me more about this conversation the other night. I want to know everything.'

Felicity shrugged. 'We just had Harry and Tristan over for dinner. Nothing really to report.'

Andrea's face fell. That clearly wasn't the right thing to say.

'Nothing? Didn't he… they… didn't they mention me?'

Understanding dawned at last. 'Do you mean, did my long-lost father talk about you? Is that what you're asking?' said Felicity. She couldn't help scowling just a little bit.

Andrea had the good grace to look a little bit awkward about it, as she nodded. 'Yes. I just…'

'Are you in love with him?' said Felicity, taking both of them by surprise.

'Am I what?'

'You heard me.'

Her boss looked stunned.

'Don't tell me you're lost for words,' said Felicity, incredulously. 'You've never ever been lost for words in the whole time I've known you.'

Andrea turned away and pretended to wipe the counter. 'I'm locking up in a minute,' she muttered under her breath. 'Time to go.'

Conversation over then.

Felicity nodded and headed for the door. Then she turned, and spoke quietly to her boss's back. 'Sorry, I hope I didn't overstep the mark there.'

Andrea's shoulders sagged a little, but she didn't turn. 'Not at all. We're practically family.'

'Ew,' said Felicity.

Andrea turned to face her then, a smile just twitching at the corner of her lips.

'Not like that. I mean, you and I are practically family, that's what I meant.'

Felicity resisted the urge to go and hug her. 'I know what you meant. I feel the same. But still, I shouldn't have said it.'

'Don't worry about it. See you tomorrow.'

'Yeah, see you. Glad the whole Diana Edwards thing hasn't put you off.'

'Quite the opposite if anything,' said Andrea.

'Ew,' said Felicity again, with feeling this time.

As she drove back to the house that night, rain pattering on the windshield of her old beat-up Mini Clubman, Felicity couldn't shake a weird feeling of doom.

She knew she should be happy for Andrea, she had dated a lot of men since Felicity had known her and she had never ever seen her like this before. If she was happy, if she was in love with Harry, who was Felicity to stand in their way? It wasn't like she even had any kind of father-daughter relationship with him.

So why did she feel so peculiar?

Perhaps it was jealousy. Perhaps seeing Andrea and Harry bonding when it was meant to be Felicity and Harry bonding (though not in exactly the same way – ew) was making her jealous? She thought about this for a few minutes and then dismissed it. No. That wasn't it. She was pleased they had met, if anything. Deep down, anyway. Andrea was the closest thing she had to a mother figure in her life and Lord knows the mother she was born with had been anything but motherly, or even vaguely competent, for most of Felicity's life.

So why, then, was her stomach in knots at the thought of Harry and Andrea together?

She racked her brain, humming along to "Birdhouse in Your Soul" on the radio as she did so, and wondering for the umpteenth time how a song about a nightlight shaped like a canary could be quite so damn catchy.

And then it hit her.

The impending doom was Harry himself.

Felicity may not have seen him for years but he had run away on Boxing Day and moved in with another woman when Felicity was just six years old. Jocelyn had been cheating on him, fair enough, but Harry had still betrayed their trust and left them completely bereft, just when they really needed a father. Felicity couldn't help but feel he was only going to let her down again at some point. Once an abandoner, always an abandoner, right? It was the reason she was only letting him get so close right now. That revelation made her gasp. She had been holding him off. Not letting him hug her and not sharing too much of her own life with him. Even as an adult her subconscious was protecting her from getting too close. She knew he still had the ability to hurt her deeply if she let him.

What if he did the same to Andrea? How could she sit by and let dear Andrea get hurt?

And then it hit her square between the eyes. She was a terrible friend. She was already letting exactly the same happen to Bex.

I have to do something, she told herself, as she pulled her crappy old car into the driveway next to James's fancy red Mustang and his "save the planet" electric number. *I have to protect both of them from making terrible mistakes.*

But how?

And was she too late to save either of them?

CHAPTER 37

Felicity was running out of time.

The big day was practically here and she still hadn't decided what to do about Bex, or how to do it. In a little over twenty-four hours her best friend would be getting married to the same man who had broken her heart multiple times. And at this rate, Felicity was going to let it happen. What kind of friend did that make her?

To make matters a million times worse, Felicity was the damn chief bridesmaid, which meant everyone she knew would be watching proceedings with an extra layer of interest. Hoping for a bit of drama. A touch of gossip to take back to their dull little lives. Ironic, really, given that less than two years ago Felicity's life had been the dullest of all. And although she wouldn't (really) have swapped it, at this moment she wanted to crawl back under the covers and sleep until Monday. She lay for a moment staring at the ceiling and then, finally and with a monumental effort, she dragged her reluctant body out of bed and down the stairs. Her phone was already buzzing with an endless stream of WhatsApp messages so Felicity threw it into the cutlery drawer, dumped some biscuits into the cats' bowls and then sat at the kitchen table clutching a mug of hot tea and trying to put her thoughts in some kind of order while they munched noisily beside her.

Everything was organised, of course, because Sophie existed, and right at this moment Felicity could not have been more grateful for that fact. Her friend had somehow known that this would all be too much to contemplate and had quietly and discreetly taken on most of the maid of honour duties, something Felicity would merrily spend the rest of her life thanking her for. What she wasn't so thankful for, was the fact that they were due to leave shortly for an Airbnb for the night before, a pretty former mill-house by a river just a few minutes from the venue, which was a converted barn with beautiful high-beamed ceilings and an overwhelming aroma of – what did Bridget Jones call them? – "smug marrieds" around every corner.

And before the horrors of the wedding there was the Getting Ready. In other words, spending a miserable Friday with all the other bridesmaids she still hardly knew, Sophie (thank God) and Bex. All Felicity had to do was pack a bag and get in the car and head to the house they'd rented for the weekend for the girls to get ready in, but as she sat there that morning, the silence of the house surrounding her, her gorgeous James asleep two floors above her, the prospect was almost crippling. She very nearly rang her therapist but she knew Hattie wouldn't thank her for a phone call at 6.47am and besides, there wasn't time. This one she was going to have to handle on her own.

This time on Sunday, she repeated over and over like a mantra, *this time on Sunday it'll all be over. Either you will have told Bex not to marry Adam or you will have watched her marry your ex and doom herself to a life of unhappiness.*

What would Felicity's world look like then?

'Darling Felicity,' said Bex, throwing her arms around her neck as soon as she arrived, still bleary-eyed from the early start. Felicity gave her back a cursory pat.

'It's nearly time, how are you feeling?'

Bex waved a hand. 'Fine, just fine. I'm fine.'

Felicity raised her eyebrows. 'Erm. Are you sure about that?'

Her friend's face crumpled just a little. 'Yes… I think so.'

'Do you need a chat?' *Why did I say that?* 'I mean, if not with me then I can find someone I'm sure…' *Or that?*

Bex put her head on one side, her lips drawn into a perfect pout. 'No, actually, you'll be perfect.'

'Okay…' said Felicity, although this was very much not okay.

They nestled into an alcove in the capacious Airbnb lounge which meant their knees were touching and Felicity didn't know where to put her eyes. She ended up focusing on the bookshelf on the opposite wall – it had a ladder and everything! – just so she didn't have to really look Bex in the eye from this acute angle. She remembered something funny she'd seen online, pointing out that Beauty would have actually happily slept with the Beast in his beast form just to get a library with a ladder. Felicity loved books. She loved libraries with ladders too. But maybe not quite that much.

'Shoot,' said Felicity, wrapping a foot underneath her and trying to focus on being in the present moment.

Bex took in a long slow breath. 'I'm so glad you were the first one here, Fliss.'

Felicity gave a wry smile. 'Maid of Honour Extraordinaire, that's me.'

'Yes, well, I'm grateful because I wanted to talk to you.'

'Okay…'

'Stop saying okay like that. You make it sound like you think I'm some kind of ogre.'

Felicity felt her face flush a little. That was exactly what she thought. 'Nonsense.'

'Of course you do. And who could blame you? I am marrying Adam, after all.'

Acid began bubbling in Felicity's stomach and she cursed herself for not bringing the Rennies. 'What's that supposed to mean?'

'You know exactly what it means,' snapped Bex.

The sharpness of her tone took Felicity's breath away. 'I'm afraid I don't. I can't tell if you're implying you think I still have feelings for him or…'

'I'm not implying anything. I'm saying it.' Bex was properly scowling now.

Felicity stood up and started pacing back and forwards across the room. She felt like she'd been ambushed but she wasn't sure how it had happened, exactly.

'Saying what? That you think I still love Adam? You must know that's not true. How could that ever be true? After what he did? After what you both did?'

Bex shrugged. Actually shrugged. 'The heart wants what the heart wants. Isn't that the line?'

Bile rose in Felicity's throat and she had to swallow three times, which at least gave her a moment to think.

'Let me get this straight,' she began. 'On the day before your wedding to my ex-boyfriend, the man who you cheated on me with for years and have now elected for some unknown reason to tie yourself to for eternity, you are accusing me of being still in love with him? Do I have that straight?' Felicity knew the hot flash of anger was visible on her pale cheeks but she no longer cared.

To her surprise, Bex burst into tears. Great, lashing sobs that shook her whole body. Felicity stood paralysed, only able to watch as her friend, or whatever she was, tried to get herself under control. She had never ever seen Bex cry like this.

'No,' Bex said, sniffing, 'that's not it at all.'

'But you said—'

'I know what I said,' Bex cut in, swallowing another enormous sob, the tears rolling freely down her cheeks. 'I know what I said but I didn't mean it. I'm so sorry, Felicity.'

Felicity sat back down in the alcove with a thump and patted Bex's knee.

'What did you mean then?' she said, trying to keep her voice even.

'I know it's not your fault,' said Bex. 'And I know I'm the worst person in the whole world for even thinking it but I think Adam still loves you. And I hate you for it. And I'm so sorry.'

Felicity rubbed at her forehead. 'There's no way that's true,' she said, after a few moments' thought.

Bex looked up at her, hope flashing in her eyes. It was kind of pathetic. Felicity suddenly felt really sorry for her. Maybe she really did love Adam.

'You don't think so?'

Felicity shook her head. 'No, I don't think so. I'm being truthful. I've barely seen him since you two got engaged so I have no idea where you even got this from.'

'Because he said…'

Felicity held up a hand at that. 'I actually don't want to know what he said.' *Even though she really did.* 'I can't see how that's going to help anyone, is it?'

Her friend's shoulders slumped. 'No. I suppose not.'

'Forget what he said. He says a lot of things. And the thing is, we did talk about this when you got engaged if you remember. You said you knew he might always have some feelings for me but you were going to go for it anyway. Do you remember that?'

Bex frowned. 'That doesn't sound like me.'

'Well, that's what you said. And I'm not saying he does still have feelings for me, or anything like that, but you went into this with your eyes wide open. You know what kind of man he is. Are you sure you want to marry him, Bex?'

There. She'd said it.

Bex spun to look at her.

'So, you don't want me to marry him. I knew it.'

Felicity held up her hands. 'That is very much not what I said.'

Bex's eyes narrowed. 'I knew you'd try and sabotage this. I'm going to go through with it. And there's nothing you can do to stop me.'

Felicity stood up but this time her feet carried her all the way to the door.

'Then you're going to have to do it without your maid of honour. I quit.'

She opened the door to three of the bridesmaids whose names she couldn't even remember. Kirsty or Kristy or something, wasn't it? Felicity felt the tears well up as she looked at their surprised faces but she just swallowed and pushed past them. 'Good luck,' she muttered, pulling out her phone to tell Sophie what had happened.

It was the right thing to do. Of course it was. So why did she feel so rotten?

CHAPTER 38

Felicity was sitting at home that night, licking her wounds, while Bobby Charlton purred away on her knees doing his best to cheer her up, when the doorbell rang. Standing on the front step was Bex, face lined with streaks of make-up, eyes red.

Before Felicity could even say a word Bex had thrown her arms around her neck. She resisted the urge to push her away.

'Fliss... I'm so very sorry,' Bex was murmuring into her ear, over and over again. Her long dark hair tickled Felicity's nose. She patted Bex's back tentatively – Bex was another non-hugger in her life so this was still relatively new territory – and waited for the hug to end.

'It's okay,' said Felicity eventually, even though it wasn't.

Bex pulled back and looked at her. Felicity couldn't read her expression but then she had long felt like a stranger.

'Come in,' said Felicity, and led her friend, or whoever this person was, through to the kitchen to put the kettle on.

'Is James here?' said Bex, wiping her eyes.

'No, he's at work late today so he can be free for the wedding tomorrow. It's just me.'

'Oh. Good. I mean, not that I don't want to see him of course.'

'I know.'

They took their cups of tea through to the lounge area and Bex perched on the edge of the squishiest armchair, her feet placed neatly together on the floor, still sniffing. Felicity curled up on the sofa and tucked her feet underneath her. Immediately little Holly the cat came and sat on her lap. Felicity absently stroked her ginger-and-white fur and waited for Bex to speak.

'I'm getting married tomorrow,' said Bex, eventually.

Felicity huffed a laugh. 'I know that.'

'And I really need you to be there.'

'I don't think that's appropriate, do you?' Felicity had already planned a Saturday of sofa-surfing and a marathon of the BBC's *Pride and Prejudice* if James would tolerate it. Her go-to hiding-place show.

Bex started to cry. Not dainty barely-there crying like her usual but more of those big racking sobs that shook her whole body. Felicity wondered if she actually wasn't coping. Something was very wrong. 'You're my maid of honour,' she said between convulsions, trying to get her breathing under control.

'Not anymore,' said Felicity. And then she felt bad. 'I mean, I'm sorry. I just don't think I can do it.'

'But you're my friend. I need you beside me,' said Bex and something in her tone broke something inside Felicity's soul. Tears sprang to her eyes. Time to speak the truth.

'Bex, you're marrying Adam. My childhood sweetheart—'

'I know that, but—'

Felicity held up a hand. Bex's eyes widened.

'No,' said Felicity firmly. 'This time you are going to let me finish, Bex. You are marrying my childhood sweetheart. You expect me to stand beside you as your maid of honour as you do that. And, bizarrely, you seem to think I'm going to be fine with all that. News flash. I'm not.'

Felicity paused, waiting for an indignant outcry that never came. Bex just nodded dumbly.

'And that's not because I'm in love with Adam or anything ridiculous like that,' Felicity went on. 'Just to be clear. There is no love lost between Adam and I. Right?'

Bex nodded harder.

'But that doesn't mean I'm thrilled about this wedding. And that's okay.' Felicity knew as she said it that it was true. It was okay for her to feel like this and she didn't need to apologise for it. It was the first time her brain had caught up with her gut.

Bex was still nodding.

'You're right,' she said, her long red-painted fingernails tapping vigorously on the arm of the chair. 'I have asked you to do something completely unfair.'

'I'm glad you can finally see it.' Felicity's heart was thumping but she tried to keep her tone calm, neutral. It was the night before Bex's wedding after all and the next few words were critical.

'I can see it.' Bex took a deep breath. 'I know you're worried about me and I have to say I haven't always been but I'm super appreciative of that now. You've always been a great friend to me, Felicity.'

Felicity shifted uncomfortably on the sofa. 'I've tried to be,' she said in a small voice.

Bex inhaled deeply. 'But I am still going to ask you to be there tomorrow. Please, Felicity. I know it must be hard but you're one of my only real friends and if I don't have you there it'll be like I don't have your blessing.'

'You don't.' Felicity crossed her arms.

Bex waved a hand. 'I know that and you know that and Adam knows that but no one else knows that, do they? They'll all be watching…' Her voice tailed off.

Realisation hit Felicity like a freight train. 'So you want to make it look like I approve? Is that what this is all about?' Her voice was rising in pitch. Just when she thought things were getting better. She finally understood the phrase "tearing your hair out".

Bex nodded once. 'Yes, of course it is. I want – no, I *need* everyone to see that you're okay with this. Otherwise I'll always worry and my family will be worried too and we don't need that. You know? I love Adam and I don't want any whispering tomorrow about the fact he used to be with you. I need you there so they can see it's all okay between us.'

She paused.

'It is all okay between us, right? I mean, aside from me puking on you at the hen do that is.' Bex gave a weak smile.

Felicity looked at her for a long moment.

'Let me get this straight in my head. You want me to come and be your maid of honour and show the world I'm fine with you marrying Adam?'

'That's exactly it, yes,' said Bex, relief palpable.

Another long pause while Felicity considered her options. There weren't many. She could lose Bex's friendship forever or she could stand up there tomorrow and show the world she thought Adam wasn't the most terrible guy on the planet. Even though he was. And even though Bex's friendship was hardly worth saving.

'Fine. I'll do it,' she said, regretting the words even as they left her mouth. Bex started crying all over again.

It was just one day, right? How bad could it be?

Pretty bad, as it turned out, although it mostly wasn't Felicity's fault, in the end. Mostly.

CHAPTER 39

The day of the wedding dawned bright and sunny. The birds were singing outside her bedroom window as Felicity got dressed in her teal-coloured chiffon maid of honour dress, put a tiara in her hair, did her make-up with a shaking hand, and tried to get her thoughts into some kind of order. Teal had won out, in the end.

'You ready, beautiful?' said James, sticking his head round the bedroom door, his voice like balm against her agitated mind.

She turned and he inhaled sharply.

'Wow, you really do look beautiful. Even, er, even more beautiful than usual I mean.'

'Ha ha, sure. At least she didn't go with rose, not the best colour to go with ginger hair. I swear she was just doing that on purpose to tease me.'

James laughed, then came towards her and pulled her into a hug. He didn't need to ask who "she" was.

'You're a knockout,' he whispered into her hair.

'I can't do this,' she said into his chest.

'There's still time to back out. I can make some excuse. Say you're ill. Say you've suddenly moved to Australia. Whatever you want.'

She breathed against him. In. Out. In. Out. The dress's corset was tight against her skin and the fabric was itchy. She didn't remember it being this itchy in the shop. Had it been this itchy in the shop?

'No. It's okay. Let's just get it over with.'

He gave her a squeeze and then loosened his grip. She appraised him for a moment. Navy suit, cream shirt, navy tie. He always did scrub up well.

'Damn, you look pretty good yourself,' she said.

James gave her a lingering look, then shook his head. 'No time for that now, Brooks, we've got to go. Plus I don't want to muss up your hair.'

She giggled in spite of the butterflies swirling in her stomach.

'You never stop, do you, Penguin Man?'

'Not if I can help it.'

The plan was for Felicity to be dropped off at Bex's house an hour before the ceremony. Which would have been fine except Felicity's sudden attack of nerves meant they'd had to go back to their own house three times already to check the curling tongs were off and the cat flaps were open and the house had been locked, even though they had to unlock it anyway. You know, to check it was locked.

They arrived fifteen minutes late in the end, but fortunately Bex was too busy having a last-minute meltdown of her own. The other bridesmaids and Bex's mother Petunia were circling her like she was some kind of caged beast, hands raised, voices soothing, while Bex screamed and hurled clothes around the lounge, ostensibly because she'd lost the bracelet Adam gave her. Although Felicity wondered if it just felt good, burning off some nervous energy, letting it all go while she still could. Felicity could do with a bit of hurling herself.

When she saw Felicity, Bex's face relaxed into relief.

'You came,' she breathed, coming forwards to take Felicity's hands in hers. She really did look incredible. The creamy skirts beneath the red corset were made of pure silk, with tiny pearls sewed in swirls across the fabric, and it rustled extravagantly when she walked. The contrast with the teal of Felicity's dress, it was even more perfect than she imagined.

'Couldn't miss the party of the century, now, could I?' Felicity grinned with some effort, trying not to catch Sophie's eye from across the room.

At this Bex's forehead crinkled.

'It would be the party of the century,' she wailed, 'if I could only find my damn bracelet.'

'What, this one?' said Sophie, holding up something sparkly.

'Where did you find that?' said Bex.

'It was down the side of the sofa,' said Sophie, coming forwards and bending to attach it to Bex's arm.

'What would I do without you two?' said Bex.

Bex and Felicity looked at each other over Sophie's hand, and for one special moment it felt absolutely right that Felicity was here. Just like old times. The three of them together, as they had always been.

For one moment, anyway.

Felicity felt rather differently an hour later when they were walking solemnly down the aisle to a piece of classical music she couldn't remember the name of. She was too busy trying not to catch the eyes of what felt like a thousand people all turning to stare at her as she passed. Felicity's face heated to approximately a thousand degrees under the burning scrutiny of those stares.

'Ignore them,' hissed Sophie from beside her, but how could she? What were they staring at?

Felicity had to swallow down the physical temptation to turn and run, which was almost overwhelming. She looked over the heads of the crowd until she found James. He was staring at her with something like awe, and when she caught his eye he nodded, just once, almost imperceptibly, but it was enough. She could do this.

Just don't look at Adam.

Whatever. You. Do.

A murmur ran through the crowd as Bex arrived behind her in the doorway and for a moment, all eyes turned towards the bride. Without any signal between them Felicity and Sophie's walk got a little faster until finally, finally, finally they reached the front and could take their places in the front row. Felicity's sigh of relief as she sat was so deep her ribs strained the corset of her dress and she winced.

Adam was standing right in front of her now, his expensive aftershave almost overpowering. She could stare at him freely for a moment, as his attention was finally elsewhere. Felicity had felt his eyes on her all the way down the aisle but she didn't want to think about what that might mean.

Annoyingly, he was even more handsome than usual, in a silver-grey suit and teal tie to match the bridesmaids. His dark hair was slicked back and his brown skin was almost luminous in the light of the church. She watched him smiling that full-toothed smile across the room at Bex as she took slow deliberate steps down the aisle. For anyone else it would have seemed like the perfect romantic moment. Only Felicity could see that the smile wasn't reaching his eyes.

An awed hush settled over the room as Bex reached the altar and Adam leant over to whisper something in her ear. She really did look stunning, her dark hair in an elaborate twist and studded with pearls, her high cheekbones even more accentuated in the pseudo-daylight of the church. But there was a sickly pallor to her skin that Felicity hadn't noticed back at the house. She wondered vaguely if Bex was pregnant.

The vicar stood up. This was his moment. He cleared his throat and began with the famous "dearly beloved" line and Felicity wriggled back as far as she could on the pew and started to relax a little. It felt slightly surreal in the way that weddings often do. She'd seen so many on television and in films perhaps that it didn't feel quite like reality now she was actually there. As he spoke the familiar words, Felicity let them wash over her. Tears prickled behind her eyes. It was happening. After all the excruciating waiting the ceremony was finally happening and soon she could go back to her life and she'd never have to see Bex and Adam again if she didn't want to.

Sophie reached across and patted her hand. James was in the row behind but she could feel his presence and that was a comfort too.

Suddenly there was some sort of kerfuffle from halfway down the church.

'Wait.' The word rang out strong and true and the whole congregation fell silent.

The vicar covered his eyes and scanned the room.

'I'm sorry, did someone speak?'

'It was me,' came the voice again, strong and confident and female.

The vicar almost laughed, perhaps from shock or nerves. Bex and Adam exchanged anxious glances.

'And what can I do for you?' said the vicar, his voice shaky.

'You have to stop the wedding,' came the voice, and there was a loud gasp from the crowd.

Felicity turned to see a young black woman with the most incredible dark glossy hair pouring down over her shoulders, standing up now in a row about halfway back. She was dressed in a simple and very elegant silk burgundy dress, little more than a slip, really, and her eyes were big and dark-brown and sincere.

'Tabitha?' said Adam, his voice catching in his throat. 'What the hell are you doing?'

'That's Tabitha?' squeaked Bex, turning towards him.

But he didn't respond. Just stared at this interloper, along with the rest of the room.

'I'm afraid I can't do that,' said the vicar, whose face had turned a sort of greenish colour.

'But what about if anyone knows of any lawful impediments?' said Tabitha, her eyes never leaving Adam's face for even a second.

'We haven't got to that part yet,' said Bex, tossing her head.

But the vicar was frowning. 'Do you know of any?' he asked her. 'Is one of these persons already married and they haven't declared it? Is this marriage taking place under duress, to your knowledge?'

Tabitha looked a little shaken for the first time.

'I...'

'It has to be *legal* impediments, you witch,' said Bex, her face like thunder now. 'Otherwise you can sit the fuck down.'

Petunia, sitting in the second row, came to life then. She tutted at Bex's use of the F-word and Felicity made a mental note to use that word as much as possible in future. Then Bex's mother turned to Tabitha, cool as you like, rolling her eyes as if Tabitha were a small child having a tantrum. 'Do sit down, dear, you're making a spectacle of yourself.'

The vicar looked at her gratefully. Felicity wondered if he was going to ask her to run the service next.

'Wait.' Another voice came ringing across the room. A little less confident than the last perhaps but still unmistakably female.

The vicar was looking like he might actually be sick now.

'I'm sorry, who is that please? Do you have something to say? Shall we go into the vestry and discuss all this in a calm manner?'

Adam turned to him. 'Is this some kind of a joke?'

'I'm afraid not, I'm sorry, er, Adam, this has never happened before. Um, just bear with me and we'll get to the bottom of things.'

'We may not know of anything legal,' came the voice. Felicity turned and squinted. Right at the back of the room was another woman, this time dressed all in black. 'We may not know the rules but we can tell you a few home truths about Adam here.'

Petunia let out a little scream and covered her mouth with a gloved hand.

'Oh my days,' whispered Sophie as more gasps came from around the room.

By now the vicar was frantically flicking through the *Book of Common Prayer* as if that was going to hold the answers for what to do in such a scenario, even though Felicity was fairly sure this had never happened before in the whole history of time. Not in real life, anyway.

'I'm sorry, Bex or whatever your name is, but you have to know.' Tabitha was speaking again now. 'This man you are marrying cannot be trusted.' She seemed to be trying to get in there ahead of the mystery woman at the back.

'Damn straight.' That was the one at the back chiming in. 'He's scum.'

Felicity glanced at Bex, who let out one long, ear-splitting wail and sank to her knees at the altar. Sophie and Felicity leapt out of their seats and tried to help her up but she pushed them away. Even Petunia's cool façade had cracked and she was dabbing at her eyes with a tissue.

'Bex, listen to me,' Felicity found herself saying. 'He's changed, I'm sure he has.'

Adam turned and nodded. 'I have, I've changed, Felicity's right.'

'He hasn't changed,' came the voice from the back, and now the mystery woman in black was walking towards them down the aisle. Felicity's blood was pounding in her ears. *What was happening?* 'He hasn't changed and I can prove it.'

'This is my *wedding day.*' Bex was properly sobbing now, the tears pouring down her face.

'Not if you know what's good for you,' said Tabitha loudly.

The vicar held up his hands and tried to get some kind of order but no one was listening to him anymore.

The mystery woman came right up to the front. Felicity didn't recognise her but that didn't mean much, she knew Adam had a history. Tabitha, she had known about. Tabitha had been the original intended recipient of the Tiffany ring that had afterwards been given to Felicity and now adorned Bex's finger too. It had history, that ring, and Tabitha they had both known about all along. But this? This new arrival could be anyone.

Bex reached out her arms and her friends pulled her to her feet. *Good on you,* thought Felicity and then vaguely wondered if the three women were going to fight.

'Get out of this church right now,' Bex spat, tears still staining her face.

The woman ignored her completely, turned to Adam and slapped his face, hard, a ringing slap that reverberated off the stone walls. Adam, thank God, didn't fight back, didn't even respond really, although his eyes watered and a large red mark started appearing on his face almost immediately.

There was a long pause while the whole room held its breath.

'What are you doing here?' he said finally, his voice cracking.

'I'm saving you from yourself,' said the woman, her head lifting, jaw flexing. Felicity caught James's eye and he gave her a surreptitious shrug. *He's bloody enjoying this,* thought Felicity.

Bex went right up to the woman, her face right in hers and Felicity inhaled sharply. Bex put a hand out as if to touch her shoulder, then thought better of it.

'Clearly you are not well. Why don't we call someone to take you home?' she said in her most charming voice. Just like her mother. Trying to seem like the reasonable one.

The woman recoiled from her, took a step backwards, then turned to face the congregation. The poor vicar actually took a step back too, whether in solidarity or perhaps he'd realised he had totally lost control by this point.

'This man is a fraud,' said the woman, pointing at Adam, her blue eyes flashing with hatred as she scanned the crowd. 'He was sleeping with me less than two weeks ago and then had the audacity to tell me he was getting married today. It might not be a lawful impediment or whatever the word is but there's no way this wedding should be going ahead, today or any other day.'

At her words, all hell was unleashed.

CHAPTER 40

All around them was total pandemonium. Petunia had fainted or, at least, someone nearby was fanning her with an order of service. Some people were shouting at the woman in the black dress. Other random relatives were shouting at Tabitha. Still more were shouting at the vicar. Adam was shouting at himself, weirdly, his hands gesticulating wildly as if berating himself for ever having been born in the first place. As well he might.

'Get. Me. Out. Of. Here,' hissed Bex as Felicity and Sophie dithered backwards and forwards as if someone had hit pause on an old-fashioned video, neither quite sure what the hell to do.

Eventually James jumped up, waving his car keys. 'My car is just across the road, let's go,' he said. Felicity almost had time to appreciate how hot he looked when he took charge.

Bex nodded grimly. Tears were openly falling onto her silk dress, causing tiny little watermarks. Sophie went to dab at it with a tissue but Bex batted her away. 'Don't bother. I don't need it now, do I?' she muttered, grimly.

Sophie nodded, her jaw set in a tight line. She hated any kind of confrontation. 'Let's go then.'

All around them was noise and chaos. Petunia had been moved to the side of the church and someone had found her a chair. Relatives on both sides were putting their coats on and tutting, others seemed to have taken it as an excuse to air their own dirty laundry and there were little mini-scenes happening all over the church. The poor vicar had come over all faint, too, and someone had gone to fetch him a brandy. Adam was marching up and down the aisle, still berating himself, while the woman in black followed him, shouting abuse at his back as she did so.

As they made their way down a side aisle towards the door, Felicity realised Tabitha was right in front of them, also beating a hasty retreat.

'Yeah, you better run!' screamed Bex, speeding up her steps and reaching out to pull the woman's hair. Sophie grabbed her hand.

'I don't think that's a good idea, do you?'

'Don't tell me what's a good idea,' spat Bex. 'Why did no one tell me? Why did I have to get to the bloody altar before someone had the guts to tell me what I was dealing with?'

At that, Felicity lost the plot.

'I do hope you're joking,' she said, trying to keep her voice calm even as her blood pressure rose to boiling.

Bex turned to her at the door, looking blank.

'I told you, Bex. I tried. God, how I tried.' Tears filled her eyes.

They blinked at each other. Then Bex's face changed. Softened just a fraction. Or was that resignation? 'You're right. I think you might be my only friends in the world, you two. You did try to warn me. And now look what's happened.' She dropped her hands to her sides as if to say the whole world was ruined, then smoothed her skirts absent-mindedly. Her skin was even paler than before and Felicity wondered if she was going into shock.

As they headed outside the church, Bex muttered quietly, 'What was I thinking?'

'There'll be plenty of time for the post-mortem later,' said James, from behind Felicity's right ear. 'Right now, we need to get you the hell out of here.'

'I'll take her home,' came a stern voice, and they turned on the steps to find Petunia standing behind them, looking grim.

'Mum,' said Bex, collapsing into her arms. 'I'm so sorry.'

'You have nothing to be sorry for,' said Petunia, stroking her daughter's hair a little awkwardly. 'This is not your fault, my darling. I blame those awful women.'

James scoffed. 'Don't you think you ought to be blaming Adam?'

Petunia waved a hand. 'Men will be men,' she said. 'But to bring it up on my darling's special day, that's just cruel.'

Felicity and James exchanged a look.

'I'm sorry,' said Felicity. 'Did you just say, "men will be men"?'

Petunia raised her chin defiantly. Her perfectly coiffured hair had slipped forwards giving the appearance she was wearing a bad wig. Perhaps she was. 'I did say that. And I stand by it. Anyone with any sense knows that men cheat. But as long as they are loyal when it counts, that's what matters.'

Bex's mouth dropped open. 'You cannot be serious right now,' she said, jaw clenching.

'We'll discuss this at home, come along now, Rebecca.'

And with that, she took Bex's arm and led her across the street to her waiting car. Behind them, guests were pouring out of the church doors, their voices raised in excited discussion, and Felicity guessed the vicar had finally managed to call it a day.

When Bex had gone, Sophie, James and Felicity looked at each other, their faces grim.

'Well, that went well,' said James after a moment.

'Perfect,' said Felicity. She was shaking with what? Shock? Relief? Some combination of the two?

'Swimmingly,' said Sophie, with a light laugh. Then she stopped and ran a despairing hand down her face. 'What a bloody mess,' she said.

'At least we've given this lot something to talk about,' said Felicity, nodding to the heavy wooden doors. Wedding guests were still pouring through, blinking in the afternoon sun like giant moles, even though they'd only been inside the building for less than thirty minutes.

'What now?' said James.

'Pub?' said Felicity.

'Pub,' said Sophie, nodding. 'I'll drive.'

'How are you feeling?' said James, passing Felicity her drink and slipping into the booth beside her.

Felicity pondered this for a second or two, pulling at her corset. Her dress was made of cheap fabric that still itched whenever she moved. She couldn't wait to get it off. How was she feeling? This was the outcome she had wanted, deep down. She wanted Bex to know the truth about Adam and now she did and she supposed she should be happy but all she could think of was those little dark tear-stains on Bex's beautiful cream dress. Her heart, torn in two. Felicity had been through break-ups herself, of course, always with Adam incidentally, but to be so humiliated in front of all those people like that. Felicity couldn't even imagine how Bex must be feeling right now.

'I'm fine,' she said, coming back into the moment.

'Yes, me too,' said Sophie.

'Me three,' said James lamely, and they attempted a polite laugh, which died swiftly on their lips.

'Good, glad we're all fine,' said Sophie.

'Poor Bex though,' said James.

Felicity put her head in her hands and gave an anguished groan. 'That poor girl. I should have tried harder. I should have done more. Hell, I should have locked her in her house so she never even had the chance to get there. So he never had the chance to do that to her.'

James rubbed her back absent-mindedly.

'To be fair to the guy, even he couldn't have predicted that would happen.'

'Talk about your past catching up with you. Literally,' said Sophie.

'Your very attractive past,' said Felicity. 'That Tabitha was stunning. Did you see her? Wow. Those boobs, my goodness.'

'I'm glad you're the one who said that,' said James.

Felicity leant her head on his shoulder. 'Thanks for pretending not to notice them,' she said, with a feeble attempt at a smile. He turned and placed a kiss on top of her head. It sent a warm shiver down her spine despite the circumstances. 'You're welcome.'

'Gross,' said Sophie.

'Anyway,' said James, 'what happens now do you think?'

'We have to see if Bex is okay. What if she's not okay? How can we just sit here drinking, when she's in all that pain?'

Felicity half stood as if to go right that very second but Sophie reached out and put a hand on her arm. Her honey-coloured hair was still bound up in its bridesmaid's plait but her make-up had slipped. She looked tired.

'Do you think you're the best person to go to her?' she said to Felicity, gently.

Felicity sat down again. 'I suppose you're right.'

James nodded his agreement. 'She doesn't need to be reminded of you right now, I expect.'

It was a kind of relief.

'I'll go,' said Sophie. 'James, can you take Felicity home?'

'Sure,' he said.

Sophie turned to go, then turned back to the table, downed the last of her half pint, and grimaced. 'What a crappy day,' she said.

'Way to put it mildly,' said Felicity. 'Good luck, Soph. And thanks.'

CHAPTER 41

To this day Felicity will never know why she did it.

But that night when they got back to the house, she tried to blow things up. Not physically of course, that would be weird. And illegal. No, instead, Felicity did her damn best to put a torch to everything she'd built with James and he very nearly let her.

It started innocently enough.

'I don't deserve you,' she said, as they were moving around the kitchen, making cups of tea, grabbing sofa snacks, pouring drinks, the cats roaming round their legs, rubbing against them, hoping for an early dinner or a late lunch or whatever time it was.

'Why are you saying it in that voice?' said James, pouring boiling water over teabags.

'What do you mean?'

'Well, it's not your usual voice. You sound… weird…'

'Do I?' said Felicity distantly, a bag of supermarket-brand Doritos in her hand. They had both ditched their wedding gear in favour of pyjamas and had planned an evening of movies and tortilla chips in an effort to block out the horrors of the day. But Felicity just couldn't stop thinking about it.

'You know you do.'

Felicity waved a hand. 'I was just thinking how lucky I am, that's all. I don't deserve to be with someone as amazing as you.'

'Erm, I'll be the judge of that, thanks very much,' said James, with a grin. He stirred the tea, added milk, spooned the teabags into the bin. Turned to look at her with that piercing stare.

Felicity gave a weak smile and leant back against the counter. 'It's just…'

James's eyes widened and she could see the muscle in his jaw clenching. She cursed herself for what she was about to say, but somehow she couldn't stop.

'What?'

'All that pain, you know? All that trauma. It's astonishing how much two people can hurt each other.'

'Where are you going with this, exactly?'

Her voice caught in her throat. 'Well, I can't help thinking I should let you go now, and get it over with.'

What the hell is wrong with you? said the voice in her head.

'I'm sorry?' said James, frowning.

'To avoid the inevitable heartbreak when you eventually figure out that I'm a total deadbeat,' she said, staring at the floor so she didn't see his face crumpling in pain.

James's voice was gruff now. Raspy. 'Is that a joke? It *sounds* like a Felicity Brooks joke but it doesn't *look* like a Felicity Brooks joke if that makes sense?'

She didn't smile even then. Where once her head had been full of him, her thoughts were now black and despairing. Even now, only eighteen months in, she couldn't bear to think about how she would (or wouldn't) cope if the man she loved was taken from her, at the altar or anywhere else. Perhaps it would be better just to end it now before it became totally impossible to extricate herself without causing permanent harm.

She crossed her arms. 'When I was a kid, right, this random relationships expert came into our school and told us about how sleeping with someone is like putting two bits of cardboard together to make it corrugated or whatever the word is. For some reason I never forgot it.'

'What are you going on about?' He smiled, hoicking himself up onto the counter opposite her.

'Bear with me. So… once you make corrugated cardboard, right, it's super strong but if you try and rip the layers apart again it's nearly impossible to do without leaving pieces behind.'

'Okay…'

'I mean, I think the teacher was trying to just encourage us all to become nuns or monks or something, but the point still stands, right?'

'I'm not following.'

'Once you've connected to someone like that it's almost impossible to separate again. Or not without a whole world of pain.'

James folded his arms. 'Don't think I don't know what you're doing,' he said, a little sharply.

'I'm not doing anything, I was just thinking out loud.'

James hopped down off the counter again and came towards her. He put a hand on either side of the counter where Felicity was standing and leaned in. She could smell his aftershave, his shampoo, his scent, and it was so distracting she almost lost her train of thought completely. *Focus, Felicity.* But it was too late.

'I'm not letting you do this,' he said. 'Do you hear me?'

She tried to feign innocence and failed. His face was inches away now, and his eyes were flicking back and forth from her eyes to her lips. She had to look away again. Felicity had never been very good at eye contact.

'Do what?'

'Destroy us.'

'I'm not.'

James sighed, long and low. 'Do you remember what I said to you when we first got together? That I loved you and there was no way in hell I was ever going to let you go? Well, I meant it. And—' Felicity went to interject but he held up a hand. 'No, Brooks, wait. I know you have trust issues and I told you I would stick by you until you learnt to trust me, didn't I? And I think we made good progress, all things considered, but now you're trying to blow it all up because you've seen the damage that two people can do to each other more times in your life than anyone ever should and you're trying to protect yourself from the same thing happening. Am I right?'

Felicity looked up at him. He actually had tears in his eyes. Her heart clenched in her chest at the sight.

'You're right,' she said. 'How the hell did you know that?'

He sighed again. 'Because I get it. I've been there too, remember. I've had my heart ripped out and stamped on and when you've been through something like that and then you meet someone new it's hard not to spend every day in absolute terror of it happening again.'

Felicity swallowed a lump in her throat and shook her head. 'Seeing Bex and Adam today. Her face. My God, I never want to go through something like that.'

He inched closer to her. 'I would *never* do that to you. I mean it. Never.'

'I know that,' she whispered. 'I mean, my brain knows that rationally, like, you're a good guy and we have something great here… but I'm still scared every single minute.'

'I get that. And listen, right, if you really want me to go and leave you to turn into a proper Crazy Cat Lady, I will. I'll do whatever you want me to do. I just want you to be happy.'

'You're making it very hard for me to concentrate right now,' she breathed as he drew closer until he was a heartbeat from kissing her.

'Tell me to go and I'll go,' he said, his lips millimetres from hers.

Her heart was thumping for different reasons now. 'I don't want you to go. It was a stupid wobble, that's all.'

James bowed his head and she put her hands into his messy blond hair. He wrapped his arms around her waist and groaned with relief, pulling her to him.

'Say that again,' he mumbled into her chest.

'It was a stupid wobble.'

'Not that bit.'

'Oh. I said I don't want you to go.'

He let out a grim laugh and she could feel his body vibrate against hers. 'Thank God. Please don't scare me like that.'

She giggled in spite of herself. 'I'm so sorry, that was really mean.'

'It was really mean,' he said, lifting his head and looking into her eyes once more. 'And now you need to be taught a lesson.' He gave her a cheeky grin.

'Ooh, I like the sound of that,' she said, as he lifted her onto the counter and pressed his body between her thighs. Her hands were on his shoulders and her heart was in her mouth.

'You better believe it,' he said, his voice a low purr.

'Are you going to punish me?' she whispered in his ear and he moaned once more, then covered her mouth with his and kissed her deep and soft and slow till it was her turn to moan.

And then his hands were lifting her pyjama vest over her head and running all over her skin and she had her hands on his taut stomach and they were kissing each other urgently and all Felicity could think was *please, please, please never leave me.*

Fortunately, she couldn't embarrass herself by actually saying the words out loud or begging him to stay with her forever. After all, her mouth was busy.

CHAPTER 42

*B*ex was in a bit of a pickle.

By all accounts, Sophie had spent the rest of the weekend camped on her sofa, mopping her up on a regular basis, making sure she was dressed, trying to get her to eat a few morsels of food, brushing her hair. It was like having another child, she said. Felicity had never heard her friend sound so worried.

On the Monday, Felicity took her turn. Bex had done it for her, after all, all those years ago. As she let herself into Bex's flat with the key from Sophie, the first thing that struck her was the smell. It was the smell of eco-cleaner which seemed to permeate the whole place. Eucalyptus and rhubarb or something like that. It was overpowering.

She found Bex curled up under a duvet on the sofa.

'What is that smell?'

No response.

'Bex. Are you under there? What's that awful smell?'

She shook Bex's shoulder, or at least, where she thought her shoulder should be under all those feathers, and felt a stab of fear go through her when there was no movement. And then, very slowly, Bex pulled down the duvet just far enough that she could turn her head and look at Felicity. Her eyes were red and swollen and her skin was blotchy. Felicity couldn't remember ever having seen her without make-up before, let alone looking like this.

'Sophie's been cleaning,' she said quietly, and her voice was rough as if she hadn't spoken for a while. Which, according to Sophie, she hadn't.

'You're not kidding,' said Felicity, attempting a laugh. 'It smells like she's cleaned the whole place with a stick of rhubarb. I do hate rhubarb.'

She was hoping for a small chuckle with that one, but there was nothing. Felicity perched on the edge of the sofa and put a hand on the duvet pile.

'How are you?' she said gently.

'Why are you here, Felicity?' said Bex then, her voice sharp.

'I had to see you, to see if you're okay.'

'What do you think?'

'If I had to guess I'd say… you're not?'

The body under the duvet snorted with disdain. 'Funny that.'

'Do you want me to get you some lunch?'

'Not hungry.'

'Okay. Is there anything else you need?'

At this, Bex threw the covers back completely and Felicity stood up and moved to the opposite sofa to give her some room. Bex sat up and rubbed her hands across her face but she didn't reply.

'Bex, I'm so, so sorry. Can I do anything?' said Felicity, attempting to sound patient and understanding.

Her friend looked across at her, her expression blank.

'Can you turn back time? Can you send me to a desert island where no one can ever find me? Can you take away my memories? Any one of those would do me.'

Felicity sighed. 'I'm sorry, Bex. I can't do any of those things.' Then she brightened. 'But we are having an open day at the centre on Saturday. Why don't you come? It might do you good? You could come see the cats and dogs. We've got the most adorable puppies.'

'So you want me to turn into Crazy Animal Lady now, do you?' Bex practically spat.

'No, not at all. I just thought…'

'I appreciate it,' said Bex, with a sarcastic smile. 'But I'll pass.'

Felicity stood up. 'Look, it's obvious I'm not being much help. I'll just get you some lunch and then I'll get out of your hair.'

'I said I don't want any lunch.'

'Fine, then I'll just go.'

'Fine.'

Felicity was almost at the door when she turned back.

'Bex?' she said. Bex was crawling back under her duvet and didn't even turn at her name.

'What?'

'I did try to warn you.'

As soon as the words were out of her mouth, she knew they were a mistake. What a cruel thing to say. She felt sick.

'I know you did,' said Bex, with a bitter laugh. 'And I thought you were trying to break us up so you could have him. When all along he'd found someone else anyway. Two people maybe. He can't keep it in his pants long enough to make it through a wedding without someone wanting him, apparently.'

'He never deserved you,' said Felicity quietly.

Bex sat up again. 'You're right, he didn't. Why are you here, Fliss?'

Her words were sharp and they cut Felicity almost physically.

'I'm your friend,' she said, her voice catching.

Bex scoffed. 'Some friend I've been to you.'

'It's okay,' said Felicity.

'It's not okay. I'm a terrible person and now I've got what I deserved, haven't I?' Again, that bitter laugh.

Felicity took a step towards her, then stopped. 'No one could deserve what he's put you through,' she said.

'Please don't mention it. I can't even think about Saturday, I'm so embarrassed.'

'No, of course not, sorry.'

'Do you think he ever even cared about me at all?'

Felicity shifted from foot to foot. 'Honestly? I don't know, my lovely. He's your classic narcissist. I don't know if Adam is capable of loving anyone but himself, and he doesn't even do that very well.'

'I wondered if he was a sex addict, you know, like that actor.'

'That was never proven, was it?'

'Still.'

Felicity considered this for a moment. 'I mean, I suppose that could be true. He probably ought to be better at it though,' she ventured, then grinned at Bex and to her delight, Bex answered with a giggle. There was the friend she knew.

'It's good to see you smile.'

Bex shrugged. 'Can't let the bastards get us down, can we?'

'That's my girl.'

On her way down the stairs, Felicity's phone buzzed in her pocket.

Sophie: How's the patient?

She stopped on a landing and tapped out a reply.

Felicity: You know, I think she's gonna be ok.

Sophie: I really hope so.

Felicity: What do we do about Adam?

Sophie: Shall we burn his house down?

Felicity: I mean, I was thinking more like talking to him, but ok, let's go straight to arson. In fact, I know a guy who can probably do that for us.

Sophie: Why don't you get Penguin Man to talk to him?

Felicity: Are you mad?

Sophie: I'm serious. He's a spy, he's got all those negotiation skills and whatnot.

Felicity: He's not going to waterboard him if that's what you mean. And for the hundredth time, my boyfriend is not a spy. He just works for the government.

Sophie: Same thing. And surely just a tiny bit of waterboarding would be fine.

Felicity: Do you even know what waterboarding is?

Sophie: Not really. Is it like surfing?

Felicity: Love you.

Sophie: Love you. Thanks for going today. That must have been hard.

Felicity: It was.

And it had been. So hard to see Bex in such a state and also really hard to take the brunt of her simmering hatred when in reality, Felicity had been "this close" to never even being at the wedding. How part of her wished she'd been brave enough to stay home and watch Jane Austen in her pyjamas.

And then it hit her. Would it have all played out the same if she hadn't been there? Had her presence actually stirred up the hornets' nest instead of making things better? There was no way to know.

Felicity: I'm so glad you were there.

Sophie: Me too.

CHAPTER 43

Saturday morning was sunny for September, but a sharp northerly wind bit at Felicity and James's cheeks as they got out of the car. Today was the open day at Animal Saviours, and Felicity and James had arrived super early to hang bunting and sweep floors and make frantic phone calls to find alternative food vans when two of the ones they booked broke down on the same day.

By 10am all was calm. They were ready. The centre looked beautiful. Clean, beautiful… and empty. Even by 10.30am not a single guest had arrived. Andrea came and stood next to Felicity by the front doors, where she was staring out into space willing people to come walking round the corner or pull into the car park.

'They'll be here,' said Andrea, in her weird, slightly chipper voice that she only used when she knew Harry was coming to visit.

'They'd better hurry,' muttered Felicity. 'Maybe it's too cold. Maybe they're all hibernating.' And then a thought struck her and it struck her so hard and fast that cold ice ran down her spine. She edged away from Andrea, slowly.

'Just got to go and check something,' she said hastily, and then turned and ran before Andrea could even reply.

Felicity burst into the staff room where Charlie and James were obediently laying out cups and investigating the ancient urn they'd borrowed from Charlie's dad to see why it wasn't boiling yet. Which basically involved tapping the light on the front and frowning.

Charlie's face lit up when she came in.

'Morning, Charlie.'

'Morning yourself,' he said with a wink, and James threw him a look.

'Er, James, can I borrow you a second?'

James raised his eyebrows but obediently followed her. 'Come here,' said Felicity and dragged him by his shirt into the cat room.

'I really don't think we have time for this, Felicity,' he said suggestively.

She shook her head. 'Honestly. What do you think I am?'

'Insatiable?'

'Stop it. Look. I've got a major problem.'

'What is it?'

'Ooh, I feel sick.'

'Tell me.'

'Just give me a minute, I think I might throw up...'

James moved to stand beside her and rubbed her back. 'Please tell me what's going on.'

Felicity took three deep breaths, then gritted her teeth. Waves of nausea and embarrassment washed over her. 'Don't be mad, okay?'

'With you? How could I ever be mad with you?'

'You haven't heard what I'm going to say yet.'

'Well, try me.'

'Oh, James. Help. I've forgotten to actually send out any invitations. No one knows this is happening. I'm such an idiot.'

Pins and needles were creeping into her fingers and up her

arms and Felicity wondered if she might be having a panic attack. James, however, just threw back his head and laughed.

'Keep your voice down,' hissed Felicity, trying to shake the pins and needles out of her hands.

'Sorry,' said James, still laughing.

'It's *not* funny,' she said firmly.

'It is a bit.'

Felicity peered at him. 'Okay, it is a bit. Or it will be later I'm sure, but right now, stop laughing and do something.'

James put his hands on her shoulders and looked her square in the eye. 'Don't throw up on me please.'

Felicity's stomach roiled as if in protest.

'You don't need to worry,' he said, still looking her right in the eyes. It was something they'd been working on, on her therapist's advice. Maintaining eye contact. All she had to do was not look away. *Don't look down.*

'I'm quite worried actually,' she said. 'No one's going to come. This is going to be a disaster and Animal Saviours is going to have to close and it's all my fault.'

'Right, but you see that's the opposite of not worrying.'

Felicity nodded.

'You don't need to worry,' he went on, 'because your dad will come and he's the only person we actually need to come. He's told all his readers. Or at least, all of Diana's readers. Blessed Diana and her followers can save the day all by themselves.'

'That's true I guess.' She shrugged.

'But also, you don't need to worry because you actually asked *me* to do the advertising, and I sorted it.'

'You did?'

James smiled. 'I did.'

'Felicity!' came a shout from the corridor. It was Andrea. 'Come quickly. There are loads of people coming. Action stations, everyone.'

Felicity's heart nearly stopped in her chest. She kissed James full on the mouth and he laughed and pulled her into a hug. 'I delegated that job,' she whispered. 'I forgot.'

'Yes, you did.'

'And you did it.'

'Yes, I did.'

'Thank God for you, James Cowley.'

'He did do a spectacular job with me, it has to be said.'

'That He did,' said Felicity, smiling. 'Plus, you always did look hot in an Animal Saviours top.'

'This old thing?' said James, gesturing down at himself in the rather tight-fitting polo shirt, left over from his days volunteering at the centre when they first met.

'Come on, God's gift. Let's go.'

And they marched out of the door to meet the crowds James had indeed conjured up out of nowhere.

CHAPTER 44

*T*he day went by in a flash. Felicity barely had time to look up but every time she did, there was an even longer queue of people for the signing table.

The whole place looked great, the children adored meeting the puppies and kittens and rabbits, and Saskia entertained them all with her stories of daring rescues and Andrea's various antics over the years, which had them all transfixed. It was James, though, who had had the really cunning plan. They'd sourced an old room divider and set it up in front of the table with big signs about Diana Edwards and "her" work. The squeals of delight and occasional screams of not-quite-horror-but-perhaps-extreme-surprise as avid fan after avid fan turned the corner into the makeshift signing booth and came face to face with Harry punctuated the day.

They had set up some donation buckets on tables beside the queue along with back catalogue copies of Harry's books in what Felicity thought would be a vain attempt to raise a few more pennies on top of the £5.00 entrance fee. But when she went over and had a look at lunchtime, the books were almost all gone and the buckets were full of cash. Who knew authors could have such loyal and wonderful fans?

'What a day,' said Felicity, eight and a quarter hours later, kicking off her battered old Converse in the hallway of what she still thought of as James's house.

As she wiggled her toes in the soft deep-pile carpet, she winced. They ached as if she'd just run a marathon. Or at least, she assumed that's what it must feel like. Never having run a marathon, of course, or even done any running of any kind since adulthood. But in any case, her feet hurt quite a bit. The day had been a huge success, the centre was packed out and Felicity spent most of it walking about, standing, pointing and lifting small puppies and kittens out of cages so their visitors could give them a stroke. Not the most taxing of days but she had spoken so much it felt like she'd run out of words. Another unusual state of affairs.

'You okay?' said James, padding into the kitchen ahead of her and flicking on the kettle.

'All good,' she said, scooping up their little black cat Bobby Charlton and hugging him to her chest. He immediately started purring and rubbing his soft face on her chin. Felicity giggled. 'Hello, gorgeous boy,' she whispered into his fur, carrying him through to the lounge and lowering herself gingerly onto the sofa, praying he wouldn't jump off as she did so. Mercifully, he stayed in her arms but he did look rather put out when she had the audacity to move forwards a few inches so she could tuck her legs underneath her. Eventually, though, she was forgiven, and Bobby curled up under her chin and purred louder than ever against her neck. After such a long day, it was just what she needed.

'It went well, I think. Do you think it went well? I think it did,' James was saying, carrying two huge steaming mugs of tea and a plate of biscuits through on a peculiarly chintzy tray that really didn't go with anything else in that house.

'All right, Grandma?' Felicity laughed as he sat down. 'I think you forgot the tea cosy.'

'Right, let's have this out here and now, Brooks. What do you have against The Tray, exactly?'

'I don't have anything against it,' she laughed again, softly, 'it's just so… mumsy, that's all.' Felicity patted his arm (gently, so as not to upset the cat). 'So… not you. Or Erika for that matter.'

A shadow passed across his face, just for a moment, as it always did at the mention of his ex-girlfriend's name. And then it was gone. He leant towards Felicity conspiratorially, reaching up a hand to give Bobby a little scootch on the head as he spoke. Bobby responded with a little chirrup which made both their hearts melt.

'Do you want to know a secret?' said James, after a second.

'Always,' said Felicity, with a grin.

'I bought it as a present for Erika. Because I knew she'd hate it.'

'You didn't?'

'I did. Isn't that awful? We were on holiday in some tourist village in the New Forest and I saw this dreadful tea set and tray, covered in flowers and a tiny dormouse and a fox and all that, and I thought, Erika would absolutely detest having that in the house. So I bought it.'

'That's terrible.'

'It was a bit but you should have seen her face when I gave it to her. It was totally worth it.'

'I'm surprised she didn't smash it over your head.'

'I'm lucky she didn't.'

There was a pause.

'I thought you two were perfect,' said Felicity, in a small voice, trying to resist the urge to look away from those eyes of his.

James caught her eye, holding her stare. 'Far from it,' he said.

Something like relief washed over Felicity's body at that. Apart from the whole walking out on James at Christmas and breaking his heart into a million pieces thing, Felicity always thought Erika and James must have been relationship goals. This exotic Japanese beauty and her blond titan. Perfectly perfect in every way. James never really spoke about Erika, and certainly never said a bad word about her. In Felicity's mind, Erika was still really a rival, especially as she had made a play to get him back once before. To hear James actually admit she'd been a teensy bit annoying brought Felicity a disproportionately enormous amount of joy. She bit her lip to try and hide it.

'Of course, you realise you've made a grave error,' she said.

'Is that so? Do you think that's why she left me? Is The Tray really that bad?'

'I mean, it's pretty bad,' said Felicity, giggling so much that Bobby got the hump and leapt off her chest in disgust. 'But the error is that you ended up with the bloody thing.'

James nodded seriously. 'You're right. That was an error.'

'Anyway, moving on. Today went well, I thought,' said Felicity. 'What did you think?'

'I think that tray is going to haunt my dreams,' said James, taking a sip of tea. 'But yes, Ms Brooks, today went very well. Do you know the total yet?'

'We reckon about £1,000 on the door, or that's what Andrea said.'

'Plus whatever Harry's crazy readers thought to donate?'

'Plus that. I've got it in my bag. I don't dare open it.'

'Do it, do it, do it.'

'Okay, fine. Hold on.' Felicity attempted to jump up sprightly and then realised everything hurt and had to cling to the arm of the sofa for support. 'Ow,' she said, managing to hobble out of the room as the muscles in her legs seized. She hobbled back in with an envelope full of cash and flopped down on the sofa again, all the while pointedly ignoring James who was watching her with great amusement.

'You all right there, Crazy Cat Lady?'

'How come you don't seem to be even remotely sore after a day on your feet? And you have a bloody desk job. I should be used to it.'

'What can I say, I'm a great specimen of manhood?'

Felicity laughed and punched him lightly on the arm. 'All right, calm down, John McClane.'

'Open it, open it, open it,' said James, gesturing to the envelope.

'Patience.'

But her hands were shaking. She didn't even know why. The day had been a resounding success, but a thousand pounds on the door wasn't going to get them very far and even the contents of this envelope were unlikely to make that much of a difference. So why on earth did she feel so excited? Perhaps it was hysterics? Maybe she just needed a glass of wine. Perhaps it was her blood sugar. She did feel a bit light-headed, now that she thought about it.

'Get on with it,' said James, laughing.

'All right, all right, I'm doing it,' she said, giggling, and ripping the top open.

Nothing in the world could have prepared her for what was inside.

'What is this?' said Felicity, for the millionth time, turning to James and then staring back down at the slightly crumpled piece of paper in her hand.

For on top of the pile of cash was a note. Not a note, as such; a photocopy. A photocopy of a title deed. But not for the Animal Saviours centre. Oh no. It was the title deed for a certain Donkey Haven animal centre. On Guernsey. Formerly owned by one Ms Valerie Evans.

'Has my father gone stark raving mad?' said Felicity, when she'd asked the universe what it was several hundred more times. 'Was he always mad and I'm only just finding out?'

'I think he might be,' said James, as Felicity handed him the piece of paper.

'He's bought Jessica the donkey?'

'I'm not sure that's quite what this…'

'Or, Jessica's house at least? He's bought it outright and he doesn't even know if Andrea will move away from here. Or does he? Is he thinking she'll move over there? Is he planning to go with her? Is he leaving me again? When I've only just found him? What is going on?'

James stood up. 'I've not got the foggiest clue, I'm afraid. But I know how to find out.'

'What's that?'

'Let's go ask him.'

'Now? It's late, they might be... ew...' Felicity's voice tailed off.

'Ew is right but also, they might just be sitting watching Saturday night TV like a normal couple. Not everyone is as sex mad as you, Felicity Brooks.'

'Ha. You wish,' she replied, pulling on her shoes.

'Bet they're into *Gladiators*. All that Lycra.'

'Not everyone is as mad about Lycra as you, James Cowley.'

'Touché.'

'Let's go.'

So they went. And despite their earlier discussion it was with some trepidation that Felicity rang the doorbell of Andrea's modest little cottage just outside town. Immediately a cacophony of sound erupted.

'That'll be the dogs.'

'Oh, thanks, yes, without that explanation I'd have been wondering all evening.'

'Shut it.'

'She's got three, I think.'

'I love how they are all barking at a slightly different pitch and perfectly out of time. It's a really relaxing sound.'

'Isn't it?'

In all the years she had known Andrea, and it was a lot of years by now, Felicity had only ever been to her boss's house once before. It felt a tiny bit naughty.

'Please don't be naked, please don't be naked,' Felicity prayed quietly, and then let out a long breath as Andrea opened the door still fully clothed from the day. She didn't look remotely surprised to see them.

'Oh, thank God, you're dressed.' The words were out before Felicity could stop them.

Andrea's eyebrows went up into her hairline for a split-second, then she full-on grinned. 'You've just missed the floor show if that's what you mean.'

'Oh, God,' said James, making retching noises.

Andrea just giggled. 'Come in then if you're coming. Ignore the dogs, they'll calm down in a minute.'

They did not in fact calm down at all. Andrea had three spanielly-type things of varying sizes and colours, with floppy ears and extremely waggy tails. All three of them seemed to move as one creature, like a very small murmuration or shoal of fish, gliding this way and that, but occasionally they gathered into a semicircle and formed a dog barricade just the perfect height for a human to trip over. In typical fashion from the moment they walked through the door all three dogs had ignored Felicity completely and took an instant shine to James, flocking round his feet wagging their tails and trying to climb on his lap for the entire visit.

Harry was nowhere to be seen.

'Well, this is awkward,' said Felicity after a few moments. 'Where's Harry?'

'He's gone out for Chinese, he'll be back in a minute.'

'Right. So he was here. And you two are...?'

'Yes,' said Andrea with a brisk nod, only the tiniest hint of colour rising on her neck.

'Right. Well, it was him we wanted to speak to really.'

'Okay. You'd best wait then. Drink?'

'Please.'

Andrea pottered through to the kitchen and Felicity and James exchanged a look. She had always smelt a little of dog, had Andrea, but that was to be expected, given her job. The cottage, however, was ripe with it, as if the smell of dog had permeated deep into the soft furnishings. Hardly surprising given the sofa was covered with almost an entire rug's worth of dog hair. Even Felicity's hardened nose was beginning to itch.

Perhaps Harry had lost his sense of smell as well as vision.

'Thank you so much for today,' said Andrea, handing them each a smeary glass of what they assumed was white wine.

'I enjoyed it,' said Felicity. 'I love talking about that place…' She stopped mid-sentence, but couldn't think of a suitable way to change what she had been going to say.

'Felicity? Are you okay?'

'Oh, yes, sorry, I just—' She could feel her face burning.

'I thought it was a great day,' James cut in, smoothly. Felicity made a mental note to kiss the face off him later. 'I loved being back in the old AS uniform. And everyone today really seemed to love it.' He patted the logo on his chest and then remembered what they'd come about and fell silent too.

'Why are you two being weird?' said Andrea, never one to beat around the proverbial.

'Who's being weird?' said Harry, opening the lounge door with his foot. The dogs burst into the song of their people again and swarmed round his ankles. Harry very nearly went face first onto the dog-hair sofa but with some impressive manoeuvring he managed to keep the spoils, in other words a small cardboard box full of takeaway, intact.

Andrea handed Felicity the bag of prawn crackers from the top of the box without even needing to be asked. She immediately ripped the top off and began munching, batting James's attempts to snaffle one away with her free hand.

'So let me guess, this is not just a social call,' said Harry, half an hour later, when Felicity and James had polished off the prawn crackers and finished watching him and Andrea eat their chow mein and prawn balls while trying not to salivate.

'Look on the bright side. You're seeing us twice in one day, you lucky things,' said James.

'I'll be the judge of that,' said Harry. He was sounding more and more like an actual father these days, thought Felicity. Not that she really knew what one of them was meant to sound like.

'We're sorry to interrupt your domestic bliss,' she said, absent-mindedly stroking a spaniel ear, 'but, Harry… what is this exactly? We found it in the donations envelope. Is it some kind of joke?'

Felicity held out the rather smudgy photocopy and raised her eyebrows forcibly to the heavens. Harry swallowed a last mouthful of prawn ball and took it from her hand.

'Ah. Yes. This.'

Without a word, he passed the document to Andrea, then sat back casually and waited for all hell to break loose.

Except no hell really broke loose. Or not straight away, anyway. Andrea just sat and stared at the piece of paper in her hand for such a long time Felicity wondered if she'd had a stroke.

'Are you okay, love?' said Harry, eventually. 'Please say something.'

Still nothing. He looked pleadingly at Felicity.

'Andrea? Are you okay?' she said. No reply.

Finally, James got up and went over to her. 'Do you want me to read it for you?' he said in a slightly patronising tone.

She shook as if from a stupor and looked up at him. 'Piss off, you sarcastic git,' she said.

'She's cured,' said James triumphantly, and sat back down in his seat, a smug grin on his face.

'Oh thank goodness. Thought I'd given you a small break-down for a minute there,' said Harry, a smile spreading across his still-handsome features.

Andrea looked across at him. 'Is this your doing?' she said, blinking rapidly.

He had the grace to look a little embarrassed. 'Maybe. If you like it? Otherwise I'll blame Felicity.'

'Hey!'

'That's where Jessica the donkey lives,' said Felicity feebly, but Harry and Andrea didn't even respond.

'You've bought a donkey sanctuary in Guernsey? You're leaving me?' said Andrea, her forehead crinkled.

Never mind you. He's leaving me. Again, thought Felicity.

Harry's eyes widened. 'What? No. Well, yes, I've bought it, but no, I'm not leaving you, you daft cow. I bought it for you. It's a present. Your very own animal rescue centre. And of course, if you want me to come with you and run it... I'll be more than happy to do some writing from there. No hardship.'

Andrea looked as if she had even more questions than Felicity had an hour before. Did she actually have tears in her eyes? This was unprecedented. But the question that came out of her mouth first was, 'How on earth did you ever afford it? Not those smutty books, surely?'

'Ah, we should probably go,' said Felicity, standing up and edging towards the door.

'It's fine, you can stay,' said Andrea, a little absently, her eyes fixed on Harry's.

James huffed a laugh. 'Trust me, you will want to be alone for this.'

As they navigated their way past the pile of spaniels on the floor, Felicity couldn't shake the feeling she was still missing something important.

CHAPTER 46

On Monday morning Felicity crept into Animal Saviours, hardly daring to breathe.

There was no sign of Andrea, but she found Charlie with his feet up in the staff room, carefully rolling a cigarette, which always made him look as if he'd been born a century too late.

He leapt up when he saw Felicity in the doorway. 'Ah, just the person I was hoping to see.'

'I do work here.'

'Yes, I'm aware.'

'You okay, Charlie?'

'Yes, all good, thanks.'

Felicity flicked the kettle on. 'Any sign of Andrea?'

'She left a message in the office, asked us to start without her.'

Weird. A little shiver ran down Felicity's spine but she shook it off and tried to look calm and professional. 'Best we do that then I guess.'

Charlie waved a hand. 'Yes but first I need to ask you something. Tell you something, I mean.'

Felicity leant back on the counter. 'You have as long as it takes me to brew this tea.'

Charlie nodded eagerly and Felicity felt a pang of affection for him. He wasn't so bad.

'Okay, look,' he said, staring at the ground. 'I'm really sorry for coming onto you. I know you're with James—'

She cut him off hastily. 'And even if I wasn't, you'd be far too young for me.'

He went on. 'Yes, I know, and that. Although I still maintain that we could make a go of it.'

'Charlie!'

'Sorry. Okay, look, I'm sorry anyway. And I wanted to say thanks. Because this is my last week working here.'

'Oh. Er, sorry. I didn't know.'

Charlie shifted from foot to foot. 'Yeah, well, I've got to get back to college anyway. But look, I wanted to thank you because I've, well, you've... I...'

Felicity attempted an encouraging smile. *He's just a kid, remember.*

Emboldened, Charlie took in a breath and stumbled on. 'I know it might not always show but I've really loved working here and working with you. You've been really kind.'

'I don't know about that, Charlie,' said Felicity. It was taking a huge effort to keep her face neutral.

'No, you have. I'm not really used to that.'

'How so?'

'My parents are not kind.'

There it was.

Something twisted inside Felicity and tears sprang to her eyes.

'Charlie... I...'

He threw up a hand. 'No, it's okay, it's just that I'm not used to people treating me like an adult. Or like I've got something to say.' He gestured between them. 'Even this, like now, you're listening to me, you know?'

It was the most words he'd ever said in one go. Felicity felt a rush of guilt for giving him a tea-brew time limit.

She stepped forwards and before he could object, she gave him one quick, warm hug, then stepped back. He smiled but for once it didn't seem suggestive. Was he learning at last?

'Thanks…'

'Look, Charlie, I don't know how much you know about me but my parents weren't kind either. I know Harry is a great guy now but he wasn't… well, let's say he wasn't always around back then. And my mum… she was really not very good at it, to tell the truth.'

It was the first time it had occurred to her. Perhaps Jocelyn had just really struggled with motherhood. People did, didn't they? Maybe she had postpartum depression or worse, new mums even had psychosis sometimes, didn't they? She'd seen something about it on *EastEnders* once. Or maybe Jocelyn just wasn't suited to it. Perhaps the drinking was her way to cope. This all zipped through Felicity's mind in the time it took her to take her teabag out of her mug and drop it in the bin.

'I'm really sorry, Felicity.'

'Thanks. And I'm sorry about your situation.' She paused, wondering how to say it. 'They don't… hit you, do they?' she said. 'Nothing physical or…?' She left the sentence hanging.

Charlie shook his head almost violently, his black fringe falling over his forehead.

'Nothing like that. It's more like I'm completely invisible. Which seems worse but I'm sure it's not.'

'It can be just as painful, emotionally at least, and it's definitely not okay,' said Felicity. And then another thought crept into her brain. 'Is this why you did all that stuff? To get their attention?'

Charlie didn't even pretend to consider this. 'Yup. Got me lots too. Just not the right sort.'

'You know that's not the answer, right?'

'I know,' he said, dropping his shoulders in a sort of half shrug.

'So you're not going to get in any more trouble, right? Your parents love you, I'm sure, they might just not be very good at showing it. Give them a chance.'

He looked at her for a long moment then, his dark eyes almost navy under the shoddy staff-room strip light.

'I'll try. For you.'

'For me. Thanks, Charlie.'

'No, thank you.'

'Right, that's quite enough of that.' Felicity laughed. 'We'd better get on with rounds or Andrea will have our heads.'

'Bagsy the puppy room,' said Charlie, already on his way.

'You got it. I'll be there in a sec.'

Felicity sat down in a chair and took a few soothing breaths. It had been a while since she had thought about Jocelyn, her emotionally absent mother, and it always knocked the wind out of her. She still hadn't decided if it was better to have emotionally distant parents or alcoholic ones or ones that only turn up after thirty years to see if you are still alive. Or perhaps no parents at all?

At the end of the shift, Andrea finally showed up. She accosted Felicity while she was having a sneaky last cuddle with the pups.

'So, the thing is…' she began.

Felicity gave Mike's little snoot a boop. 'You're moving to Guernsey. With my father. And I need to start looking for a new job.'

'How did you know what I was going to say?'

'I can sense it. You have a different air about you already. Just please tell me you can take all these lovely little ones with you when you go.'

'You're being very calm about all this, Felicity.'

'It's hard not to be calm when you're jiggling a puppy,' she replied, nuzzling Mike's tiny little body and letting his wiggles soothe her.

'But you're not okay really.'

'I'm… not, not okay. I mean, I love this job, of course, but there are other jobs I guess. It's just… I'm not sure what I'm going to do without you. Or Harry for that matter. I've only just found him.'

'Well… That's the thing.'

Felicity put Mike down in his box amongst the other little wiggling bodies and turned to face her boss.

'What's the thing?' she said.

Andrea cleared her throat noisily. 'So, the thing is that the other day I was having a chat with James and he said why don't you both go to Guernsey too?'

'The other day? Didn't you just find out about this on Saturday?'

Andrea took a small step backwards. 'I did. That's right.'

Felicity drew in her breath, trying not to scream and frighten the puppies.

'You did just find out about this plan on Saturday, right?'

'Yes…'

'There's no way you three have been in cahoots about this all along, is there?'

'Definitely not.' Andrea's usually ruddy face was a little pale, she thought.

'That's good then. Excuse me while I just step outside for a moment.'

Felicity ran to the front door and stuck her head outside, taking a few gulps of air and mouthing a few choice swear words into the universe. Then she closed the door and made her way back along the hall, heart thumping in the top of her head, making her feel woozy. Andrea was waiting outside the puppy room for her. Looking contrite, as well she might.

'I feel like a total idiot,' said Felicity.

'It's not like we didn't tell you.'

'Isn't it?'

'It's more like we made some preparations ahead of time.'

'I don't know if you're expecting me to be grateful for that.'

'Not exactly, just trying to explain. So you don't feel like we're just abandoning you.'

'I'm used to it by now.'

'Can you at least let me say what I need to say?'

Felicity crossed her arms. 'This ought to be good.'

Andrea ran a hand down her face. Her hair was coming out of her plait all over the place so she looked even more like Crazy Animal Lady than usual. Felicity resisted the urge to pat it down.

She took a deep breath before speaking. 'I'm not sure how to put this.'

'Try,' said Felicity, a little more sharply than she'd intended.

'It's just, I guess we know Guernsey is sensitive for you, you know? So... the thing is... we didn't want to just spring this whole thing on you in case you weren't up for it. We thought maybe you might need to come round to the idea slowly.'

Felicity and Andrea were still moving as they talked. They arrived at Marmaduke's pen and Felicity picked the elderly ginger tom up and cuddled him to her chest. He instantly began purring like a freight train and she found herself wondering if James would tolerate just one more addition to their little cat collection at home.

She looked up at Andrea. 'And what's the idea exactly? You know, the one you've *all* been talking about without me even though it massively involves me.'

Andrea looked abashed. A rare moment for her. 'That we all move to Guernsey. Me, you, your father, James, and the animals. There, I said it.'

'Not, all moving in together, surely? Like some pseudo-family? Cos that's just weird.'

'God, no. Nothing like that. Harry and I, we'll move into the donkey place or whatever, and you and James… you can find somewhere to suit you. James works from home so he can work from anywhere anyway, and you can be my official donkey carer.'

Felicity's heart started to beat faster, but she wasn't sure if it was with excitement, fear or fury. 'I don't know any more about caring for donkeys than you do.'

Andrea, on the other hand, was pure excitement. 'I've already looked it up, there's a donkey welfare course we can do and everything. And Valerie's happy to stick around and volunteer for a bit. She can teach us. She just can't cope with the place anymore, wants a bungalow by the sea.'

'You really have got it all figured out.'

'Well, not everything. We still need to work out what to do with our animals here. We'll need a rehoming drive I think, try and rehome as many as we can and then take the rest with us.'

There it was.

'So you're definitely closing this place down then.'

'Harry gave me the choice. He's happy to sell Valerie's place and give me the money from that sale to pay for this place… but now I keep thinking about being with donkeys. By the sea. It's got under my skin.'

'Guernsey tends to do that. Which you'd know if you'd actually been. Don't you think this is all a bit rash?'

Andrea's eyes flashed with excitement. 'That's what makes it so exhilarating. I'm getting older and it's about time I had an adventure. It's got sea, sun, cliff walks, great food, and lots of animals to rescue. What more could I want?'

'But what if you hate it there? Not everyone likes island life.'

Andrea had the grace to look as if she was seriously considering this perspective.

'But what if I love it there?'

'Fair point.' Felicity sighed. She knew Andrea well enough to know there wasn't going to be any changing her mind now. And especially not when she saw the island for herself. As much as Felicity hated to admit it, as much as she wanted to be mad with them all right now, deep down in her heart, or maybe even further, perhaps in the pit of her stomach, there was a kernel of excitement she just couldn't ignore. Could they really do this? And how could she arrange to take Sophie and Tristan with her?

CHAPTER 47

*A*ndrea had clearly warned James he was about to be in BIG trouble because when Felicity got home that night, she found him on the floor in the lounge surrounded by sofa cushions which he had upended on all sides. In fact she could barely see him at all except for a tuft of his blond hair, but she knew he was in there because the cats were hurling themselves at the structure on all sides. Whether they were trying to get inside or knock it down was anyone's guess.

Felicity sat on the armchair and tried to keep her voice gentle. 'Did you build a fort?'

After a beat a voice came from inside. 'It's more a castle, I like to think.'

'It's very impressive. But it won't protect you this time I'm afraid.'

'Are you sure about that?' came the voice again. 'It's very well built.' As he said those words Bobby hurled himself at one corner and knocked an entire side down flat. James hastily reached to pull it back up but Felicity had already seized the moment and jumped onto it with a deftness that surprised even herself. She crossed her legs to steady herself and looked across at James, who was sitting with his back against the sofa frame, his face tense. Holly immediately waltzed in and curled up in his lap. He rubbed her little ginger ears absent-mindedly.

'Halt, who goes there?' he said, his voice wobbly.

'You look braver than you sound,' she said.

'I'm a bit worried I'm about to get a strip torn off me.'

Felicity pretended to look at her watch. 'Not straight away. I thought we could at least talk first.'

'Phew. Okay. Talking I can do.'

'Are we doing it in the fort?'

'I think so, yes,' said James. So Felicity crawled a little further in and leant against his side. He wrapped an arm around her shoulder and made a happy sighing sound into her ear. A sound she loved so much she forgot to be mad for just a bit.

'So, Mr Penguin Man. We're moving to Guernsey, huh?' she said, eventually.

'Not necessarily. I mean, only if you want to. I'm so sorry, Felicity. I should have told you. I should have asked. I should have… done it differently.'

Felicity sighed and ruffled Holly's ears. 'I know why you did it like that.'

'I don't want you to think we all went behind your back.'

'Well you did, didn't you?'

'Not in a bad way. Not really. We just thought you might not like the idea.'

'I don't know how I feel about it, to be honest.'

'So we were just exploring the possibilities before we told you, that's all.'

Felicity leaned into him, breathing in his lovely clean-laundry smell. *Be honest.* 'I get it. I do. But you also know I have trust issues. This is really not ideal for me when all the people I do actually trust in the world have been going behind my back.'

James inhaled sharply. 'When you put it like that it actually sounds terrible.'

'I know, right?'

He squeezed her tight. 'I'm so sorry.'

'So, what now? I mean, how does this even work, all this? What will you do about your job? I'm not exactly the breadwinner here. And how am I meant to cope without Sophie?'

James kissed the top of her head. 'Well, my job I can actually do anywhere, I do most of it from here, after all. I only have to go to London occasionally and there are ferries and planes and all that jazz. As for Sophie, that's a bit more tricky... but I'm sure she'll be able to visit, once we find somewhere? She can fly or even get the ferry. We just need to make sure we've got enough space on the drive for all her Range Rovers.'

'I suppose so,' said Felicity absently, her mind whirring.

'The most important thing is, we'll be together,' he whispered. 'And there will be donkeys.'

'This is true.'

'Felicity? I really am sorry.'

'It's okay,' she mumbled. 'Just no more surprises, okay? I mean it.'

'Sure,' he said. 'No more surprises.' Was it her imagination or did his voice sound a little strangled?

He may have said no more surprises, but the very next morning James told her he had to go away for business for a couple of days. 'Sorry,' he had said, over their cereal and coffee. 'I know I promised but this is for work, I've got to go to Manchester for a conference but I'll be back by Friday. Then we can talk through the whole Guernsey thing properly, okay? There's no pressure, remember. It's got to be right, for both of us.'

Felicity had nodded reassuringly. 'Of course, that's fine.' There was nothing else she could have said. But deep down inside her there lurked a familiar and rather ominous sense of doom.

246

CHAPTER 48

'I've got a bad feeling,' she said to Sophie when they met for coffee the next day and Felicity had attempted to explain all the craziness that was going on.

'He's just gone away for work, right?' said Sophie breezily. 'Nothing to worry about.' She'd been surprisingly good about the whole Guernsey thing, which had just made Felicity feel worse about potentially moving away.

'I'm sure you're right.'

'So why does your face look like that?'

'Like what?'

'All crinkly?' said Sophie gently.

'I don't know,' said Felicity. 'What if he's planning to leave me?'

'Why on earth would he do that?'

'I don't know. Maybe I wasn't enthusiastic enough about the Guernsey idea? What if this is all just a distraction anyway?'

'A distraction from what?'

'I don't know, to keep my eye off the ball somehow? Metaphorically speaking. What if I've messed it all up?'

'And what if you haven't?' said Sophie, taking a sip of her chai latte which was so strongly aromatic with cinnamon and cardamom it was making Felicity feel a bit ill.

'Fair point.'

'Just relax. It'll be fine. He's a keeper. No way he's going anywhere. Trust me.'

'I'm trying. Honest.'

Sophie raised an eyebrow. Then her perfect face crumpled. 'Seriously though, what am I going to do without you, Fliss?'

Felicity smiled. 'It's not even on the cards properly yet.'

'Oh, I think it is,' said Sophie. 'And more to the point, I think it's an amazing idea. Or at least I would if it didn't mean I had to lose you.'

'You could *never* lose me,' said Felicity, her voice catching in her throat.

'Ditto.'

'So that's fine then. I mean, we'll make it work. Anyway,' said Felicity, draining her own cup of nice plain breakfast tea, 'have you seen Bex at all? How is she?'

Sophie's perfect brow crinkled even more deeply. 'Not good. Seriously not good. I've never seen her like this before, to be honest. She's barely eating, she's lost loads of weight. She's not even washing her hair.'

Felicity let out a little gasp. In Bex's world, that was an emergency. 'What can we do?'

'I don't know. She doesn't want to see anyone, she says. She's just hiding in her flat, she's not been to work, nothing.'

'That's not like her,' said Felicity, instantly trying to think of ways to fix it.

'I know.'

'We have to give her time I suppose but how long before maybe we need to stage an intervention?' asked Felicity.

'Let's give her a few more days and then see.'

'Okay. Good plan. Poor Bex.'

'I know.'

But they didn't need a couple of days.

On Wednesday evening, Bex showed up at Felicity's house. The weather was turning colder, autumn was upon them, and there was Bex, standing on the doorstep with not so much as a jumper over her crumpled linen dress, shivering. Sophie had been right, she looked absolutely dreadful, even worse than before. Her usually glossy black hair was limp, her clothes were hanging off her and her face was tear-stained.

Felicity led her through to the living room, and sat Bex down in an armchair, wrapping a blanket round her shoulders. Bex didn't even react. Felicity headed for the kitchen area to make her a nice hot cup of tea and sent an emergency text to Sophie:

Bex is here, help!

Then she sat opposite her friend and tried to think of something to say. Bex clutched the tea as if it was a lifebelt, and said nothing. Just when the silence had gone beyond awkward into downright embarrassing, Sophie rang the doorbell. Not for the first time, Felicity whispered a silent thank you prayer for the existence of Sophie in her life. And for the speediness of her posh car.

They both sat opposite Bex and waited for her to speak.

'I've heard from Adam,' said Bex. Her voice was raspy as if she'd been crying all day again. Which, for all they knew, she had.

'And?' said Sophie, ever so gently.

'He's not in a good way. He wants to see me.'

'Really? How do you feel about that?' said Felicity, her voice wobbling. She knew from all too bitter experience that the last thing Bex should do would be to give Adam the time of day. He had a way of wheedling his way back into her heart that she'd never been able to fully explain. In this state, Bex wouldn't stand a chance.

Bex put her head in her hands. 'I don't know. I don't think I want to. But what if I tell him to get lost and he actually gets lost? I don't want that either.'

Sophie took a deep breath. 'You're not seriously considering taking him back, are you?'

Bex spoke through her fingers. 'No. No, of course not. Maybe.'

Felicity and Sophie gasped collectively, exchanging worried glances.

'You can't,' said Sophie. 'Not after that, surely. He was shagging someone a month ago. While you were engaged.'

'He's a rotter. There's no two ways about it. You need to make a clean break, Bex.'

'Like you did, you mean?' Bex practically spat the words at Felicity and she recoiled.

'That's not fair,' said Sophie. 'It was Adam who wouldn't leave Fliss alone if you remember.'

'I remember,' said Bex bitterly.

Felicity could feel tears prickling the back of her eyes. 'The thing is,' she said, trying to keep her voice level, 'you don't seem to really hold him responsible. I can't understand it.'

'It's like my mum said, men will be men. This is just what they do, right?'

Sophie and Felicity exchanged another look. 'You can't seriously believe that,' said Sophie.

Bex shrugged. 'I don't know what I believe anymore.'

'Petunia is wrong about this, Bex,' said Felicity firmly. 'You have to know that. I'm sure she means well but she's completely wrong about this.'

Sophie piped up. 'Bex. Seriously. You used to be the biggest feminist of the lot. I just don't understand what's happened to you.'

They had no time to continue the conversation as just then, the doorbell went again. Felicity looked around the room, they were definitely already all here. So who could this be? And then she realised, her palms instantly prickling with sweat.

Sophie went to the bay window at the front of the huge room and peered out. 'It's Adam,' she said needlessly.

Felicity stood up, feeling decidedly wobbly. She looked at Bex. 'Want me to tell him to get lost?' she said.

'Let him in,' said Bex, jaw clenched.

'Okay. But if he causes any trouble at all, even a modicum of trouble, even a smidgeon, an inkling, the barest whisper of trouble, I'm kicking him out.' Felicity didn't even wait for a reply. She hated the idea of Adam coming into her lovely safe haven in Chancery Downs and she was secretly hoping he'd give her an excuse to send him away. 'Brace yourselves, everyone,' she said as she walked down the hallway.

And sure enough, there on the doorstep – her bloody doorstep – was Adam, her ex-boyfriend and one-time stalker. James was actually going to kill her if she let him in.

'What can I do for you?' said Felicity, trying to sound nonchalant.

To her surprise and no small delight, Adam looked almost as bad as Bex. His usually bright skin was sallow and he hadn't washed his hair. He even had a breakout of spots on his skin, something Felicity had never seen before, not even when he was a teenager. He was still dressed to kill in chinos and a pale-green shirt but his twinkle, that Tom Cruise smile, was definitely dulled.

'Is she here?' he said, not bothering to sit on ceremony let alone stand.

'What do you want, Adam?'

'Is she here?' he replied, like an automaton.

'Yes, she's here, but...' Felicity tried to finish her sentence but Adam pushed straight past her and into the lounge.

'Hey...' said Felicity, following him through to where he had crouched down beside Bex, who was looking at him like he was a sight for sore eyes. 'Adam, I'm not sure this is a good idea.'

'Yes, maybe you should go,' said Sophie, practically wringing her hands.

'Just give us a minute please,' said Adam through gritted teeth.

'It's not up to you I'm afraid. Bex, are you happy for him to be here?'

Bex looked up at her and smiled. 'It's good to see him, actually,' she said quietly.

'Okay,' said Felicity, 'but we're not leaving the room.'

'Fine,' said Adam.

Felicity and Sophie moved over to the window to give them some space and/or eavesdrop like the proper friends they were. Adam shot them a nervous glance. He'd obviously never seen Bex like this either.

There was a long silence. And finally, 'I missed you so much,' he breathed, taking Bex's hand in his.

Bex looked at him for a long moment. 'I missed you too,' she said.

Felicity gripped Sophie's arm silently. It was all she could do not to speak up.

Adam sighed with relief, pressing a palm to his chest. 'Thank God. I'm so sorry, Bex. I don't know what's wrong with me. I think I need to go and see someone.'

Bex nodded furiously, taking his hand from his chest and holding it gently. 'I said to Felicity, I wonder if you've got some sort of addiction, you know, like that actor.'

'That was never proven,' said Felicity from across the room.

They both completely ignored her.

Adam hung his head and Bex put a hand on his shoulder.

Sophie rolled her eyes and muttered, 'How stupid can you get?' under her breath. They ignored that too.

'I'm willing to get help,' said Adam. 'I have no idea what's going on with me really but I'm happy to get help if that will make you feel better.'

'I don't think anything could make me feel better, Ads. You ruined my wedding day. I thought it was those girls, but it was you.'

Felicity held her breath. That wasn't what she was expecting Bex to say, and it was clear from Adam's expression that he felt the same.

'Hey, I'm not sure that's entirely fair,' he began to say.

Sophie cut him off. 'Let her speak,' she hissed.

'Yes, please let me speak, Adam,' said Bex, suddenly almost deathly calm.

'You're right, I'm sorry.'

'I've always known you were in love with Felicity,' began Bex.

Felicity tried not to cough or make a single sound. She was praying they'd forgotten she was in the room.

Adam opened his mouth to protest but Bex held up a hand.

'Let her speak for God's sake, man,' said Sophie again.

Adam finally nodded, got up from his crouching position and sat opposite Bex on the sofa.

'Sorry. Go ahead. I won't say anything else.'

His brow was crumpled. Felicity wondered if maybe he did have proper feelings for Bex after all. Perhaps he'd only just realised. Too little... in typical fashion. But was it too late?

'Thank you,' said Bex with a deep sigh. 'Look, I've always known you were in love with Felicity. That was one thing. You two have history and that's something I could cope with knowing, somehow. Those feelings would always be there, and I knew that but I also knew Felicity would never cheat on me or try to take you from me. I just knew.'

Adam nodded slowly.

Bex went on. 'But the thing I can't handle, the thing that really gets to me, Ads, is those other women. You were sleeping with at least one of them the whole time. While we were planning the wedding. While you were sleeping with me. While you were telling me I was the only one for you until the end of time. It's just despicable.'

Adam grabbed a perfectly primped cushion and began fiddling with the tassels around the edge. To his credit, he still didn't speak.

'And to find that out on my wedding day,' said Bex, with venom. 'To find that out in front of everyone that I love. In front of Felicity, in front of my mother of all people. To find out that you had been round the block more times than a postman.' She smiled faintly at her own weak analogy. 'To find that out, Adam. On my wedding day. In front of everyone like that. I think you've taken every scrap of any dignity I may have had left.'

'I never meant to do that,' said Adam at last.

'Why didn't you tell me before?'

'I don't know. I honestly don't. I meant to, so many times.'

Bex stood up suddenly, fists clenched. 'It doesn't matter what you *meant to do,* Adam. Surely even someone like you can see that? It only matters what you *did.* You shagged that Tabitha and that other girl and you treated them so badly that they turned up on our wedding day and ruined everything. Can you even begin to conceive of even a tiny inkling of how I feel right now?'

Adam was stammering now, looking up at his once beautiful bride, who currently looked more like a walking corpse.

'Yes, take a good look,' said Bex, walking slowly towards him. 'This is what you've done to me. This is what you did.' Tears began to roll down her cheeks. 'I can't eat. I can't sleep. I don't want to go anywhere or see anyone. I'm a wreck.'

'I'm so sorry,' whispered Adam.

'And do you know the worst part of all?' said Bex, almost shouting now. 'The worst part is I've hurt my friendship with these two,' she pointed to Sophie and Felicity, 'really badly. Most likely beyond repair. I've hurt Felicity, I've refused to listen to her, and of course, she was bloody right all along, wasn't she? And I've treated Sophie like absolute shite. I'd be surprised if they ever speak to me after tonight, so I may as well say it. They are the two people I love most in the world and you have destroyed it all. What do you say to that?'

Bex sat back down but her shoulders were heaving and she was breathing hard.

Adam shifted his feet and looked around the room. Felicity and Sophie were starting to get uncomfortable perching side by side on the windowsill but they didn't dare move.

And then he stood up. 'I was going to make some excuse,' he said. 'But when you put it like that, I have none.'

Bex's eyes grew wide.

'I am despicable, you're right,' said Adam, his jaw flexing. 'I've treated you terribly badly I know but I came here to win you back, to try and make amends. I can see now that that's not going to happen. My only option is to leave you with my apologies and an assurance that it is you and only you that I love, no matter what you say.'

With that, he backed out of the room. Felicity, Sophie and Bex looked at each other, mouths open. This was very un-Adam-like behaviour. After a beat the three women followed him out into the hall where he was hastily pulling on a pair of very expensive-looking pointed brogues. Felicity had always hated those shoes.

'I won't be back,' he said, straightening up at last and looking Bex dead in the eye.

'That's probably for the best,' said Sophie, stepping between them.

'Good riddance,' said Felicity, her voice catching in her throat. Adam glanced at her and she was delighted to find even the sight of those eyes finding hers did nothing for her anymore. She was free at last.

Adam looked back at Bex. 'I'll go then, shall I?'

'Off you go then,' said Felicity.

But still he waited, eyebrows raised. Bex and Adam stared at each other for the longest time. It was almost as if he was waiting for her to follow him. Calling her bluff. Fully expecting her to capitulate and beg him to come home. *Don't you dare*, thought Felicity.

'And don't come back,' said Bex, finally. Adam's face dropped to the floor and simultaneously, Felicity's heart leapt in her chest. Had she finally broken the chains? One day, Bex would be free too, thought Felicity, and what a day that would be.

As Adam slammed the door behind him the three friends looked at each for a long moment and then for some reason burst out laughing, Bex the loudest of all.

'Well, that was easy,' said Felicity with a grin, and they laughed some more. It felt good, somehow. Even Bex looked relieved although they had to help her back to her chair, she was so wobbly on her feet. It was a big day, after all.

CHAPTER 49

hen James came back on the Friday, something was different. Off, you might even say. Felicity felt it as soon as he came in the door. He looked tired, his handsome face a little drawn, so perhaps that was all it was but a sinking feeling appeared in her stomach and two days later, it still hadn't left. He didn't even react when she told him what had gone down with Bex during the week. Not even when she gently mentioned Adam had been in the house. This was peculiar.

'Is everything all right?' she attempted, as they sat in their favourite pub that Sunday. It was their favourite partly because it didn't just allow but positively welcomed dogs so there were always some ears to scritch, but also because their Sunday roast came with a pie on the side, "pie and slice" they called it, because everything is better with pastry. Even the vegetarian version for Felicity was absolute heaven.

'Why wouldn't it be?' said James.

'I don't know. You just seem a little bit off,' she said, waving her fork around as if it would help her put her thoughts in order.

'I'm just tired,' was his reply, which wasn't any comfort.

'You always say that when you're mad with me.'

257

'No, I don't. And surely I can also say it when I'm just tired?'

His tone was not reassuring.

'You can of course, but...' Felicity's voice tailed off. She seemed to be making things worse. She resolved to try again later and they ate in strained silence for a few agonising moments. Then to her great relief, James spoke.

'I was wondering if you might like to go away for Christmas this year,' he said, suddenly. He sounded a little nervous, but at least he was planning ahead. You didn't plan ahead if you were planning to dump someone, did you? A whisper of relief ran down Felicity's spine. *Don't be paranoid. Everything's fine,* she told herself.

'That could be really nice,' she said. 'Who would look after the cats though, it might be difficult for Sophie on Christmas Day?'

'I've sorted that already,' said James, and he went back to eating his pie in silence.

'Okay… And where did you have in mind exactly?'

His turn to wave a fork. 'Wherever you want. I was thinking somewhere lovely and festive. You know, really get us in the mood for Crimbo.'

He paused, then gave a grin and she burst out laughing. 'You know I hate that word,' she said, with a giggle.

'Crimbo? It's a classic. Right up there with holibobs, surely?'

Felicity made a horrified face and it was James's turn to laugh. 'No? You don't like holibobs?'

She shook her head furiously. 'People who say holibobs wear socks with crocs. It's a known fact.'

He grimaced. 'That should be a crime.'

'I'm fairly sure it is in about thirty countries.'

'Rightly so.'

'Yup.'

Felicity allowed herself a small sigh of relief. Here was the James she knew and loved.

'So not somewhere too Christmassy then,' said James, trying to get the conversation back on track.

'No. I don't mind a little bit festive but I need to feel like I can opt out if I need to.'

'Fair enough,' said James with a nod. 'Will you allow me to surprise you if I stick to those rules?'

'If you like.' A little rush of excitement went through her.

'Okay, that's settled.' James went back to eating his food but she could have sworn his shoulders had dropped by a good eight inches. It wasn't like James to be nervous about anything. This was all very peculiar but Felicity did the only thing she could do under the circumstances. She went back to eating a Yorkshire pudding the size of her own head and pretended everything was absolutely fine.

CHAPTER 50

*I*t was four weeks to Christmas. Everywhere there were decorations going up, trees being heaved into place in town squares, lights being switched on by barely celebrities. James and Felicity had vaguely thought about going to get a tree instead of the tiny selection of branches they'd gone for last year, and that was definite progress. It even snowed a little in late November. Only a little, not enough to cause any – shock, horror – disruption but enough to make things look wintry, which was just the perfect amount for Britain. It had had the result of leaving everyone feeling even more festive than usual.

James and Felicity were booked to go away… somewhere… on Christmas Eve, the anniversary of their meeting and rapidly becoming Felicity The Reformed Grinch's favourite part of the Christmas season. She still had no clue where they were actually going though, and it hadn't helped when he'd told her to bring a mixture of clothes because the climate was "unpredictable".

'It's not Scotland, is it?' she said a little nervously.

'Nope,' was all he said in reply.

'No offence to Scotland of course, but, you know.'

'I know.'

Andrea and Harry were busy making the last-minute preparations for their move to Guernsey which was all booked for the second weekend of December. This included navigating some very complex repatriation rules regarding Harry's long absence from the island but he seemed to be taking it all in his stride. In fact, they seemed very keen to have this semi-famous novelist back. There had been no further mention of James and Felicity going over to join them, which was weird, but Felicity just assumed they'd all decided she hated the idea. Which she didn't entirely. But she'd made such a fuss it was a bit awkward to mention it now. Perhaps they'd go and visit at some point and she could casually slip it into conversation.

Andrea was all of a flutter. It was a situation Felicity was finding highly amusing.

On this particular morning, Felicity arrived at work to find Andrea just standing in the entranceway, looking dazed. The dogs were barking their heads off but she hadn't seemed to even notice.

'Are you okay?' she said over the din, putting a hand on Andrea's arm so as not to frighten the life out of her.

'What? Oh. Yes. Fine.'

'I think the dogs want their breakfast.'

'Yes. I suppose they do.' Andrea gave no sign of moving so Felicity left her where she was, dumped her stuff in the break-room and started on the feed rounds. An hour later when it was all finished and the world was peaceful once more, she found Andrea in her office, still with that same vacant expression on her face.

Felicity sat down in the chair opposite her and studied her boss for a few moments.

'Andrea? Are you sure everything's okay?'

Andrea's ice-blue eyes finally focused on her. 'What? Oh. Yes. Fine.'

'You said that before.'

'Did I?'

This was very peculiar behaviour for anyone but especially for Andrea.

'Is there something you need to talk about?'

To Felicity's great surprise, Andrea's pale eyes filled with tears. 'I'm just going to miss this place so much,' she said, with a sob.

Felicity had never ever seen Andrea cry before and had no clue how to respond. She looked around the room for inspiration and felt tears spring to her own eyes. This place held a lot of memories. Not least, it was in this office that she and James had shared that first ever Christmas lunch together, even if it was rather accidental and most of it got bought at the garage round the corner. Yes, it was the place she'd first found James, but more than that, it was the place where she'd started to find herself after so many years of being lost.

Tears were rolling down both their cheeks now but they were smiling at each other across the room.

'It's a special, special place,' said Felicity eventually.

Andrea let out a giant sob and wiped her nose on her sleeve. 'I just can't stop thinking about all the animals that have been through here over the years. All those little faces. All the little puppies and kittens. We even had a llama dumped at the front door once, that was quite the day.'

'A llama?' said Felicity, smiling through her tears. 'You've never told me that story.'

'Haven't I?' said Andrea. 'It was quite early on. Poor thing got tied to the railing outside the front door overnight. It was here when I got to work, freezing cold and wet and skinny as hell, but he had the most gorgeous big brown eyes. We called him Inca.'

'What happened to him?'

Andrea shrugged. 'Saskia thought I was taking the piss when I called her to tell her I had a llama for her. Thought it was an

April fool or something. But she came. They brought a horsebox and took him away. Not sure what happened to him, I'll have to ask her. Wow, I'm going to miss Saskia too.'

'Perhaps we need to throw you a going away party?'

Andrea rolled her eyes. 'You know I hate parties. All those… people. Ugh. It was bad enough on the open day.'

'I know you do but other people love parties. Apparently.'

Andrea laughed then. 'You hate parties too, if you recall.'

'I do. But I'd do it for you.'

'That's sweet but honestly, I don't want any of that nonsense. Let me just close it down quietly and be on my way.'

'So, you don't regret it?'

Andrea wiped her eyes with a tissue and tossed her salt-and-pepper plait over her shoulder. 'Moi? Je ne regrette rien.'

'You know they speak English on Guernsey, right?'

'I'm not an idiot. But you said some of the official stuff still happens in French. So, I thought I'd brush up on the old Duolingo just in case.'

'Harry will be impressed,' Felicity said with a smile.

'Nonsense. He won't even notice.'

'He notices everything you do.'

'I still have no idea why.'

Felicity shrugged. 'That's what you do when you love someone. Ugh, I can't believe I'm saying that. My father, and my boss. What are the odds?'

'Have you seen your father? He's hot. In what world was I not going after that?'

Felicity stood up. 'Yuck. That's enough of the heart-to-heart, thanks. I've got work to do.'

'Damn right you have,' said Andrea, but her eyes were twinkling. 'This place won't run itself for the next few days.'

'Roger that.'

❄

And a few days was all it was. Despite Felicity's constant pestering, Andrea wouldn't consent to a party but they did have Saskia, Sophie, Charlie, Harry and James in on the last day to toast the centre and to help pack up the remaining stuff to accompany the animals on their voyage across the sea. Most of the animals had been rehomed but amongst the remainder were two of the Disney puppies, Stitch and Sully, Marmaduke the cat, three of the lop-eared rabbits and Half Pint the pigeon.

'No pigeon left behind,' said Harry for the seventeen-hundredth time that day.

'It wasn't funny the first time,' said Felicity, but her voice was full of affection. She had a dad who made terrible jokes. Life goal achieved at last.

They said their goodbyes with promises to see each other soon, and then Felicity and James headed home that night to make their own arrangements.

Soon enough it was Christmas Eve, two years to the day since Felicity and James first met, and it was time for kissing the cats goodbye and heading off to East Midlands Airport, which was decorated to within an inch of its life. Felicity was even starting to feel a little bit festive for once, although she was still none the wiser as to where they were heading. James had refused to even drop a hint. He at least seemed a little bit more upbeat than he had been. Upbeat, or still a little nervous, or perhaps both at once.

The airport was clearly feeling a bit festive too, and there was not one or two but three fake plastic Christmas trees standing in the entrance foyer. *Shame no one's thought to actually decorate them,* thought Felicity grimly. James collected their tickets from the fancy machine and made a big show of hiding them from her but she knew he'd have to cave and tell her soon. He couldn't exactly smuggle her onto the plane without her hearing any boarding calls or seeing the screens, could he?

They dumped their numerous bags full of Christmas presents and myriad clothing at the baggage drop and got through security with no toothpaste-related mishaps. It was only a small airport and the security queue opened straight into the Departures lounge where the information board was ticking over slowly. A few flights were cancelled due to freezing fog but they were still flying to some lovely places. Alicante, Barcelona, Berlin, Geneva, Antalya, Channel Islands, Lanzarote, Cyprus, Naples, Rhodes, Santorini... *Wait. Go back.*

'We're not going to Guernsey for Christmas after all that, are we?' said Felicity with a laugh as she stared at the list of gorgeous places.

She was expecting him to laugh back at her; how ridiculous, as if they'd be going to Guernsey when they could go to Gran Canaria. Right?

He wasn't smiling.

'Would that be terrible?' he said, with a sort of half smile, half grimace that didn't even remotely show off his dimple.

Felicity faltered. Her head was saying, *Don't react badly, don't react badly, smile and say thank you.* But her mouth said, 'You are joking.'

James looked at her for a long moment, then shook his head. He was looking a little green around the gills.

Felicity took a deep breath. 'We're going to Guernsey for Christmas?'

He nodded. 'We are. Is that awful? I thought it would be romantic. I thought... I thought you'd like it.'

'I do like it. It's a great idea. Lovely,' said Felicity but she knew she didn't sound convincing.

James's face fell. 'I thought you'd like to see Andrea and Harry, you know, help them get settled in.'

Felicity crossed her arms. 'We literally just said goodbye to them like two weeks ago.'

'I know. I was trying to keep a straight face.'

'I cried and everything. You total git.'

'Sorry.'

'You don't look very sorry. Stop smiling.'

'Sorry.'

'I need the loo. Wait here.' And with that Felicity marched off to find the toilets before she said something she'd regret. Guernsey. Of all places. What was he thinking? She stared at herself in the unflattering toilet mirrors and took several deep and what were supposed to be soothing breaths but they only made her feel even more cross. Cross and also excited. Maybe they were going to find their forever home. Maybe he was taking her house-hunting. Still. House-hunting at Christmas. That was new levels of *bah, humbug,* even for him.

When she got back James had found them some seats by the Channel Islands desk. He was looking suitably sheepish. Felicity sat down heavily beside him.

'Sorry,' she said. 'Didn't mean to be ungrateful. I just thought we were… going somewhere else, that's all.'

'I know. I should have told you. I thought it would be a good surprise, really.'

'I just, I haven't been on Guernsey for Christmas since…'

'I know. I thought it was high time we laid the ghost of hideous Christmas Pasts to rest.'

Felicity laughed lightly but her heart was pounding. 'I'm sure you did. It's a good idea, really. We'll have a great time. And we'll get to see Jessica the donkey again, what's not to like?'

James smiled with relief. 'See? Look at you pretending to be excited.'

'How am I doing?' said Felicity.

'Not bad. Keep up the good work.'

'Thanks.'

Well, one part was true. At least they'd get to see Jessica. Life wasn't so bad, was it?

CHAPTER 51

The Bella Dame Hotel was fast becoming Felicity's second home, but this time they'd been upgraded to a luxury room with a huge modern four-poster bed and a sitting area by a large set of French windows looking out over the garden. The whole place was decorated with taste and there were bunches of flowers, enormous fragrant white lilies and opulent white roses, on every flat surface.

Felicity ran over to look at the biggest arrangement which was sitting on the coffee table by the window.

'Are these all from you?' she said in awe.

'I wanted red roses but you're not supposed to put red and white together apparently,' said James, rubbing the back of his neck.

'What? Really?'

'It's meant to be bad luck.'

'Oh yes, I've heard that. Blood and bandages or bone or something?'

'That's it.'

'What nonsense. They're beautiful. Thank you.'

'You're welcome,' said James, coming over and wrapping his arms around her.

Felicity turned and buried her face in his chest. 'Sorry for being an ungrateful whatsit,' she muttered.

'S'okay,' said James, kissing the top of her head. 'You were only a little bit whatsitish.'

'I try. Hey, maybe that's why Bex and Adam had bad luck flowers at their wedding. Doomed from the start, right?'

'Ah no, I think in their case it was the teal that did it.'

Felicity chuckled. 'I always said they should have gone for rose.'

'Now, let's go down, we're just in time for afternoon tea.'

'Yum. I'm starving.'

'Don't let me eat too many scones though,' said James. 'We've got dinner at 6pm.'

'You've thought of everything.'

'I hope so.'

'What?'

'Nothing. Shall we go?'

After the most delicious afternoon tea they went back to their room for a nap and then it was dinner with the hotel's own gin, the most delicious home-made pasta with a festive cranberry twist and a dessert which consisted of a pile of brownies and home-churned butterscotch ice cream. They retired to bed groaning and rubbing their bellies.

'Diet starts tomorrow,' said James with a laugh.

'Don't count on it in this place,' said Felicity.

'Well, in any case it's time for my beauty sleep. We've got a big day tomorrow.'

'I nearly forgot it was Christmas Day.'

'You've forgotten to be grumpy about it too. I think it's growing on you.'

'There's still time for plenty of grumpiness in the morning, don't worry.'

'Hush now, close your eyes or Santa won't come.' James patted her hand as he lay next to her on the bed.

'That's quite enough of that,' Felicity said, laughing.

They lay in silence for a few moments, enjoying the feeling of being full and warm and together.

'James…' said Felicity.

'Yes…?'

'It's two years since we met. Can you believe it?'

'Feels like forever.'

'Hey.'

'Not like that.'

'Two years since you swept me off my feet.'

'Ha. And what a two years it's been. Tell me something, did you fancy me straight away?' He always loved asking her this question.

'I mean, you were all soggy and dressed as a giant penguin.'

'That doesn't answer my question.'

'It was late at night. I thought you were going to be an axe murderer.'

'Still not answering the question.'

Felicity sighed. 'Okay, fine. Yes, of course I fancied you straight away. I mean, have you *seen* you? Even more so when you took the suit off and I saw your blond hair all messy and gorgeous. That did it.'

They were facing each other now. James reached over and slowly stroked a strand of Felicity's red hair. 'Ditto,' he said. 'In fact, I can still remember how you looked when you first opened that door. My little Christmas miracle. You looked so hot even in that ridiculous Animal Saviours T-shirt. But it was when you took me out to rescue the cat in the ditch and put your shoe right into a huge muddy puddle that I properly lost my heart.'

'I'm so smooth,' said Felicity.

'So… you liked the hair, did you? Wanted to climb me like a tree, did you?' said James, one eyebrow quirked.

'James Cowley. That is terrible.'

He moved closer. 'You did, though, didn't you? Admit it.'

Felicity's face went hot like lava. 'I may have. I mean, actually when you came down the corridor in that tight white T-shirt, I didn't know what to do with myself.'

'Tell me what you wanted to do to me.' His voice was low, suggestive, and Felicity wriggled with anticipation as he moved so his lips were inches from hers.

'You know I'm no good at all that.'

'I'll be the judge of that.' His eyes were on her lips and it was all she could do to find any words at all.

'I… wanted… to… sorry. I'm crap at this.'

James chuckled softly. 'Just forget it, and kiss me instead,' he said, then covered his mouth with hers in a deliciously deep kiss that sent delightful shivers down her spine. Before she gave herself to the moment completely, she paused and put her hand on his chest.

'Climb you like a tree, eh? How would that go, exactly?'

'Aren't you getting bold?'

'It is Christmas.'

'Nearly.'

'Well,' he chuckled softly, 'why don't I show you?' And with that he lifted her gently and pulled her on top of him and she kissed him again and wondered how she could keep living in this moment forever. Surely it couldn't last. Could it?

CHAPTER 52

Christmas Day dawned bright and frosty. Felicity opened her eyes, stretched her arms above her head and stared at the ceiling, revelling in the fact she could even do that on this particular day without feeling completely depressed and miserable. There was only a slight pang this year, the best it had ever been really. She looked across at James, and ran one hand idly down his chest, face flushing as she remembered their antics of the previous night with pleasure and more than a little discomfiture in the cold light of day.

'Morning,' said James, with a lazy smile, blinking in the daylight.

'Morning yourself,' said Felicity.

'Happy Christmas,' he murmured, turning over onto his side so he could face her.

'Happy Christmas yourself,' whispered Felicity, taking in the nearness of him. He was so damn broad.

James reached across and tucked a strand of hair behind her ear.

'I love you,' he said.

'I love you, yourself,' said Felicity. 'Wait, that one doesn't work.'

'Ha, got you,' said James.

Later, James and Felicity ordered a room service breakfast and opened what presents they'd been able to bring in their suitcase on the enormous super-king bed. Felicity had new pyjamas with cats on, even though James knew full well she'd never give up the old tartan ones without a fight, and James had to settle for a Jason Bourne box set because she couldn't find a decent enough Bourne costume.

Then they ate an extravagant and extremely expensive Christmas lunch in the restaurant with a few families and several dowagers and their entourages and retired to their room for a nap. At 4pm there was a knock on the door and a somewhat shy member of hotel staff delivered a tray heaving with festive cakes and cookies and although there was meant to be a late supper at 7pm in the restaurant they both had to admit defeat by then. They elected to stay in bed instead because, why not? It was Christmas after all.

'I've never been so full in my whole life,' said Felicity with a groan.

James just moaned in response.

They were propped up against the squishy cushions watching *Die Hard* because they'd missed the opportunity to watch it the day before and with cats named Holly and Gennie (Gennaro) after the character in the film, it was now a yearly ritual.

'Remember when you dressed up as John McClane?' said Felicity.

'How could I forget?' said James in that low, sexy voice of his.

'Do you, um, still have the outfit?'

James looked horrified. 'I mean, I do, but you're not suggesting…?'

Felicity grinned. 'God, no. Not now. I can barely move to a sitting position let alone anything… else.'

'Thank God. Me too. Christmas Day is officially the least sexy day of the year. Also, I didn't bring it.'

Felicity traced an idle circle on his stomach with one finger. 'So that means you do still have it.'

'I might.'

'The vest and the gun and all that?'

'Maybe.'

'Then that's happening when we get home, right?'

'Right you are. Or should I say, yippee-ki-yay?'

Felicity laughed and snuggled against him. 'Yes. You should. Perfect.'

The following morning Felicity woke early. The light seeping through the gap in the thick curtains was still grey and soft and she lay for a time staring at the ornate ceiling rose, listening to James's steady breathing beside her.

When it was clear all hope of going back to sleep was lost, she threw back the pillowy duvet and pottered around the room as quietly as she could manage. Realising there was no hope of actually getting the noisiest wardrobe in the world open without waking James, she eventually settled for pulling one of his woollen jumpers over her fancy new cat pyjamas and strapping on her walking boots.

The cold air hit her as she crept out of the hotel's heavy front door and padded down towards Moulin Huet Bay in the semi-dark, and she shivered as she walked down the quiet lane, exchanging a wry smile and a whispered "Happy Christmas" with a pink-cheeked woman clad in pyjamas and welly boots who had clearly had the same idea a little earlier.

The walkway down to the water was steep and slick with frost but something was pulling Felicity to the sea and she walked with purpose, not really clear what that purpose was but certain it would reveal itself at some point.

Reaching the bay, the sun just barely peeping over the horizon, she closed her eyes for but a moment and breathed the salty tang on the air, listening to the waves softly lapping at the beach below. A bench had been set up to the side of the path just a few metres from the sand, and she sat gratefully, wrapping her arms around herself and wishing she'd been brave enough to open the creaky wardrobe and grab a coat.

This was the view that inspired Renoir, she thought. Perhaps not on such a misty cold morning, but still, even now it had a bleak kind of beauty. There was something about the sea that always seemed to speak to her soul. Perhaps everyone felt like that. There were practical reasons too, of course, but perhaps humanity always populated the coastlines first because they had a spiritual need to, somehow.

Boxing Day. She had survived another Christmas with James and he hadn't walked out and left her. More to the point, she hadn't ruined it by being grumpy and sad and Eeyore-ish. In fact, this time she had positively relished their Christmas Day, and she wondered vaguely whether they could get away with sneaking off to Guernsey every year. Would anyone notice, or mind?

The bench was cold through her pyjamas and seeping into her bones and she knew she should probably head back to the hotel but something… something was nagging at her. But what was it? Nothing bad, that was for sure. She couldn't remember ever feeling this happy in fact. So what?

And then it hit her. That's what it was. She was happy. She was actually happy for the first time in ages. Perhaps – and Felicity cringed at her own dramatic flair – for the first time ever. She was in love. Properly, completely, fully in love and more than that, she was happy in her own skin. In her life. In where she was. She had people who loved her back and not just because they had to or in a surface way but fully, completely, loved her.

James loves me.

I love him.

More than that, she thought, *I trust him.*

I'm not constantly expecting him to leave.

I'm not expecting him to leave at all.

That last thought hit her like a thunderbolt. *I trust him.* For Felicity, who had never been able to rely on a single person for her whole life, except perhaps Andrea, to fully and completely trust someone felt like an almost impossible achievement.

A little laugh of delight escaped her lips and she looked guiltily around to see if anyone had heard, but the bay was deserted, the rising sun just barely creeping across the sea and touching the tips of the rocks, giving the whole vista a strange almost eerie look. Did she dare say the words out loud? She tested them in her mouth – *I trust him* – over and over again until at last they came whispering lightly over her lips and the salty air carried them out across the sparkling sea.

And then a thought dawned. And it was a big, bold thought that nearly stole the breath from her lungs. Felicity knew in that moment that trusting James was a decision, not a feeling. She could decide to trust him, and maybe she'd have to decide every day to do that but she didn't need to be led by her feelings. No matter how many wobbles she had, how many times the betrayals of her past came back to haunt her, Felicity could decide each and every morning that this man was worthy of her trust. She knew him. She knew it to be true. Just like with forgiveness – and she knew she still needed to work at forgiving Harry, of course she did – but in the same way, she could decide this. It was within her power to change the game. And that, thought Felicity, breathing the sea air deep into her lungs, that was everything.

Felicity practically skipped back to the hotel, but when she got back to their room, she opened the door as quietly as she could, half expecting James to be right where she left him, snoring softly. But no, he was up and pacing the floor.

'Where the heck have you been?' he said, rushing over to her.

He looked so serious, so grave somehow, that her heart gave a lurch. The irony, she thought, forcing herself to remember her little revelation. *You can trust him. Everything is fine.*

'Sorry, I went for a walk down to the bay. I couldn't sleep. Are you okay?'

'Yes, of course, sorry,' he said. He was smiling but she could see tension in his jaw. 'I just woke up and you weren't there. I got… scared.'

He looked almost sheepish. Her shoulders sagged in response.

'I really didn't mean to scare you. You were out for the count when I left. It's still early, want to go back to bed?'

She raised her eyebrows at him in what she hoped was a suggestive manner but if he noticed, he didn't react. His eyes flicked to his watch.

'Actually, we do have somewhere to be today. You might want to take a shower.'

'Oh… it's like that, is it?' she said, taking a step towards him.

He looked distracted, and her stomach flipped. What was wrong with him?

'Not like that. I mean an actual shower,' he said, a little sharply. 'You'll have to trust me on this one.'

Now she was getting paranoid. She recited the words from the beach in her head like a mantra. *I trust him. I trust him. I trust him.*

'Okay, so now you're making me paranoid,' she said, in another attempt at levity. 'Don't you like the smell of the sea?' She tried a winning smile. This time his lips twitched and she relaxed, just a little.

'I would love you even if you were actually wearing a dress made of mussels and clams,' he said, with a grin, 'but that's very much not the point right now. Go and have a shower and then I'll explain.'

'A dress made of mussels and clams. How would that even work?'

'I panicked, okay? That's all I could think of at short notice. But it's also very much not the point right now. You need to go and get ready. We have somewhere to be.'

'Don't tell me you're going to make me *go outside* again,' said Felicity with a grimace. 'It's cold out there.'

'Felicity Brooks… don't make me double-name you.'

'I think you just did.'

'Get in that shower.'

'Fine, I'm going,' said Felicity, heading for the bathroom, cheeks burning. She must smell. That must be what it was. She washed herself twice over just to be sure.

When she came out of the bathroom, wrapped in a soft white towel, James was sitting on the bed, tapping a foot on the deep carpet.

'There. Happy now?' she said, dropping as civilised a curtsey as she could manage without totally disgracing herself in the scanty robe. James didn't even react. Something was definitely up.

'I've got something for you.' James swallowed, handing her a large white box that had been resting on the bed beside him. His eyes were wide with excitement or, was that worry? It was hard to tell.

Felicity sat down next to him on the bed and blinked. 'Where did that box come from?'

'It was in the wardrobe.'

She ran a hand over it absently. 'No, but I mean, how did you get this here on the plane without me seeing it?'

'I have my ways.'

'Sneaky thing.'

'I know,' said James a little proudly, although his voice was strained.

'What? Why does your face look like that?'

'All will become clear. But first… breakfast.' James stood up, opened the door to the hotel room and picked up a tray which must have been sitting there a while. He placed it on the little table by the hotel room window and lifted the silver cloche with a flourish. Underneath it was a plate piled with a full English vegetarian breakfast plus a little rack full of toast, a glass of orange juice, a mug of coffee and even a little flower in a vase.

'Eat this, then put that on and meet me in the lobby,' he said, indicating the box. 'And it must be in that order. Do not under any circumstance attempt to put that on before you have eaten. Promise me.'

'What? What's going on?'

'Promise me, I said.'

'Fine, I promise. Aren't you eating?'

'I'll get something downstairs. Take as long as you need, I'll be reading the paper.'

'James, you're scaring me. What are you up to?'

'Just do it.'

Felicity's blood was beginning to pound in her ears. What in the name of a room service breakfast was going on here? *I trust him, I trust him, I trust him. And also, oh God, please don't let him leave me.*

She waited until he'd pottered around the room a bit more.

Eventually James left and went downstairs, still with that same look on his face.

Heart thumping, Felicity took the lid off the box.

Inside was the most exquisite dress she had ever seen in her life. It was ivory satin with buttons and sequins sewed into the bodice and a long extravagant skirt. She lifted it up and gasped at how the material flowed, soft and silken and very, very expensive. If Felicity didn't know better she'd think it was a…

'This is a wedding dress,' she said in a wobbly voice, although there was no one in the room.

A voice came from the other side of the door.

'Put it on.'

'You're supposed to be downstairs.'

'I know. I knew you'd bloody open the box first. Eat your breakfast. Then you can put the dress on. Don't think, just do it.' There was a long pause while Felicity's stomach did a series of mini-somersaults. 'I love you. Just remember that, okay?'

'I love you,' she said to the door.

'Go on, get eating. We're on a clock here.'

'Okay, okay, I'm doing it,' said Felicity, her pulse beating wildly now. What had he done?

CHAPTER 53

When she was finally satisfied that he'd actually gone downstairs, Felicity sat down at the little table, but her appetite had vanished.

I'll eat a bit later, she thought, and then hurried into the bathroom to do her make-up. What on earth was she meant to be making herself up for, for goodness' sake? Surely that wasn't a wedding dress, was it?

Felicity pulled it over her head and nearly gasped out loud at the sight of herself in the mirror. The satin creation fit her perfectly, accentuating her minimal curves the best it could and even giving her a tiny bit of cleavage, which was unheard of. *This must be Sophie's influence,* she thought. James was good but even he wasn't that good.

Her hands were shaking as she brushed and dried her hair and found a hair clip to pin it up on one side, the most effort she ever went to.

When she'd finally completed a frantic transformation, her eye turned to the food.

Just one mouthful, she thought.

She piled her fork high with a combination of egg, beans and tomato, and very carefully brought it up to her mouth. At the last moment, a lump of egg wobbled off and dropped down the front of the dress and Felicity let out a little scream.

'What?' came a voice from outside. James was still bloody out there, wasn't he?

'Don't come in, don't come in, everything's fine,' said Felicity, frantically rushing to the bathroom and locking the door.

'Do you need me?' came James's voice, more distant now.

'No, bugger off,' she yelled.

'Are you sure?'

'Go downstairs, will you!'

Felicity looked in the mirror, aghast. Her beautiful cream silk dress now had a trail of egg yolk down the front of it.

'Bugger, bugger, bugger,' she said, staring at her own reflection. 'You bloody idiot, Felicity, now you've done it.'

'Room clean,' came a distant voice from the door. Higher pitched this time.

Felicity threw open the bathroom door in a panic. 'I know that's still you,' she yelled. 'Stop pretending to be a cleaning lady.'

At that, the door opened and an actual cleaning lady stuck her head in. She was elderly and her face was lined and pale.

'Are you okay, my dear?'

'Oh, I'm sorry, I thought you were...' Felicity couldn't even finish the sentence. Tears began rolling down her cheeks.

The woman looked down at her dress and let out a little yelp.

'Oh, good Lord. What have you done?'

'It's egg,' said Felicity, her face crumpling. 'I don't know what to do.'

Like some kind of miraculous fairy godmother, the woman rushed forwards, waving her hands frantically. 'Don't touch it,' she said. 'And whatever you do, don't put hot water on it. Just trust me, okay? Wait here.'

She rushed out of the room. Still sniffing, Felicity stuck her head out of the corridor behind her but thankfully, James was nowhere to be seen. But she knew it was only a matter of time before she'd have to come clean, pun intended.

He's going to kill me, she thought, sitting down on the bed despondently. Why was she such a klutz? Fair enough, James had known this practically from the start, when she properly fell over right in front of him on their first proper date and he had to patch up her knee with a sticking plaster, but this? This took the biscuit.

Five long minutes later, the lady was back, carrying a tray of cleaning products.

'Right, off with the dress,' she said, coming over and pulling it straight over Felicity's head.

Felicity was too shocked to even object. She wrapped her arms around herself to disguise the teeny tiny underwear she was barely wearing.

'You,' said the woman, tucking the dress carefully over her arm and pointing at the congealing breakfast by the window, 'You eat while I sort this out.'

Felicity opened her mouth and out came a sob she wasn't expecting.

The woman's face softened. She had hazel eyes and dark-grey hair swept off her face. She stepped forwards and put a hand on Felicity's cheek. She seemed nice but clearly had no boundaries whatsoever. Felicity was very conscious she was barely clothed.

'It's going to be okay,' said the woman. 'You'll see. You are going to look perfect.'

Felicity nodded, choking back a sob and also resisting the temptation to take a step backwards. The fairy godmother lady gave her arm a squeeze and then turned and vanished into the bathroom with the dress, leaving Felicity shivering in her under-wear and wondering what the hell was happening and why she couldn't just follow simple instructions.

She took a mouthful of toast and chewed rapidly. James was going to kill her.

✳

'Ta-da,' came a voice from over her shoulder as she finished eating.

Felicity spun, and her mouth dropped open.

The woman was laying the dress out on the bed. Not a jot of egg yolk in sight.

'It's a Christmas miracle,' she said, turning to Felicity and giving her a massive smile.

'How the hell did you do that?' said Felicity, leaping to her feet and giving her a huge hug. 'Also, thank you, and what's your name by the way?'

The woman laughed lightly. 'It's Anna,' she said. 'And you're more than welcome. I used to be a dry cleaner, can you tell? I know all the tricks. Just never put anything hot on an egg stain or you'll cook it into the fabric.'

'Gross,' said Felicity.

'That's nothing compared to some of the sights I've seen, my dear.'

Felicity hopped from foot to foot. 'I bet. I really want to hear those stories too but right now...'

'We need to wipe that ketchup off your face and get you dressed.'

Felicity scrubbed frantically at her cheek. 'Yes please,' she said. And then, 'I am an adult, honest.'

Anna laughed again, a lovely tinkling sound. 'I believe you. And soon to be a married one if this dress is anything to go by.'

As Felicity got dressed, she told Anna the whole story of how she'd met her Penguin Man and as much as she knew of what was happening now – which wasn't much. By the end, Anna left the room clapping her hands together excitedly, determined to tell everyone in the hotel what was going on. So much for the surprise.

CHAPTER 54

*A*t last, she was ready. But when Felicity went downstairs, egg-free and finally feeling glamorous and less like a disaster zone, James was nowhere to be seen.

Felicity stood in the reception for a few moments wondering whether she'd taken too long with the whole egg-gate episode and what the hell to do, when the hotel manager approached with a small bunch of roses in his hands, the same pure white as the ones in their room.

'Miss Brooks?' he said. He had dark slicked-back hair like Hercule Poirot and a small immaculate moustache. His eyes were kind.

'Yes?' Felicity's voice had gone all wobbly.

'You look absolutely exquisite.'

'Oh. Thank you,' she said, her face heating.

'I've been asked to tell you that Mr Cowley has gone on ahead. He's requested that you get into this car and it will take you where you need to go.'

He led her outside the hotel to where a long black vintage car was waiting. It had white ribbons tied on the bonnet. A whole row of staff was standing alongside it ready to wave her off.

There was Anna, right at the end, waving frantically. Felicity's heart leapt into her mouth. So then. Her fairy godmother-cleaning lady was right. This was her wedding day. Strange. She didn't even remember being proposed to.

'Madame, are you well?' said the kindly manager.

Felicity nodded. 'Yes, erm, I think so I mean. Just a little bit shell-shocked I suppose.'

The manager smiled and opened the car door for her and Felicity mechanically got in, all the while wondering if she should have done more with her hair. Or painted her nails. Or any of that stuff brides normally do. Her heart was pounding so hard she could barely hear herself think.

'Morning, miss,' said the driver, who was smartly dressed in a cap and suit. He watched in the rear-view mirror as Felicity put on her seatbelt then patted her hair nervously, before he switched on the engine and eased the car out of the hotel driveway.

'Morning. Do you… er… happen to know where we're going?'

'As a matter of fact I do, miss. We'd be in trouble if I didn't,' he added with a chuckle.

'And can you tell me?'

'That I cannot do I'm afraid. Mr Cowley was very strict about that. He said you'd ask and he said under no circumstances was I to tell you.'

'You don't have to do what he says you know. Go on. Tell me. Live a little.'

'He said you'd say that. Forgive my rudeness, miss, but he told me to tell you that it wasn't far and that that was all you are getting.'

'Nothing's far on Guernsey,' said Felicity, a little intrigued and also a bit turned on that James knew her so well.

'Well, exactly, miss.'

They fell into an easy silence then, the driver concentrating on the narrow roads while Felicity watched the beautiful stone walls and cute cottages fly by the window. Every so often she'd even get a glimpse of the sea but otherwise it was easy to forget they were on a small island in the English Channel. She finally understood the phrase, "my heart was in my mouth". Where were they going? She tried to think of all the churches on the island and at one point even wondered if they were going to get married in the tiny Little Chapel, a marvellous curiosity made out of clinker and decorated with seashells and pottery pieces, which was extremely popular with tourists.

But no, by now they had gone past the Little Chapel and were heading for the west side. People waved from the side of the road as she went past and it took a moment to realise it was because it must look like a wedding car. The ribbons. What was going on? She was completely unprepared to marry James but then, at the same time, totally ready. He was the one, after all. There could never be another. She had told herself after just a few months that if he upped and left her as she had always expected he would, she would just morph into full Crazy Cat Lady which to be honest she had been on the verge of anyway before he came along. Nothing wrong with being a crazy cat lady after all. It was a fine ambition. A jolt of excitement ran down her back. What exactly was going on?

As fields and cottages and decrepit old greenhouses from the days when the people of Guernsey were tomato-farming fanatics flashed by, another thought began to dawn. *Could it be? No, surely not.* Surely they were not going to the...?

'Here we are, miss,' said the chauffeur. And sure enough, he pulled the car up to the entrance to Le Manoir, and turned up the drive. Felicity gasped. It looked incredible. The long gravel drive was hung with poles every few feet, and fairy lights were strung artfully between the poles, with white ribbons and bows positioned between them. As they crept along, with the gravel crunching under the car wheels, she could see a crowd of people gathered outside the front of the house under a gazebo also covered in fairy lights and draped in white ribbons. There were balloons, too, and two enormous Christmas trees, one either side of the door, decorated to within an inch of their short lives with lights, baubles and ribbon, all matched to the theme which so far seemed to be white. For what? Purity? *Hardly*, thought Felicity, blushing a little. Because somewhere, somewhere in the midst of all this, there was her James.

The car pulled up in front of the group of people gathered on the gravel, all cheering and waving as they came to a stop. Felicity was overcome with the urge to see James immediately. She had always hated crowds and even though this was a very small one made up of – from what she could see – all the people she knew and loved in the world, she just didn't want to face them without her Penguin Man by her side.

'Where is he?' she said as she opened the car door. Andrea, who was for once not wearing a fleece and actually looked like she wasn't even covered in cat hair for the first time ever, grabbed her hand and helped her out. Her navy-blue dress made her eyes even more sparkly than usual.

'You're not going to kill him, are you?' she hissed under her breath. 'He did all this himself. For you.'

'He had a bit of help,' said Sophie, coming up beside her dressed in an incredible deep-red velvet slinky affair, 'but it was all his idea. Please don't kill him.'

'At least, not on your wedding day. I'm no expert,' said Bex, appearing behind Sophie, 'but I believe that's considered bad form.'

Felicity smiled and her friends let out three huge sighs of relief as one. 'I'm not going to kill him,' she said. 'I just want to see him.'

'He's inside,' said Sophie. 'He's waiting for you to marry him.' She grinned a huge grin and then grabbed Felicity's arm. 'If you want to, that is. He was very strong on that point. If you don't want to that's completely fine, he said. I've just got to tell you to get back in the car and he'll see you back at the hotel and that will be that.' She stopped and looked at Felicity properly for the first time. 'You look amazing, by the way.'

Felicity looked down at herself. 'Did you choose this dress?'

'I may have,' said Sophie, kissing her friend on the cheek. 'Bex helped me. Do you like it?'

'Like it? I never want to take it off. Please don't ever make me take it off.'

Andrea piped up. 'James might have a few words to say about that, it's your wedding day for goodness' sake.'

'Hush now, they can do it with the dress still on,' said Sophie with a wink.

'You two,' said Felicity, blushing hard now. 'Please. It's my wedding day. Have some decorum.'

The four of them looked at each other and then squealed. Bex's reaction was more muted than the rest but Felicity was so relieved to see her at least partly back to herself.

'It's my wedding day,' said Felicity again. 'Am I dreaming?'

'Nope but you might be late. Hurry up and get in there and let him know you're not going to kill him, for God's sake,' said Andrea.

'I've never seen him so nervous,' Sophie said, grinning. 'Go and put him out of his misery.'

'Okay, okay, I'm going,' said Felicity, picking up the hem of her dress and moving towards the front door of Le Manoir, which had been painted a deep-red colour for the occasion, just as she remembered from her childhood.

Tristan stepped forwards wordlessly and gave her an enormous hug. Very un-Tristan-like behaviour. Pete appeared behind him and she waved excitedly, probably rather over-excitedly, as the reality of the situation started to hit.

Two children peeped out from behind them. The boy looked decidedly unbothered but the girl's eyes were the size of saucers as she looked up at Felicity.

'This is Sammy and Zoe,' said her brother. 'And this,' he went on, turning to the children, 'is your half-sister, Felicity.'

'Hey, guys,' said Felicity, a little shyly, wondering if she was going to be able to cope with any more excitement in one day.

'Hey,' they said in unison.

'We'll talk later, okay?' said Felicity, in her best big sister voice.

The children nodded silently.

'They hate me already,' she said, turning to Tristan.

He grinned. 'Give them time. They don't know you yet.'

'Exactly,' said Felicity.

'See you after the thing,' whispered her brother in her ear.

'Thanks for being here,' Felicity whispered back. And she meant it.

Just as she got to the door she was accosted by Valerie and a very smart-looking Jessica the donkey with a little friend she recognised as Eeyore.

'There you are,' said Felicity, flinging her arms around the little donkeys' necks and feeling suddenly overcome with emotion. 'It wouldn't be the same without you two.'

'You'll spoil your dress,' said Valerie from somewhere behind her.

'I don't care,' she said, face buried in fur. Jessica's familiar warm smell tickled her nostrils. 'Besides, you didn't see what happened to it earlier. Don't tell James I said that, whatever you do.'

'You look wonderful, darling,' said Valerie. 'Jessica and Eeyore are going to follow you in. She has the rings.'

Felicity thought her heart might burst right out of her chest. For sure enough, there around Jessica's neck was a little white velvet pouch on a silver ribbon. 'Already the best day ever,' she whispered, half to herself.

CHAPTER 55

As she reached the door and peered in, a familiar figure reached out a hand. It was Harry, looking dapper and ever so slightly Mafia-ish in a dark suit and white tie.

'You're here,' she breathed, taking his arm.

'Even Jessica the donkey couldn't have stopped me,' he said, looking her over with tears in his eyes. 'You look incredible.'

'What is happening?' said Felicity with a laugh as they walked into what had once been her childhood home.

'I've no idea but coming back here to walk you down the aisle was not on my life bingo card,' quipped Harry, but he looked thoughtful.

'Me neither,' said Felicity, gripping his arm. 'It's weird, that's for sure. But good to see it full of life again.'

For the house looked very different to last time she had been here, finding a stray donkey in the kitchen. Everywhere had been swept and painted. The dead leaves and broken furniture had been removed and it had been cleaned to within an inch of its life. Everywhere smelt quite strongly of furniture polish and lavender. For the new owners, she supposed. At least they'd obviously let her use it for this first. Her wedding.

Her insides did a little flip at that thought. They did a much bigger flip as they reached the end of the hallway and she saw James standing by the fireplace in the enormous living room with a Christmas tree in each corner, waiting for her like the gift he was. James was dressed in a charcoal-grey suit with a dark-blue tie and white shirt. On anyone else it might have looked like a school uniform but on him... he looked positively edible. His blond hair had been gelled but was still suitably mussy and his face... on his face Felicity thought she could count at least five emotions at once. He looked terrified and awestruck and deliriously happy all at the same time. And handsome. Was that an emotion? He looked ridiculously handsome too. Of course he did.

Music began playing from somewhere unknown. "Kiss Me" by Sixpence None the Richer in fact, a personal favourite. As she started walking towards James, she was vaguely aware that there were other people gathered on chairs on each side of the room and that others were following her in, including the little donkeys, who still hadn't put a hoof wrong. Jessica knew this place of old, of course. There was little Harper, James's niece, with her mum and dad, wearing the most beautiful little pink sparkly dress, and at the front, James's mum and dad were looking on proudly. Rita and Jim lived in Scotland so they never saw them much but they had always been so kind to her and they were giving her the warmest smile right now. *Fancy them coming all the way over to Guernsey,* Felicity thought vaguely as she walked.

But despite everything in her peripheral vision, Felicity really only had eyes for James. Her gorgeous, kind Penguin Man, who had always seemed too good to be true and now, he'd proved it. In fact, it was only when she had almost reached him that she realised he wasn't alone. Standing in front of the fireplace was a small woman with grey hair and red-rimmed glasses. She was holding a black folder and wearing a black suit and looked as though she should have been officiating a funeral not a wedding but Felicity didn't care. Half Pint and his merry band of pigeon mates could have been flying around her head and she wouldn't even have noticed.

Harry gave her arm a squeeze as they reached the fireplace and she forced herself to look away from James just for a moment.

'Thanks… Dad,' whispered Felicity into his ear.

'That's the first time you've called me that in a very long time,' said Harry, beaming.

'I know,' said Felicity. And then, 'I'm glad you're here.'

'Really?'

'Really.'

'I don't know what to say.'

'Just wish me good luck,' she said.

'Good luck, my darling girl. Thanks for letting me be part of your day.'

It wasn't everything. But it was a start.

'You look unbelievable,' said James as Felicity moved to stand beside him, glowing with pride and excitement. 'Is this okay? Tell me this is okay?'

Was she okay? Her face felt hot and her palms were sweating but she couldn't remember ever feeling so happy.

'This is incredible,' she breathed, taking his hand in hers. 'I mean, officially I'm mad with you but wow. You've blown my mind.'

James looked like he'd won the lottery, which only made her heart swell even more.

'You understand, there's no pressure, right? Sophie told you? I mean, I know there's a lot of pressure but you don't have to do anything you don't want to, okay?'

'I think you mean, will you marry me?' said Felicity calmly.

James smiled a huge smile then, his dimple dimpling away to full effect.

'You're right. Or should I say, *I do*.'

'*I do too*,' she whispered, her eyes filling with tears.

He winked at her, turning to the crowd who were all on their feet now, breaths held. Only Jessica the donkey looked like she couldn't care less that it was Boxing Day and a wedding day all rolled into one.

James took a deep breath. 'On behalf of Felicity and myself, I'd like to thank everyone for coming, especially for giving up your Boxing Day for us. We are so grateful and we love you all.'

Rita started sobbing in the front row while the rest of the crowd cheered and jumped up and down and then realised there were donkeys in the room and toned it down a little. But the donkeys thought this was a great game and decided to join in, putting in some deafening hee-haws to the amusement of them all. James had to wait an awkwardly long time before he could make himself heard again.

'I realise,' he went on when things had quietened down, 'that this was a risk. Felicity is not good with crowds and she doesn't like a big fuss so I nearly gave up on this whole idea but I can't think of anyone who deserves to have a big fuss made of her as much as she does. So, basically I thought, screw it.' The crowd tittered. 'Screw it, let's damn well make a fuss of her and give her a surprise she'll never forget and she'll just have to lump it and deal with it and it was only this morning that I wondered what the hell I had done. Bit late to stop it all by then.' More titters.

'But I'm delighted to say that the future Mrs Cowley has forgiven me for all my conniving, and – I hope – will consent to be my wife. Willingly, I hasten to add.'

He turned to Felicity. All eyes were on her and she knew her face was burning. But as she looked up into the face of her Penguin Man, she realised something extraordinary. As he looked down at her, his eyes wide, and full of hope, it occurred to her that no one in her whole life had ever known her or loved her like this. And this was how he was showing her. James knew she would have hated the planning. He knew her so well that he knew she would have detested trying to choose a dress or having people poke and prod at her, just as he knew Christmas was a really difficult time for her. He knew all that, so he'd tried to find a way to give her new memories. To give her hope. From now on, this day would not just be the source of the biggest trauma in her life, Christmas would also be a point of hope, of a future, of pure joy. Forever her wedding anniversary. Something that couldn't be taken from her. And what was Christmas all about if it wasn't joy? Hell, maybe James was also coming round to the season too.

As her eyes roved the room, something caught her eye, and she took a deep breath. In the corner of the room was an empty chair with a jar of white lilies on the seat. Balanced above it was a framed photograph of her mother. There was Jocelyn. Beautiful, complicated Jocelyn. Looking down on her. Giving approval in absentia.

Felicity's heart gave a lurch. It was so incredibly sad – beyond sad, really – that her mother wasn't here to see this, had missed so much of Felicity's life, but the fact that James and Harry had thought to include a tribute to her, it meant such a lot. She sent up a silent prayer for Jocelyn, wherever she may be.

James took her hands between his, gently bringing her back to the present. She blinked up at him.

'Felicity Brooks. Will you marry me?' whispered James, his face pale.

Felicity looked up into his eyes and beamed, eyes glistening. 'I will,' she said.

The crowd went wild and even Jessica and Eeyore began to join in again which sent them all into fits of giggles. As she watched them all howling with laughter, Felicity wondered if her heart would burst.

CHAPTER 56

*T*hankfully, her heart didn't give out, and twenty minutes later it was done. Felicity and James were husband and wife. It felt like a dream. Perhaps it always would feel that way. Perhaps that was always the intention.

As the registrar declared their knot officially tied, Rita and Jim wrapped their arms around them, and the rest of the guests leapt from their seats, cheering and shouting with joy. Felicity's heart swelled in her chest at the sound. As Felicity and James turned to walk back down the makeshift aisle, avoiding the discreet pile of donkey droppings on the way, James held up a hand. He was fighting a losing battle but eventually... eventually they began to quieten down enough for him to speak.

'I have one more announcement. Well, two announcements really. One is that there's absolutely loads of food and drink in the next room, Christmas-themed of course and no, not made by me, you'll be pleased to hear, but by a wonderful catering company who didn't seem to mind coming out on Boxing Day – so please be nice to them, everyone. And help yourselves.'

'And secondly,' he said, giving Felicity's hand a squeeze. 'Damn, I should have said this one first,' he added as the volume of the murmuring in the room went up considerably. 'Never mention food first, rookie mistake.'

Sure enough, people were already drifting away into the next room. James and Felicity stood there for a moment wondering if anyone was even going to stay for the second thing. A few folk lingered at the back, but it was clear they were just being polite and secretly couldn't wait for the buffet. James turned to Felicity and smiled down at her.

'This one's really for you anyway,' he said, then leant and whispered in her ear. His breath made her whole body tingle.

'I didn't catch that,' she said, mainly just to make him do it again.

'I said, how would you feel if I said this was our new home?' he whispered, a little louder this time. Felicity blinked at him.

'I'm sorry, Mr Brooks, could you say that again?'

He let out a low chuckle.

'"Mr Brooks". I like that. I said, how would you feel if we lived here?'

Felicity let out a high-pitched squeal and threw herself into his arms.

'Are you kidding me?' she said, as he lifted her up and held her close.

'No, I'm not kidding. I mean, unless you don't like the idea in which case I am absolutely one hundred per cent kidding. Because, you know, I get that it might be weird.'

Felicity looked at him, looked deep in his blue eyes and wondered how she ever got so lucky.

'It's not weird. It's perfect,' she said. And she meant it. She hadn't realised until now just how perfect it would be. Like her life had come full circle, but this time she intended to live it to the full.

'Oh, thank God for that because I've already paid the deposit,' said James, with a breathy laugh.

'What? How the hell did you afford it?'

'I had some savings. Okay, I had a lot of savings. Turns out it pays to be a very poor imitation James Bond.'

Felicity squealed again.

A polite cough came from someone in the doorway. 'So sorry to interrupt but it's time to cut the cake,' said a man in an apron, presumably one of the caterers.

'There's a cake?' said Felicity, impressed.

'It's made of doughnuts,' said James, a little sheepishly.

'Even better,' said Felicity with a smile. 'God, I'm going to get so fat being married to you. Get ready for Cankle City, Mr Cowley.'

At this, James beamed. 'We'll be there in a moment,' he said, and the man nodded and backed away. James turned to Felicity, who was still in his arms. 'Now excuse me while I kiss my wife,' he said, and she threw her arms around his neck and he kissed her until she saw stars.

'I love you, Mr Penguin Man,' she said when she came back up for air, her entire body fizzing and popping with excitement and longing. She wondered vaguely if there were any beds upstairs. Perhaps James had sorted that too. Her face and neck flushed crimson at the thought.

'I love you, Mrs Penguin Man,' said James, brushing her hair from her face and placing her gently back down on the floor.

'I'm Mrs Penguin Man,' said Felicity, her eyes filling with tears.

'You are. You always were,' said James with a grin. 'But you can still be Crazy Cat Lady too.'

'That's why Sophie couldn't cat-sit for us,' said Felicity, as realisation dawned.

'That's why. But don't worry, we can bring them with us when we come. It's all arranged.'

'This is why you went away?'

'This is why.'

'You didn't go to Manchester?'

'I didn't go to Manchester. Sorry about the whole lying thing. I was putting up bunting for three bloody days straight. I mean, how much bunting does one wedding need anyway?'

'I think you're forgiven. I bloody love bunting.'

She reached up, pulled his head down to hers and kissed him, then breathed against his lips. 'Thank you for this incredible day, and Happy Christmas.' Her voice was wavering. 'Oh, and by the way, I dropped egg down myself while I was getting ready.'

James roared with laughter. 'Of course you did.'

'Of course I did. Sorry. Can't expect me to ignore a fry-up, can you?'

'Happy Christmas, and thank you,' he said hoarsely.

'For what? I did literally nothing.'

James laughed again and kissed her forehead. 'You really have no idea, do you? Just by turning up today, just by agreeing to marry me, you've given me everything,' he said. 'You've given me a home. Scratch that, actually. You are my home. You're everything, Felicity Brooks. Or should I say, Felicity Cowley?'

Felicity's heart was about to burst right out of her chest, for real this time.

'Say it again,' she whispered, awestruck.

James beamed at her again. 'Felicity Cowley.'

'I love it.'

'Me too.'

And right there and then Felicity knew the truth, once and for all. That home was not a place, but a person. This person. Her incredible, wonderful Penguin Man. Her James.

Her husband.

Her home.

Her family.

Felicity's face was aching from smiling. Her hand hovered lightly over her stomach, then quickly dropped down to her side.

Her secret news could wait just one more day.

THE END

300

ALSO BY NICOLA KNIGHT

The Night Before Christmas

Felicity Brooks hates Christmas. But when she meets a man dressed as a giant penguin on Christmas Eve, could it spell a change of heart, in this laugh-out-loud festive romance?

'Amazing... You have to read it.... I can't do my review justice but this is one of my books of 2024.' — NetGalley Reviewer

BUY NOW

ACKNOWLEDGEMENTS

Writing a second novel is famously not an easy thing to do for so many reasons, mostly because you have to navigate a whole river of insecurity and self-doubt. But in my case, despite dipping my toes in that river on numerous occasions, getting the chance to return to the world of Crazy Cat Lady and Penguin Man for this book has been an absolute delight.

Felicity Brooks was the character who first encouraged me to embark on this writing lark in any serious way and she will always be very special to me. Her story originated as an entry into a writing competition, where you had to write a 'Christmas Love Story'. Back then all I had was one miserable scene where Felicity was staring out of a window on Christmas Eve, hating Christmas and feeling generally very sorry for herself. In a weird way I loved that moment, because I knew something she didn't. In just a few moments a certain man (not Santa!) was going to knock on the door and change her life forever. All I had to do was start writing. And that's the absolute joy of putting words on a page and somehow turning them into a story. I hope you found just as much joy from reading it.

Felicity's story has changed my life too. After that competition I began to hope this might be something I could actually do. I began to knock on doors myself. Some of them even opened. Ultimately Felicity made my dream of becoming a published author a reality and I owe her so much.

I owe lots to many other wonderful (non-fictional) people too.

Sincere thanks must go to my fantastic publishers Bloodhound Books, especially Betsy, Tara and Hannah who have offered such incredible support and love for Felicity's story, and to my brilliant editor Ian Skewis whose notes of encouragement were completely life-giving... and whose knowledge and enthusiasm for the Die Hard movies put mine to absolute shame!

I must mention my friends and work colleagues (sometimes both) who have supported me on this journey, reading extracts, discussing ideas, making me laugh, buying me Percy Pigs, keeping me going and of course buying my books under only a tiny amount of duress. I really hope you know who you are. Special mentions for Jude, Georgia, Jennie, Katie, Rachael, Helen, Charlotte, Leanne, Lydia, Steph, Debbie and Lynn at Redwings and Diane, Imogen, Ellen, Claire, Jane, Gemma, my Mum and Dad, Sarah and Stuart, and to my Aunties Gill and Pam who always believed I could do this and have inspired me constantly over the years.

And finally, to the whole gang at Hope Church in Diss who came in their droves to my first ever book signing and show up for me time and time again.

Thank you too to the numerous industry professionals who have given me their support on my writing journey, from the Romantic Novelists Association who shortlisted my first book for Debut of the Year, to fabulous local retailers like Halesworth Bookshop and Diss Publishing who have welcomed me into their world with open arms. From wonderful authors like Jenni Keer, Heidi Swain, Stephanie Butland, Jenn Ashworth, Joanna Cannon, Elly Griffiths, Jo Thomas, Sue Moorcroft and Laura Shepperson for their kind support and invaluable advice, to my writing buddies for their calming words when the self-doubt river starts rising.

Final thanks go to my darling husband Dan, ten years not out! Thank for your love and patience.

And to you, dear reader. For reading of course, but also for your kind reviews and messages of support, which mean the world to me and have saved me from the river more times than I care to mention. I hope we meet again.

ABOUT THE AUTHOR

Nicola Knight is a former journalist and chartered public relations professional, who works in communications at Redwings Horse Sanctuary, a national animal welfare charity.

Her first novel, *The Night Before Christmas*, also published by Bloodhound Books, was shortlisted for Debut of the Year at the RNA's Romantic Novel Awards.

In 2023 Nicola published a chapter which formed part of a collection of stories around mental health called 'Will You Read This Please?', edited by Dr Joanna Cannon and co-authored with renowned writer Jenn Ashworth.

Nicola lives in South Norfolk with her husband, young daughter and three* chaotic cats.

(*number correct at time of going to print 😁).

A NOTE FROM THE PUBLISHER

Thank you for reading this book. If you enjoyed it please do consider leaving a review on Amazon to help others find it too.

We hate typos. All of our books have been rigorously edited and proofread, but sometimes mistakes do slip through. If you have spotted a typo, please do let us know and we can get it amended within hours.

info@bloodhoundbooks.com

www.ingramcontent.com/pod-product-compliance
Lightning Source LLC
Chambersburg PA
CBHW050545190726

48283CB00007B/2017